THE PRINCESS SEARCH

THE PRINCESS SEARCH

A RETELLING OF THE UGLY DUCKLING

MELANIE CELLIER

For everyone who wrote to tell me that
the Crown Prince of Lanover also needed to find true love

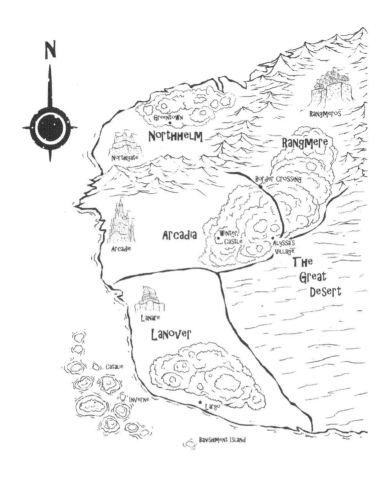

Royal Family of Lanover

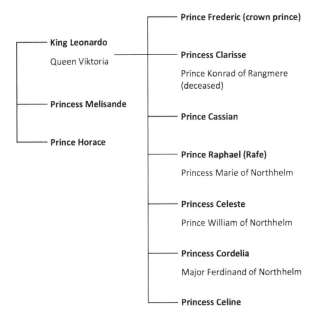

King Leonardo
Queen Viktoria

Prince Frederic (crown prince)

Princess Clarisse
Prince Konrad of Rangmere (deceased)

Prince Cassian

Princess Melisande

Prince Horace

Prince Raphael (Rafe)
Princess Marie of Northhelm

Princess Celeste
Prince William of Northhelm

Princess Cordelia
Major Ferdinand of Northhelm

Princess Celine

THE PALACE OF LIGHT

"*T*he trouble in Lanover grows closer by the minute."

The gray-haired woman twitched her wings and frowned at her companion. "Yes, indeed, and what of it?"

The first godmother, her hair more white than silver, shifted uncomfortably. "Are you sure your goddaughter is up to the challenge?"

"She never had a Christening. Officially, she isn't my goddaughter."

The white-haired one rolled her eyes. "Don't quibble. You know she's still your goddaughter. Although I'm sure she thinks everyone has abandoned her."

The gray-haired godmother put her hands on her hips. "I may not have rescued her outright, but you know why. You know we've been weaving the threads into place for this moment for decades. Don't tell me you've gotten cold feet now!"

"Not cold feet, exactly." The first sighed. "It's just that my charges—all seven of them—have been through a lot lately, and I hate to leave them unaided at such a moment."

The second godmother frowned. "And my goddaughter has been through a lifetime of troubles. A lifetime she's about to be

1

forced to revisit. Nothing about this is going to be easy for any of them. But they're not unaided because they have each other. Such challenges are not supposed to be easy. If they are to rule the kingdom someday, they must endure the difficulties before them and prove themselves worthy."

"Yes, you're right, of course." The white-haired one sighed again. "Only I do so enjoy helping to pave the way to true love."

The other shook her head. "If you find yourself so restless, why not pay a visit to Rangmere? I hear your widowed goddaughter there is on the painful path to love. And then you won't be tempted to interfere where you should not."

The first smiled. "Perhaps you are right. An excursion will be a great deal better than all this waiting."

The gray-haired woman twitched her wings again, observing the empty space where her companion had stood a moment before. Now that she was alone, her face lost some of its earlier assurance. "I do hope I haven't misplaced my confidence in the girl," she muttered to herself. "Or else a great many things will be lost that should not be, and it may take us generations to get things back on track."

PART I
THE CAPITAL AND THE ISLANDS

CHAPTER 1

I didn't need the tinkling of the bell above the door to tell me someone had entered my shop. For all she was only fifteen, Princess Celine knew how to make an entrance. I hurried to put down my work and greet her while my mind rushed to deal with the problem presented by her presence.

"Your Highness." I dipped into a curtsy, but the princess didn't seem to notice. She was examining a bolt of my newest acquisition—a deep midnight blue shot silk. It was certainly an impressive material, and a number of other seamstresses had already tried to prize its source from me.

Abruptly, Celine spun around. "I have a project for you. Your biggest yet." The excitement on her face made my heart sink even further.

Celine had surprising talent when it came to dress design. If she hadn't been royalty, I would have invited her to join me as a partner—her instinctive grasp of fashion would have made up for any lack of skill with a needle. As it was, her suggestions had sparked some of my most brilliant creations.

But I had received a visit the week before from no less a personage than Her Majesty Queen Viktoria herself. She had

5

been flatteringly full of praises for my work, but I was fairly certain her commission for a ball gown had been intended to soften the blow of her true purpose. Because I had also been given extremely strict parameters to follow for any future designs made for the queen's youngest daughter. It was such a pity, the queen had said, that I kept creating such masterpieces that no one ever got to see.

I had winced at her words and rushed to assure her of my compliance. In fact, I agreed with her, even without the weight of a royal command. My excitement at our shared efforts had led me to create gowns for Celine that were—strictly speaking—too old for the young princess. One or two of them I had expected to create fashion trends and had been surprised not to receive a deluge of copycat orders. Now I knew why.

I had made a name and a living for myself through great effort and toil. I had dragged myself from the muck without assistance from those who might have been expected to help me, and I had no great inclination to take orders from anyone. But I would not disobey the queen. I needed to stay on the good side of the royal family—their patronage had established me here in the capital. And I wanted my best designs to go to someone who would be permitted to actually wear them. But that still left me with the problem of the youngest princess.

Celine spun around in a giddy circle, running her hand along several bolts of soft material. "I can't wait to tell you. You're going to be so excited. It's a challenge worthy of your skill."

I frowned. I hated to disappoint her because the young princess was one of the few people who had given me reason to be grateful. She was the one who had discovered my small, newly-established shop just over a year ago, and she had always treated me affectionately despite the difference in our ranks. Without her, I might still be struggling to gain noble clients. Without her, I would certainly never have received the commission for her older sister's bridal and attendant gowns the previous summer. And since Princess Celeste was every seam-stress's dream—a girl who would look stunning in absolutely anything—I had been flooded with orders ever since her wedding.

I considered my words carefully.

Before I could speak, however, the bell tinkled again, and a different kind of figure strode into my shop. Tall, broad-shoul-dered, and with a palpable air of authority, the young man was a far cry from my usual customer. I immediately sank into another, deeper curtsy to cover my confusion at his appearance.

I looked up again just in time to see Princess Celine roll her eyes. "What are you doing here, Frederic?" She put her hands on her hips and glared at her oldest brother. "I'm busy conducting business with Mistress Evangeline."

"Mistress Evangeline?" Although he said my name, Prince Frederic's eyes regarded his sister in surprise. "Since when are you so respectful? I'd expect to hear you calling her Evie or something."

I blinked at the sound of my nickname on his lips, my surprise overwhelming my amusement at the truth of his words. She did usually call me Evie.

Celine drew herself up to her full height and looked loftily at her brother. "I treat everyone with respect."

He chuckled darkly. "My dear Celine, you don't know the meaning of respect."

I dropped my head to hide a smile since I wasn't sure the prince had meant to be humorous.

He turned to me and gave an inclination of his head. "I apolo-gize for my younger sister, Mistress Evangeline."

Celine looked as if she were about to explode at this, but I quickly dipped into a shallow curtsy in response, hoping to head off any further conflict.

I tried to remind myself that an exalted position said nothing of the person within, and that my position in the capital was assured by my own skill, not by royal patronage—however much that patronage advantaged me. There was no reason for me to be intimidated by the crown prince. And yet intimidated I must be, since I could come up with no other reason for my heart to be beating a great deal faster than its normal rate.

The prince turned back to his sister. "You're supposed to be preparing for our departure."

"I am!" She narrowed her eyes and dramatically shook her head. "Which is the biggest of the Four Kingdoms, Frederic?"

He eyed her warily, sighing when she raised her eyebrows at him. "Lanover, of course."

"And which of the kingdoms is the most diverse?"

He sighed again. "Celine."

She put her hands back on her hips. "Well?"

"Lanover." He drew the word out slowly, clearly cautious of whatever trap his sister was trying to set for him with the obvious questions.

"Exactly!" She threw up her hands. "Unlike the other kingdoms, we have many different sub-cultures here. Tell me Frederic, what are the latest fashions worn on the islands?" She didn't wait for him to respond, and he showed no desire to do so. "What about in southern Largo? Or among the jungle dwellers? What about the nomadic desert traders?"

When he still said nothing, she gave a decisive nod. "Precisely!"

My eyes lingered on the prince's handsome face. He looked almost as confused as I felt. If the princess thought she had proved her point, she was sorely mistaken.

Celine turned to me. "Men."

I had to suppress another smile at her world-weary tone.

"I'm sure, if left to his own devices," she continued, "my brother would simply pull on the first clothing to come to hand each day. Hardly befitting the crown prince of the most fashionable kingdom in the land! Which is why it's such a good thing his sisters have always taken responsibility for his wardrobe. Only now that all the rest are married and gone, I'm the only one left. And the high and mighty Frederic doesn't like to admit that his baby sister knows more about some things than he does."

"Really, Celine. Please." Frederic cast an uncomfortable glance in my direction. I tried to maintain the blankest expression possible. Coming between squabbling siblings was always a bad idea, let alone when royalty were involved.

"Oh, don't mind Evie," said Celine. "She's my friend. And if you want this Royal Tour you've got planned to be a true success, then we need her. Because you're not going to remind all our different communities of the might and glory of the crown if we show up looking out of fashion and dowdy. And never mind impressing them enough to put an end to these rumors of a new rebellion."

"Celine!" Now Frederic sounded both shocked and angry.

His sister remained unaffected. "Oh, come on. You can't think I don't know the true purpose of this Tour. I'm not an idiot. And I already told you. We need her. And it's in our interest for her to understand how important this Tour and her role is. You put me in charge of the royal wardrobes for the Tour, and I'm here to beg her to close up shop for the season and come with us. Because we're going to need someone who can assess local fashions and ensure we're the most impressively dressed everywhere we go." She stared her brother down. "And that's no easy feat. Do you know any other seamstress up to the task?"

From the hopeless look on Prince Frederic's face, I doubted he could name any other seamstresses at all. He had probably only given Celine the role of wardrobe mistress to placate her, but despite her earlier accusations, he now looked ready to accede to her points. In fact, he looked quite struck by them.

"So, what do you say, Evie?" Celine turned to me eagerly. "Will you come with us? I know it's a lot to ask. We leave in only a week."

A week! I gulped. I had heard some talk in the capital about the crown prince's Royal Tour of the kingdom, but I hadn't realized Princess Celine was going too. And I hadn't expected it to affect me much, other than perhaps creating a quieter season given the absence of some of the royalty and nobility. It was a break I had welcomed after the hectic pace of the last year.

But now the princess was asking me to finish all my current commissions in the space of a single week so that I could then embark on an even bigger challenge. And she was asking me to leave the capital just when I had finally established myself here.

But this could be your chance, whispered an internal voice. *Your chance to prove your worth once and for all. If you succeed at this, no one could ever question if you deserve your place again.*

I bit my lip as I looked between the two royals. Celine was watching me with hope-filled eyes, Frederic with curiosity. Something about his expression roused a defiant determination in me. I could do this. I would do this.

"I am honored to serve the crown in any way I can."

The shadow of surprise in the prince's expression filled me with satisfaction. I would show him what I was capable of—him and everyone else.

"We are the ones who are honored, Mistress Evangeline." Something about the prince's grave voice inspired my imp of mischief. No wonder Celine couldn't resist teasing her oldest brother—his serious demeanor was almost irresistible.

"Oh, come, Your Highness," I said. "Surely you're not going to pretend familiarity with my designs. I suspect you didn't even know my name before your sister used it."

Frederic froze, and Celine giggled.

"Thank goodness you're coming, Evie," she said. "Frederic's picked all the oldest, most stodgy courtiers to accompany us. Every single one regards me with horrified judgment, I assure you."

"Celine," said Frederic stiffly. "You shouldn't speak of them that way. They are loyal supporters of the crown."

She sighed. "Of course they are. But they're also hideously boring." She shuddered comically, her eyes twinkling. "Which means I would have been entirely stuck with you and Cassian for the whole Tour."

Dawning horror spread across Frederic's face, and he gave me a half bow. "On behalf of myself and my brother, I must thank you again Mistress Evangeline. It seems we have many reasons to be grateful to you."

Celine winked at me behind his back, and I gave a small chuckle, looking up through my lashes at the tall prince. "Please, call me Evie, you might find it easier to remember."

He looked down at me, an arrested expression on his face. After a pause, he said, "Very well, Mistress Evie. Please report to the palace in six days' time. We appreciate your assistance."

He stepped back and grasped his sister's arm, attempting to drag her from my shop. She caught at the door frame and looked back at me. "I'll come past tomorrow to talk some more and arrange a time for you to inspect our current wardrobes."

I nodded, but the prince had tugged her away before I could actually speak.

I sank down into a convenient chair, my knees a little wobbly. Had I really just flirted with the crown prince?

Well, why not? asked that same inner voice. *He's a person, just like anyone else.* Only this time my internal dialogue sounded far too mischievous.

I had long ago decided that pain was best pushed from my mind—life was easier if viewed light-heartedly. But that didn't mean it was a good idea for me to offend the most powerful family in the kingdom.

But the thought of my past pushed a far more gripping concern to the front of my mind. I was about to have a great deal more to worry about than a prince who seemed as serious as he was handsome. More important even than preserving my secret source of extraordinary fabric and ensuring no gown I created contained any poor stitching. Because I had just agreed to a full tour of Lanover.

Which meant the royal family—my most important clients—were about to find out exactly what had driven me to the capital the previous year. How long would it be before even Celine regretted befriending a commoner who she knew almost nothing about?

CHAPTER 2

*S*ix days later, I entered the royal palace with some trepidation. A servant had already disappeared with my mountains of luggage, and I had no sooner watched him go than I had begun second-guessing how much I had packed. I had some experience of the fashions that dominated in the various parts of the kingdom, but fashions could change quickly, and I wanted to be prepared. I grimaced. Even so, I had probably brought an excess of fabric. Hopefully I wouldn't receive a reprimand from the steward who was overseeing all the practical arrangements for the Tour.

"Evie!" Celine almost tripped down the stairs in her haste to reach me. "You've arrived. Oh, thank goodness! I need you to talk some sense into Frederic."

She grabbed my arm and towed me back up the stairs. "He has the most ridiculous notions. And our first couple of stops are going to be near the capital. I need you to convince him that his current outfit just will not do."

I breathed an internal sigh of relief to hear we would be starting with the towns directly south of the capital city, Lanare. I had passed through several of them briefly on my way to the capital, but no one there would know me. My relief turned to panic, however, when I recognized where she was taking me. Celine had given me a tour of the palace when I had visited earlier in the week, and we were now in the wing containing the royal suites. I pulled back against her.

"Your Highness!" I whispered. "I can't go into the prince's bedchamber."

She threw me an impatient look. "We aren't going into his bedchamber, just his dressing room. And you're going to have to get used to it, Evie. You'll be dressing all of us on this trip."

I stopped resisting and gave a low chuckle. "Not actually *dressing*, I hope."

Celine giggled. "You know what I mean. Frederic takes his responsibilities seriously. We just have to convince him that dressing well is serious royal business."

She flung open a door, and a quiet voice I didn't recognize floated out, making her pause. "We should be heading straight south all the way to Largo. Or the Great Desert, at least. That's where these rumors are coming from, not from the nearby towns or the islands."

"I want to tackle the threat head-on as well, Cass, you know that," said Frederic, identifying the other speaker as the second Lanoverian prince, Cassian. "But you also know that Father is sending us on this Tour for a variety of reasons, and we can't leave out any of the regions."

"Yes." Cassian sounded dejected. "Apparently we can't hope to have you accepted as king one day unless you've been paraded in front of each and every one of our citizens like a performing monkey."

"Oh, not just me, brother," said Frederic. "They all need to eyeball their future Royal Chief Advisor as well. Naturally. It's why I assured Father you needed to be included."

I blinked. Was Frederic making a joke? Teasing his brother? It was hard to tell when he always sounded so serious.

"So why did you ask for Celine to be included, then?" asked Cassian dryly. "Don't tell me she's going to be your Second Advisor one day."

Celine, who had been listening with interest and without shame, made a face and bustled me through an opulent sitting room and into the connected dressing room.

"Oh, don't be ridiculous, Cassian," she said breezily. "There isn't enough gold in even Lanover's treasuries to pay me to do a job like that. I'm heading off for adventures just as soon as Mother decides I'm no longer a child. But for now, I'm the Tour's Wardrobe Mistress. And this is my seamstress."

She pushed me forward, and I dipped into a curtsy.

"Mistress Evangeline," said Frederic with a respectful inclination of his head.

Cassian regarded me curiously while Celine dismissed Frederic's words with a wave of her hand.

"This trip is going to require a lot of different garments," she said. "Evie and I are going to have to work superhumanly fast to continually prepare and adjust all of our outfits."

"By which I assume you mean she's going to be working hard?" Cassian's dry voice didn't hide his amusement.

She put her nose in the air and ignored him. "We'll all be seeing a lot of each other for fittings and such things. So you might as well dispense with ceremony now. Her name is Evie."

Frederic regarded his sister silently and then turned to me. "How do you feel about that?"

I shrugged uncomfortably, although I was touched by his consideration. "Evie is fine, Your Highness."

"That goes for you, too, Evie," said Celine. "It's going to get horribly confusing otherwise, what with us all being Your Highnesses."

"But, Your Highness..." My voice trailed away.

"Exactly!" she said triumphantly and then glared at both of her brothers as if daring them to protest.

Neither prince appeared in the least perturbed by her dismissal of formality.

"Well, that's that, I suppose," said Cassian. "Welcome to our inner circle, Evie. If you haven't learned it by now, you'll soon discover that Celine is a force to be reckoned with. Once she has an idea in her head, there's no getting it out."

I blinked several times. I knew Lanoverian culture was far more relaxed than the other kingdoms, but I still wasn't at all sure about a seamstress being included in any sort of royal inner circle. Surely they were joking and would expect proper respect when I next crossed their paths.

But when I glanced at Frederic, I found him watching me with a relaxed expression on his face. I had to admit that nothing about him gave me the impression he was the sort of flighty person who frequently changed his mind or forgot what he had said the previous day. Or even the previous month.

And yet, I couldn't shake the feeling of discomfort. The Lanoverian princes and princesses didn't really have an inner circle of friends. I knew that much at least from the noble girls who visited my shop and often gossiped as they chose their fabrics, oblivious to my presence. The younger royals were friendly with everyone at court, but with seven of them, they had always relied on each other for their closest companionship. Except now Prince Rafe and Princesses Clarisse, Celeste, and Cordelia had all married foreigners and moved to other kingdoms. The oldest princes, Frederic and Cassian, and the youngest princess, Celine, were the only ones left.

I supposed the departure of all her sisters might explain why Celine was looking to her seamstress for friendship. Unaware of my inner qualms, Celine grabbed my arm and pointed accusingly at her brothers. "You can see the problem, Evie."

"Celine," said Cassian patiently. "You know that we'll be riding for the first part of the Tour. We have to wear practical clothes."

"No one needs to wear clothes that practical," Celine muttered to me.

I bit my lip on a laugh.

"You know how close the nearby towns are to both the capital and each other," Celine told her brother in a louder voice. "It's a parade as much as a ride, so you need to look appropriately princely. We wouldn't want anyone to think the royal treasury is starting to run dry."

Cassian opened his mouth and then closed it again, an arrested look in his eyes.

Frederic threw his brother an amused glance. "Sometimes it's hard to remember she's not ten anymore. She's actually been making some good points lately."

Celine scrunched up her face. "Older brothers."

I stepped in as diplomatically as possible. "The Tour doesn't leave until tomorrow morning. If I get started now, I can modify one of your current outfits to be both comfortable and fashionable if you like."

"Would you?"

Frederic's surprise made me chuckle. "That *is* why you're bringing me along, remember."

"Don't worry, she's a genius with a needle," said Celine.

I smiled at them all, but it faltered a little. *No pressure*, I thought to myself. Needlework was something that had always come easily to me, and I had worked hard over the years to cultivate and extend my skill. But her words still made me nervous, and I appreciated the reminder not to get too comfortable with these strange royals. They might have chosen to adopt me, like a pet or a mascot for their trip, but they would change their minds.

Everyone always did.

I tossed uncomfortably in my bed, gripped by a dream that

followed all too closely with my true memories, despite the years that had passed. I had dreamed thus every night since my foolish agreement to accompany the Tour. Lanover held too many places I didn't care to revisit. Too many places from my past.

This night was one of my more unusual dreams. I huddled in a small woodshed trying to block out the sound of the other children hammering on the thin boards that made up the walls and calling taunts. I clenched my hands into fists, determined not to let the tears fall. If only I were bigger, or stronger, or not alone. Then I wouldn't be hiding in here in fear. But I was alone. And in here was safer than out there. At least until one of them grew bold enough to knock down the door and face their mother's wrath over the destruction.

The dream veered suddenly away from reality as a flicker of heat touched my side a moment before bright flames consumed the wall of the shed. I gasped and scrambled away from them. The knocking grew louder and more frantic until I awoke with a jerk to stare stupidly around an unfamiliar room. A second later memory returned, and I slid out of my bed in one of the guest rooms in the palace's servants' wing. Flinging open the door, I had to half-catch a serving maid who almost toppled inside. The young girl looked half-terrified, half-thrilled, and the candle in her hand told me my mind hadn't deceived me—morning hadn't yet broken.

"What is it?" I asked. "What's wrong?" I had been up late working on an outfit for each of the princes, and my mind felt sluggish.

"The Tour is leaving at once. It's one of the towns. Tolon. Or possibly Medellan. I can't remember now. But everyone is gathering in the gardens in front of the palace. The steward nearly forgot about you, so you'll have to run or be left behind."

Her final sentence killed the questions hovering on my tongue. I almost slammed the door in her face as I scrambled back into the room, nearly tripping as I threw myself into my clothes. I was thankful now that I had taken the time the night before, despite my fatigue at the late hour, to deliver the princes' outfits to the appropriate places and lay out my own garments.

My personal bag took only a moment to assemble, and then I was racing through the corridors. I burst out into the pre-dawn night in time to see the princes ride out at the head of two columns of riders. The ground in front of the palace, lit by countless lanterns, churned with wagons and carriages. Despite the beginning of the train already departing, chaos still reigned at the back. I looked around frantically until I heard a voice call, "Evie!"

I turned to find Celine riding toward me. "There you are! The steward almost forgot you, the idiot. Can you ride? I hope so, since I've ordered them to saddle a horse."

I nodded, still catching my breath, as the princess beckoned a groom forward. Celine, obviously unsure of my riding skills, had selected a placid-looking mare, and the groom threw me up into the saddle before I had time to gather my thoughts. A moment later, I was trotting out the gate beside the princess.

Everything had happened so fast that our procession had made it half-way through the dark, quiet city before it sank in that I was leaving the capital. The strength of the pang I felt at my departure surprised me. Lanare had been a refuge for me where I had found—if not friends—at least success and security with my dressmaking shop.

I tried to comfort myself that I would be back soon enough—the Tour was scheduled to last months, not years. But my mind couldn't force my emotions to believe it. I had plenty of experience at leaving homes, but I had never returned to one.

When I had arrived in Lanare, my expectations had been low. But I had surprised myself by how much I enjoyed life in the sprawling capital. The air here didn't have the same suffocating heaviness that it did down south in the jungles, but it still carried enough moisture to prevent the burning dryness of the Great Desert that ran the length of eastern Lanover. And while it didn't have the beauty of Largo, or the turquoise seas and pristine sands of the western isles, it had a beauty all its own. I had become accustomed to the reddish sandstone of the buildings. And the bright flowers and greenery that still burst forth wherever they could find root reminded me of the jungle without over-whelming the buildings with their presence.

Even the palace was constructed of the same sandstone, a single-story building without even a wall to protect it like those apparently surrounding the palaces of the northern kingdoms. Instead it was placed on a large hill, encircled with living gardens instead of stone, the views encompassing the entire city. And, best of all, commoners making deliveries to the palace were permitted to wander around the gardens at will. I had often delivered my royal commissions myself just so I could spend an hour soaking up the view and the colors on my way out.

But despite the unexpected emotion, my thoughts could not linger long on Lanare. Not when I had still received no proper explanation of our rushed, early morning departure. The maid had mentioned Tolon and Medellan, two of the towns directly south of the capital, but I had no idea how either of them could precipitate this unexpected haste.

I was considering the question when Celine, who had ridden up the line to talk to her brothers, returned to position her horse beside mine.

"I'm so glad you can ride, Evie. Just think how awful it would be to be cooped up forever in one of those carriages with all the fusty old nobles." She wrinkled her nose and shuddered at the thought.

"Your Highness…I mean, Princess…I mean…" I gave up on the correct address altogether. "What has happened? Why are we rushing?"

Celine stared at me. "Didn't anyone tell you?"

I shook my head, and she sighed. "Because you were forgot-ten, I suppose. You must have had to rush even worse than the rest of us." Her expression grew somber and still. "Medellan has burned."

I gasped. "How…how much of it?"

She turned saddened eyes to me. "All of it."

"All…" My voice trailed away as I considered the horror of it. I had passed through Medellan on my way to the capital. While it was considerably smaller than a regional center like Largo, it was one of the larger towns close to the capital, home to hundreds of people.

Questions ran through my mind, but it took me a moment to decide which to ask first.

"The people?" I asked eventually, voicing my primary concern.

"The messenger who reached us didn't know anything for certain." Celine swallowed audibly. "But he seemed to think the losses were minimal given the level of destruction. We don't understand what happened yet, or how a whole town could be lost. But they requested a large contingent of royal guard to assist them."

Her hands on the reins twitched. "With so many guards already committed to the Tour, Father and Cassian didn't want to leave the capital too depleted. Not after the attempted coup last year."

She looked down at her mount's head, her brow furrowed, and I remembered hearing rumors that she had been involved in foiling the despicable plot against her family. I had been newly arrived in the capital then and had heard only distant tales of the clean-up required to sweep out the traitorous members of the guard. City gossip said the royals were still rebuilding the guard numbers.

Celine looked up, recovering some of her natural bounce. "Frederic said there was no need to empty the capital or delay the Tour when we could simply leave immediately and begin our travels in Medellan. What better way to show ourselves to our people than by arriving with assistance in their hour of need?" She stilled slightly. "It was a good thought."

It was a good thought, and I admired the prince for it. Not all nobles, let alone royals, were so willing to get their hands dirty.

"Someone's supposed to come along with some food soon, something we can eat in the saddle," Celine added. "The main food wagons will be trailing some way behind us. They stayed back so the steward could organize the loading of extra supplies."

"Thank goodness it's spring," I muttered, and Celine nodded in agreement. We might never be besieged by snow every winter like two of her sisters in Northhelm, but it still got chilly at wintertime this far to the north of Lanover.

Our conversation was interrupted by a harassed looking rider with oat cakes, and we descended into silence as we munched.

CHAPTER 3

The smell of Medellan reached us long before the sight. The acrid odor of smoke mixed with smells so awful I didn't even want to consider their source. I had to fight to keep the long-gone oat cakes inside my stomach. I already dreamed of bright flames many nights; I feared now that my nighttime visions would start to include a smell so terrible it would wake me screaming.

When the road turned a slight corner and the town spread out before us, all thought of myself fled my mind. Medellan's sturdy wooden walls were largely gone, giving us a clear view into the wasteland inside. Piles of ash lay everywhere and floated fitfully through the air on the slight breeze. Here and there whole walls or chimneys still stood, streaked with soot, but I couldn't see a single intact building.

I swallowed twice and gripped my reins until my knuckles turned white. Celine, still beside me, gasped and then drew a deep steadying breath. I forced myself to survey the town, refusing to turn my eyes away. Bearing witness was the least I could do after what these people had been through and what still lay before them.

Collapsed buildings and blackened debris forced the many people moving through the town to tread slowly and carefully. Here and there a small spot of orange drew the eye, but with no fuel left to burn, these spots were small and far between. Most of the people seemed to be picking through the remains of the structures, but a few carried motionless burdens that brought tears to my eyes.

A large group of people, mostly consisting of the young and the elderly, gathered in a clearing outside what must once have been the gates. A row of figures lay on the ground along the line of what had been the wall, their faces covered with handkerchiefs or jackets. There weren't even any sheets left to cover their dead.

A cry went up from within the burned town and people converged around it. A man riding near the front of our columns spurred his horse forward until he reached the collapsed wall. Jumping down, he abandoned his mount to the youngsters there and sprinted into the ash.

"One of the royal doctors," murmured Celine. "He is accompanying the Tour in case of accident or illness."

By the time the main columns reached the edge of the town, he was overseeing several people who carefully carried a woman between them.

"She will live," one of them called wearily, and a sigh of relief blew through the gathered townsfolk. They looked as if any more bad news might knock them down. And, once down, they might never rise again.

I shook off the dark thoughts. No. These people were stronger than that. They had been knocked down by life, but they would rise from the ashes. Literally. I surveyed the town again, and some of my attempted optimism died. But I reminded myself that it had come true for me. All those times I had used the same line on myself, and now here I was, riding with royalty. If I could do it, the citizens of Medellan could do it, too.

Most of the older nobles in the carriages remained in place, but the riders swung down and made their way through the stunned townsfolk. Three wagons pulled up, and servants and guards alike began to dispense blankets and skins of water. I saw some of the remaining oat cakes being passed around and hoped the wagons of food would arrive soon. These people needed something more substantial than trail fare.

I stayed in my saddle, sure I would only be in the way on the ground, and watched the three royals drift through the crowds: comforting, reassuring, and pledging the support of the crown. Everywhere they went, hands reached to grasp theirs, muted thanks spoken softly or conveyed with a look. Many gazes lingered on Frederic, as did mine. The air of command I had first noticed in my shop was even more palpable here. His naturally serious demeanor fit the occasion, and the solid conviction of his tone brought reassurance to the people that their monarchs had not forgotten them. They would remember it when he was crowned, I would wager.

A bitter tone—softly spoken but hard and out of place with the rest of the scene—caught my attention, and I swung my horse around to find the source. A sizable group of townsfolk stood slightly apart from the rest. Some had blankets draped around their shoulders, and others carried oat cakes, but I saw no palace folk among them. I edged my horse closer and focused my attention on the man who spoke.

"Kind words are all very well," he said, his voice pitched just loud enough for this group to hear, "but where were the royals when our town burned? And where will they be tomorrow or in the months to come when winter returns? We pay our taxes, but for what?"

Some looked uncomfortable at his words, but many others nodded, the anger burning in their eyes. I knew that look. They were filled with grief and rage and despair, and they wanted somewhere more satisfying to direct it than the impartial, uncaring flames.

I looked back over my shoulder at the members of the Tour who still circulated among the other townsfolk, my eyes catching on Celine who held an infant in her arms, tears running down her cheeks. Without thinking it through, I pushed my mount forward into the middle of the angry group.

"Shame on you," I said, meeting as many eyes as I could. "Whose blankets are around your shoulders? Who gave you the food in your hands and mouths?"

Some looked away, unwilling to meet my gaze, before slinking off to rejoin the main group. Others looked away but stayed in place, and still others looked back at me defiantly.

"And who might you be, Mistress, who take such a fine interest in our affairs?" asked the original speaker, measuring me with a mocking look.

I ignored his question and continued to focus my attention on his audience. "How could the royals have stopped the flames, do you think? And tell me, if you hadn't paid those taxes, would that extra gold in your homes have held back the heat? Your houses have been gone mere hours, and already the royals are here in person to offer you help and promise you future support. If you are too grieved for gratitude, you can at least offer them your silence and cease this treasonous talk."

I gazed down at them from the extra height my horse gave me, pleased to see that the only one who would now meet my eyes nodded to let me know he accepted the truth of my words before disappearing back toward the town. One by one, or in groups of two or three, the others followed him, until only the speaker remained. He watched me with narrowed eyes for an extra moment and then disappeared into the crowd himself.

I sighed. I could not blame these people, fresh in grief as they were. But I did wish I had heard the speaker's name, at least. Celine had mentioned whispers of a new rebellion, and Cassian had believed them to be isolated to the south. Should I tell them what I had overheard? Or would they overreact and bring further grief to these people?

I considered the question as I finally dismounted at the request of the groom who had been assigned to care for my mount. As he led her away, I turned to wander through the people. Many of them wore nightclothes, and only half had shoes. As I walked, a thought came to me, and I directed my path toward the supply wagons that had been sent with us before dawn. Peeking into the one that had held the blankets, I smiled for the first time since I had smelled Medellan on the breeze.

I ran my hand along the inside, my fingers lingering on the contents, and then I hurried further down the line looking for the wagon that held the personal supplies of the Tour participants. There turned out to be several, but after some searching, I located the one that held my belongings. Rummaging through it, I produced a small bag, which I tucked under my arm.

Returning to the group of bereft townsfolk, I began to walk among them, my eyes assessing each of the older girls with special attention to their fingers. Whenever I spotted what I was looking for, I tapped the girl on the shoulder and directed her to follow me. Not one raised a protest, and I soon had a string of youngsters behind me. Many of the older women seemed occupied with the care of the children, but any that stood idle were added to my string. When I had counted out the precise number that I needed, I began to issue further directions.

～

"Oh, there you are, Evie..." Frederic stopped and regarded us with astonishment.

I had set my team up in a nook between several wagons where we would not be disturbed, and we had been hard at work for most of the day. I snipped a thread neatly and climbed to my feet.

"I'm sorry, Your Highness, were you looking for me?"

"Frederic, remember?" he said absently, his eyes still on my assistants. "What are you doing back here?" He paused. "Are those blankets?"

"Not anymore," I said proudly. Several of the younger girls smiled shyly at the prince, the haunted look in their eyes having abated somewhat now that they had a way to be useful.

"The sewing is rough, I'm afraid, but the wool is good quality, and the clothes will be hardy. I just hope the good people of Medellan like gray."

Several of the older girls scrunched up their noses, but the elders shook their heads. "It will wear well," one of them said, "and that's what's important. We've plenty of hard work ahead of us before we'll have use of party finery."

The girls ducked their heads as if cowed, but I noticed several of them exchanging wry smiles. Frederic drew me away from the others.

"I just wish I'd brought more needles," I said as I followed him. "But it never occurred to me that I would have need of so many. Thankfully most town girls are taught at least some proficiency, and the fingers of the most experienced always give them away. I —" I stopped abruptly and looked up at Frederic, a sudden worry filling my mind. "I checked with the steward, Your Highness, and he said all the blankets were for the use of the townsfolk. The guards had already handed them out to anyone who wanted one, and with the weather so mild at the moment, I figured they had more use for clothes than…"

"It's Frederic," he said, halting my flow of words. "And you are perfectly in the right." He frowned. "I just wish we had such a simple way to produce shoes for them all. I don't see how they are to clear the ground of debris and raise new buildings bare foot." He shook his head and looked down at me. "But none of that is your problem. You are already doing far more than I could have hoped for and proving once again that my little

28

sister is right. Not yet a full day, and you are showing your value."

I flushed and dropped my eyes away from his face. They fastened instead on his shoulders and chest, and I almost smiled at how well his clothes fit his broad frame. Their line looked regal and elegant but had obviously stood up to a day of harder work than any of us had anticipated. My night's labor had been well worth it.

I frowned at the new soot stains and hoped the Tour's washerwomen could get them out.

"Evie," he said, and I looked back up, reminded he had come looking for me.

"Oh, I'm sorry," I said, dismayed that I had been neglecting my primary duty. "Did you need me for your own clothes? I hadn't even thought, but you can hardly wear that again tomorrow."

"Stop," he said firmly, holding my gaze with his. "I don't need fashionable garments for breaking down fire damaged walls or caring for those with smoke sickness. I can wear one of my old outfits tomorrow."

He shook his head. "I came looking for you to ask if you could discuss ideas with the town mayor's wife for replacing some of the burned clothing. And here I find you're already halfway toward solving the problem yourself."

I rolled my eyes. "Thank you, but you're being far too complimentary. Even with so many assistants and keeping the clothes as simple as possible, we're far from clothing half of the townsfolk."

"Some managed to grab a few items on their way out, and most who managed to do so have agreed to share with their less fortunate neighbors."

I raised my eyebrows. Some hadn't agreed? I almost felt sorry for them. I had lived in enough communities to know that some things were universal. Anyone who refused to share in such a situation was likely to find their position within the group in peril.

"Yes," said Frederic wryly, apparently reading the unspoken thought on my face, "perhaps they'll change their minds in time. For now, will your assistants be all right without you? I would appreciate it if you could come and talk to the mayor's wife, anyway. She will be able to help you best distribute your new creations."

I nodded and, after a few words to my team, followed him. My legs welcomed the stretch after spending so long hunched over cloth, and the sight in front of me told me how many hours had passed while I worked. The confused mass of people had disappeared to be replaced by a semblance of industry and order. A small city of tents had sprung up in the fields around the town, and several large fires wafted delicious smells around this new camp. My nose turned toward one of them, my stomach growling in response, and Frederic immediately waved down a passing servant.

"Have someone deliver warm meals to the workers sewing behind that wagon," he directed, pointing back toward my assistants. "And then have someone deliver a plate to Mistress Evangeline."

"Certainly, Your Highness," said the servant with a bobbed curtsy before disappearing.

We resumed walking while I observed the prince out of the corner of my eye. He took his responsibilities seriously, and I admired that in him. I could not fault his treatment of me in even the smallest way. And his somber air befitted this situation. I just wished I had heard him laugh. Not now, of course, but previously. He didn't look like the sort of person who spent enough time laughing, a strange thing for someone who had spent most of their life with the dramatic Celine.

My contemplation was interrupted by our arrival at the tent of the mayor and his wife, and Frederic took his leave as soon as he had handed me over. The mayor's wife was unexpectedly young and pretty, but any reservations about her fitness for such a role soon disappeared. She seemed wise beyond her years, and her energy would be needed for the long road ahead.

Between us we had soon dispersed all of the clothes already crafted and allocated as many again from our anticipated next day's work. I dismissed my team to a well-deserved rest and was just wondering where I would be sleeping when I noticed a small figure following me.

I stopped and turned, placing my hands on my hips and raising one eyebrow. "And what are you wanting, young master?"

The short lad grinned at me. "I'm no master, and I reckon you know that. I been watching you, and you seem a knowing one."

His face looked familiar, and after a moment I placed him from his clothing. He had been the recipient of one of the outfits we had made, and he had sorely needed it, though his original garments had appeared to be clothes—of a sort—rather than a nightshirt. My estimation of the mayor's wife had risen when she used the opportunity to re-clothe an obvious street urchin.

"I never had new clothes before."

I smiled. "I'm only sorry I didn't have the time to fit them properly for you."

"Naw." He smiled charmingly. "Fitted clothes aren't for the likes of me."

"Don't be ridiculous. Everyone deserves at least one set of new, well-fitted clothes." It was this belief that had first driven me to pick up a needle at a young age. Without my own efforts, I would likely never have had clothes that fit.

The boy shook his head. "You have some funny ideas, miss, but you seem like one of the right sort."

"The right sort?" I shifted uncomfortably. What exactly had he seen while he was watching me?

He rocked back and forth on his heels as if gathering his courage. "I heard what you said to them people before."

"Which people?"

"The ones who were complaining. When you lot first arrived."

Those people. My eyes narrowed. If that was what he meant, perhaps he hadn't seen what I feared.

"And I saw you earlier with the prince. He gave me an oat cake with his own hand." He shook his head again. "Well, it seemed to me that you grand folk might be interested in what I saw."

Grand folk. If that was what he thought of me, I was surprised he had come to me at all. He shifted on his feet, watching me with wary eyes, and I wondered if he intended to bolt without sharing his information with me after all. I bit my lip. If he had approached me, it must be important. More important than my desire to keep my past to myself.

"I like to walk the streets at night," he said in response to my look of inquiry. A defensive edge entered his voice. "It's safest to be on the move, plus I like the quiet."

He paused, apparently reconsidering continuing. I drew a deep breath and crossed both arms across my chest, fists clenched. "Ain't that the truth."

His eyes widened, and a slow grin spread across his face as he returned the universal street urchin salute. "I knew you were a right one! Wouldn't have picked you for one of us, though."

"I'm not," I said quickly. "Not exactly, anyway."

"But you once were." It wasn't a question.

I shook my head. "Not exactly."

He grinned again and shook his head. "Full-sizers. You can never give a straight answer when you could give a round about one instead."

I rolled my eyes, but offered no further clarification, unwilling to go into my full past with this stranger. "So tell me, what did you see?"

He frowned. "Normally my nighttime walks be real peaceful like. It wasn't peaceful last night, though. Not once someone started ringing the fire alarm bell. Really going at it, he was. He rang the tempo to get the whole town up. For a raging fire out of control. Which was a funny thing."

He paused again, so I prompted him. "Funny how? It was a raging fire, sure enough."

"Aye, but not at that point it weren't. I hadn't even smelled any smoke yet. Not a whiff in all my strolls. Nor seen no flames neither. But the people started pouring out the doors, of course, and it must have been seconds later and the whole place was ablaze. Every building in the town."

He shifted on his feet. "And it seemed to me that maybe no one got a real good look at whoever it was rang the bell. They were all too busy running for their lives at that point. 'Cept for me." He chuckled darkly. "I ran for my life, too, o'course. But I was just around the corner when the bell started, and I took off sprinting toward it, I can tell you. I got a good look at the man. Hadn't seen him before which struck me as odd. But I seen him since. He was the man you stared down earlier. And a right good job you did, too, miss."

I blinked several times, struggling to get my head around his revelations. Had he just suggested the fire had been planned in some way?

"This sounds too big for you or me," I said. "Would you come talk to the prince? Tell him your story?"

The boy shook his head and began backing away into the crowd of tents. "Talking to royalty? Surely you know better'n that. Urchins don't stay out of trouble by mixing with royalty."

I tried to protest, but he had disappeared behind a stretch of canvas.

I had almost forgotten the treasonous talk from the morning while I was busy sewing. But it seemed my dilemma had been solved for me. I couldn't keep what I had heard from the royals now.

CHAPTER 4

*N*ight had fallen, however, and despite their assurances of friendship, I couldn't imagine what would happen if I tried to gain entry to any of the royal tents in the dark. My news would have to wait for the morning. After my almost nonexistent sleep the night before followed by a full day's work, I could barely keep my eyes open to track down the steward. I eventually found one of his assistants and learned that I had actually been remembered this time. My assigned cot was in a shared tent with several other young women, and I collapsed gratefully onto the bed that someone had kindly assembled for me.

I didn't even stay awake long enough to worry that I might have nightmares and call out in my sleep, disturbing the other inhabitants of the tent. And, indeed, I turned out to be so tired that I slept without stirring until the rising sun woke me in the morning. The other women had already departed, their cots left neat and tidy, so I did my best to straighten up my appearance and follow them. Someone had delivered my personal bag to the tent at some point which made the task a great deal easier.

I joined a line for porridge and ate quietly, standing among a group of strangers. As soon as I had scraped the last morsel from the bowl, I went back to my work site of the day before. Most of my assistants had already assembled and begun work, and I greeted them with a pleased smile. Most called back greetings of their own, though no one spoke of a good morning. How many days or weeks would it be before one of them forgot for long enough to issue the traditional salutation?

Once I had seen they had no need of me, I reluctantly turned my steps in the direction of the royal tents, easily recognizable from the flags that flew above them. I would have much preferred to spend the time sewing, but I couldn't put off delivering my intelligence any longer. I wasn't sure how much good it would do, when I didn't even know the name of the man in question. But I only had to picture Frederic's face to know he would want all the information he could get.

Thankfully I found both princes outside their tent, saving me from the task of convincing the guard at the entrance to let me through.

"Evie," said Frederic, a small movement almost like a smile touching his mouth. I bobbed a quick curtsy.

"My brother has told me of your excellent work," said Cassian. "We thank you."

"You are the ones who brought me here and who pay both my wage and the cost of the blankets, so the thanks are truly owed to you."

"A gracious thought," said Cassian with an inclination of his head.

I took a deep breath. "But I haven't come to discuss clothes, I'm afraid. I have something rather unpleasant to impart."

Frederic's eyebrows lowered as he examined my face. "In private, perhaps?"

I nodded reluctantly. It didn't seem like the kind of conversation to have where anyone might overhear.

"What's that?" A bright young voice spoke from just behind me before Celine popped into view. "A private conversation? My favorite kind!" She smiled sweetly at her brothers. "You weren't planning to leave me out, were you?"

Frederic weighed her with his eyes. "No, indeed," he said at last. "I suppose you had better join us."

Celine smiled with satisfaction and led the way into the tent shared by the two princes. Cassian followed while I hung back, ready to enter last. But Frederic held the flap open for me with a courtly gesture, so I gave him a small smile and entered the structure.

"You know, I'm surprised the Duchess of Sessily isn't with us," Celine was saying to Cassian. "It's almost as if Father thinks we're safe to be let out without our minders."

Frederic, coming in behind me, raised his eyebrows. "Somehow I don't think it was you he felt didn't need a minder."

She glared at him and then sighed. "No, I suppose you're right."

I knew the duchess's name, although I had never seen her in person. She was almost as well known in Lanover as the king, her shrewd negotiations often turning treaties in our favor. I had also wondered if she might be sent along on the Tour. Perhaps Celine was right, and King Leonardo intended to test the abilities of his children. Of course, that didn't mean none of the old guard were included. We dragged a bevy of older nobles with us since their ties throughout the kingdom would be of value to the young royals.

"Still," said Celine, brightening, "we'll have more fun without her one way or another."

"Is fun all you think of, Celine?" asked Cassian, with a significant look toward the tent flap.

"No, of course not," she said quickly. "This whole situation couldn't be more awful." Her face fell into such a woebegone expression that I wanted to go over and put my arm around her shoulders. But I didn't quite dare. I hadn't forgotten the sight of her the day before weeping over the infant, and I hoped her brothers understood that she joked and made light of things so she wouldn't cry. It was a strategy I had used many times myself.

Frederic ignored his siblings, focusing instead on me. "What is it you wanted to tell us, Evie?"

Three pairs of royal eyes trained on me, and I gulped.

"It's something I overheard yesterday. And then something one of the townsfolk told me." I quickly relayed the way the unknown man had attempted to rile the crowd—downplaying my own involvement—and then repeated the story shared by the street urchin.

"What?" gasped Celine. "You mean…"

Cassian ran a hand over his chin, his eyes hooded and thoughtful.

Frederic rocked back, his face paling a shade. "Could you point out the man in a crowd, do you think?"

"I…" I chewed the inside of my cheek, wanting to say yes but not sure in all honesty if I could. A lot had happened the day before, and I had been running on very little sleep. "I don't know. Maybe?"

"I think we need to talk to this boy," said Cassian. "Not that I don't trust your recounting, Evie, but I would like to assess his character for myself. Did he look the type to make up such a story just for mischief?"

Here I felt myself on surer ground. "No. I didn't get that impression at all. He seemed grateful for the assistance you brought. I think he wanted to repay you the only way he could." I took a breath. "I believe him to be a street urchin, Your Highnesses. He probably isn't used to gifts of clothes or food. And they have a strict honor code, for all it differs from that of an ordinary citizen. If they incur a debt, they will balance it, as well as they are able."

"Hmmm…" Cassian looked skeptical, but Frederic weighed me with an all-too-knowing look. My eyes fell away as I fought to keep a flush from rising up my face. I reminded myself that he knew nothing of my past.

"But…what does it mean?" asked Celine, seemingly less concerned about the source of the information. "Ringing the alarm bell early doesn't seem like the work of an arsonist."

"An entire town burned," said Frederic. "And if it happened at the speed this boy claimed—a story that aligns with other comments I have heard about the fire—then it must have been the work of a large team of arsonists, all standing ready to act in unison."

Cassian met his brother's eyes. "A team who wanted the town to burn, not the townsfolk."

"Could the bell-ringer have been a rogue arsonist?" asked Celine. "One who had a last-minute change of heart?"

I frowned. "He didn't exactly seem the type for that when he was riling the townsfolk to anger."

"Dead people cannot be whipped into a fury against the crown," said Frederic softly. "And they cannot spread out looking for new homes in other towns, taking their anger and hatred with them."

"Perhaps they bargained on Father not sending help," suggested Cassian. "Perhaps they thought we would continue with the Tour and send only a small contingent here."

"If so, they bet wrongly," said Frederic, steel in his voice. "Which shows they don't know us at all." He rubbed a hand across his eyes. "I didn't expect it to start so early. All the other talk came from the south…"

"It seems Father has some wiles left in his old mind, after all," said Cassian wryly. "Apparently no part of the kingdom is safe."

"No." Frederic sighed. "For all the assistance we have offered here, if the Tour is trailed by disaster, it won't help our standing in the kingdom."

Celine hopped up from her seat. "We'll just have to be on the alert, then, and make sure no more danger finds our people."

Cassian and Frederic exchanged a look that was all too simple to read. *If only it were that easy.*

≈

At the princes' request, I tracked down the Medellan urchin to ask if he could point out the rebel arsonist to me. But after thoroughly searching the survivors, he returned to inform me the man had disappeared.

I could read the disappointment in Frederic's and Cassian's eyes when I reluctantly passed on the information. Neither of them spoke any recriminations, but my insides roiled anyway. For all I knew, the man might have disappeared immediately after our confrontation the first morning. But perhaps he had not. Perhaps if I had gone to the royals as soon as I heard the urchin's story...

But there was nothing I could do about it now.

The Tour stayed for two full weeks in Medellan, longer than we would have done in normal circumstances. We helped dig graves and wept with the local people through each simple burial ceremony. And we each contributed what skills we could to helping those who remained.

Frederic refused to leave until the townsfolk had been provided for, so instead of visiting the surrounding towns, those communities sent delegations to us. Some of the people from Medellan were unsuited to life in tents, and the visitors discussed arrangements with the royals, both for housing these individuals, and for sending workers and tools to help rebuild the town.

I had no business with the delegations, so I returned to my work with the blankets, wishing that every problem could be solved with a needle and thread. On the third day, the steward appeared and re-directed us to a comfortable tent without walls. The roof kept the sun off our heads, but the open sides allowed plenty of light in for our work. Someone had even found a couple of long wooden tables and benches, and I could see from their faces that my team appreciated the change.

On the fourth day, several large bags of old shoes, in a range of conditions, arrived at the sewing tent. Apparently, we had been designated as the center of the town's re-clothing effort. The mayor's wife followed close behind and somehow talked me into overseeing the distribution of the boots and shoes that had been donated from the capital. By the end of two full days of shoe fittings, I was more than grateful to return to sewing. For every thankful recipient, there had been an unhappy one who claimed their new boots didn't fit or who felt they deserved a better quality pair than they had been given.

On the sixth day, just before we ran out of material, a pile of new bolts arrived in a variety of materials. Their quality was inferior to the wool of the blankets, but they were serviceable and, given the heat, I was glad to have some lighter materials to work with.

Celine stopped by most days to sit for a few minutes with the girls and chat. And even Frederic came by once to thank them all gravely for their efforts. The lunch bell rang while he was with us, and he insisted on walking me to the closest kitchen tent to collect our meals.

"How are you liking your new workplace?" he asked. "It seems superior to the bare ground at least."

I looked at him sideways. "I suppose I have you to thank for it. It's very considerate of you."

"We are truly grateful for your efforts."

"In that case," I said, matching his grave tone, "I do think you might have tried a little harder. Some silken cushions would have been nice. Those benches are hard, you know! And perhaps someone to fan us while we work? It may only be spring, but it is already far too hot."

He blinked and regarded me with astonishment, seemingly lost for words.

"That would be a joke, Frederic," said Celine, appearing from nowhere just as we joined the line for food. "You're almost as hopeless as Cassian."

"Oh, surely not," said Frederic, with a slow grin. "No one could be as bad as that."

"And there *he* goes making a joke now," said Celine to me. "You can hardly tell with this one, he's as bad as Mother. Most of the time he's so placid you think every joke or witticism has gone over his head, and then he comes out with one of his own, just as straight-faced as he says everything else. At least he's not as bad as Cassian. He's so reserved and detached I despair of ever finding a girl who could attract him, let alone one who would actually be interested in him back."

She sighed and then flashed me a cryptic look that filled me with dread. What mad notion had lodged in her head?

Someone handed us each a plate of food, and a voice called for Frederic's attention. As soon as he turned away from us, Celine whisked me away to a secluded corner where we perched to eat somewhat awkwardly on an old log.

"I am not one to admit defeat lightly," she announced between bites, "but I think the task before me might be too great for even my talents. At least alone." She grinned at me. "Which is where you come in. Evie, I need your help."

I knew her well enough at this point to regard her warily. "With what? Or would I be better off not asking?"

She laughed. "Nothing terrible, I assure you. In fact, if we can manage this right, we'll probably earn the undying gratitude of my parents."

My consternation grew. I had no desire to come to the notice of the king and queen again, except perhaps as an excellent choice of seamstress for the queen's future dresses. "Is there an option to decline?"

"Evie!" Celine grasped my arm. "You wouldn't leave me alone in my hour of distress? I thought you were my friend, now!"

I regarded her through narrowed eyes. "You don't look distressed."

She laughed again and resumed eating. "Terrible, terrible distress, I assure you. The thing is, all my sisters have gotten married and moved away."

My heart immediately softened toward her, even as I dreaded whatever came next.

"And, so, you see. I need some new sisters."

"New sisters? What...oh."

"Exactly." She used her slice of bread to clean the remnants from her plate. "Frederic and Cassian are the oldest, and it's beyond ridiculous that neither of them is married yet. I suppose with so many younger siblings, no one felt the need to pressure them into producing heirs, but things have gotten entirely out of hand at this point. Think how much fun I might have with an adorable little niece or nephew, or two. They won't do me any good off in Northhelm. Or Rangmere, for that matter, since the latest rumors tell us Clarisse is being courted by a nobleman there. Not that poor Clarisse doesn't deserve a bit of happiness after her awful first husband."

She shuddered. "If they had tried to marry me off to Prince Konrad, I would have run away. And I'm sure I should have been quite justified to do so—I can't see that anyone much has mourned him. But for all I'm glad for her, it does seem ridiculous that Clarisse is widowed and about to marry a second husband, when her own twin hasn't even managed a single romance his entire life."

She wrinkled her nose. "Not that I can imagine who would want to be romanced by Cassian. But he is a perfectly respectable prince, so there must be someone. Somewhere. And that's where you come in." She turned to me. "I'm fairly certain that my parents had a secondary purpose in this Tour. I think they're hoping that Frederic will find himself a wife."

She discarded her plate on the ground and pulled up her

knees, wrapping her arms around them. "Not that they precisely asked me to assist, but clearly Frederic can't be left to his own devices in such a matter. And it seems far too good an opportunity to go to waste for Cassian, either. And he needs all the help he can get. So it seems to me the task has fallen to us."

I choked on my mouthful. "Us?" I managed to wheeze out once the coughing fit had subsided.

"Yes," said Celine, ceasing her enthusiastic whacking on my back. "That's what I said at the beginning. I'm conceding the need for assistance. Together I'm sure we will be up for the challenge."

I regarded her with astonishment. Had she lost her mind? She wanted me—a common dressmaker with no family or connections—to assist her in directing the love lives of the two oldest Lanoverian princes. My mind flashed back to my earlier jest at Frederic's expense, just as if he were not the crown prince. Perhaps I had already lost my mind, and she merely recognized a fellow lunatic. Yes, that must be it.

"Celine, I really don't think—"

"Excellent, then," said Celine loudly. "That's settled."

CHAPTER 5

*M*y team, which had grown after new needles arrived from one of the neighboring towns, had used all the material by the time the Tour broke camp. We left many of our tents in place for the displaced townsfolk, new ones from the capital having arrived to replace those we had given away. I had grown more than sick of the simple sewing patterns by then and was relieved to be on the move again. I also longed, a little guiltily, to be rid of the smell that still hung over the destroyed town.

Only two concerns marred my pleasure at leaving. The largest was our new destination. Celine had told me that we would not be trying to make our way through the northern jungles. Instead we were making for the coast and the royal yacht. The official royal vessel, as big as any of the navy frigates, had been assigned to the use of the Tour.

That almost certainly meant we were headed for the islands. Which most likely meant Catalie. A shudder went through me at the thought. The Isle of Catalie wouldn't be like Medellan. I had been there for three years, a charity case taken in as a sort of ward by the viscount who ruled over the island. The same nobleman who had driven me away in shame. I had established myself now in the capital, but the sting of that mistreatment still burned strong.

But the memory of Viscount de Villa wasn't my only concern. Celine's outrageous suggestion that I help her find brides for her brothers terrified me. How could I ever help in such a task? And what if Prince Frederic ever discovered me inappropriately meddling in his life in such a way? I would simply have to convince Celine it was impossible.

The firmness of my resolution comforted me for about thirty seconds. The royal fifteen-year-old didn't seem to be the type to be easily convinced of anything. And what if she decided one of the noble girls on Catalie would make her brother a good bride? A physical shudder ran through me, causing my mount to flick an ear back in my direction. I could never bow to one of them as my future princess and one day queen.

Maybe, after all, there was nothing wrong with supporting Celine from the background. Just to make sure she recognized those whose smiles were only skin deep.

I was riding several horses back from the royals, but I could still clearly see the straight backs of the two princes at the front of the columns. I had spent my last two days at Medellan altering more outfits for them, and it brought me pleasure to see them looking both elegant and comfortable, as I had intended. That was my true role and what I should be doing for them on this Tour.

The two brothers looked remarkably similar, both with the golden skin, dark hair, and brown eyes that set most Lanoverians apart from our pale-skinned northern neighbors. They both had the muscles and bearings of warriors—talk in the capital claimed they were diligent at their weapons' training—but Frederic was taller and broader shouldered than his wiry brother. Regarding them closely, I wasn't entirely satisfied with the sit of their waistcoats and shirts across their shoulders. They had both abandoned their jackets given the warmth of the day, but I suspected those items would have the same problem. Either their muscles had changed since the garments had originally been made, or their tailor didn't have the same eye for detail as I did. I resolved to have an actual fitting while we were on the islands.

Which brought my mind racing back to Catalie. Perhaps if I looked exactly as a Lanoverian should, like the royal family, I would have had fewer problems on the island. But my skin and hair were both a shade too pale, as if a northern ancestor had included enough honey to turn what should have been the darkest brown hair to warm caramel. The same ancestor may have been responsible for the dark green of my eyes, but they couldn't claim credit for their slight slant which suggested another ancestor from among the nomadic desert traders. Even my face marked me an outsider without a home or a people.

My worries consumed me all the way to the nearest harbor. But when the first glitter of the distant water appeared, I couldn't help the smile that spread across my face. I inhaled deeply, letting the salt in the air relax the tension across my shoulders. I might not miss the people of the islands, but I surprised myself by the deep sense of joy that the coast itself gave me. I had liked living in the lap of the ocean—I had once imagined I might be happy there forever.

The process of loading our large contingent of nobility, commoners, servants, and guards onto the royal yacht went far more smoothly than I had anticipated. Obviously I hadn't been giving the steward enough credit. Without unexpected large-scale disasters, it seemed he ran a tight ship. I smiled internally at the unintended pun.

The sailors welcomed us with subdued questions about Medellan but regained most of their cheer at our positive comments about the state in which we had left them. Before I would have thought possible, the captain was calling that it was time to catch the tide, and the buoyancy beneath my feet turned into the true swell of waves. I had registered my preference for a hammock over a bunk with one of the steward's assistants but had otherwise ignored the world below decks. Instead I found a spot tucked away on deck where I was out of the way but still able to see everything that was going on.

Leaning against the railing, I peered down at the foam which curled around the wooden sides of the ship. I watched the place where the broken water from our passage through the waves smoothed out to flow past in deep swells like the smoothest satin. I wished I could lean over far enough to dip my hand into the cool water.

Several of the older nobles clutched their hands to their mouths and weakly staggered toward the ladder below decks. I considered calling out to stop them, since they would be far better off up on deck, but I held back. The captain would advise them, it wasn't my place to do so. At least I felt no similar wave of nausea. I had never had even a hint of seasickness, regardless of the size of the waves.

The sun beat down on me, but I didn't mind. Not when a pleasant breeze blew occasional spray into my face. The seabirds cried loudly, a perfect counterpoint to the slap of the waves against the hull. Could the moment be more perfect? A sleek gray body arced out of the water before slipping back out of sight. Another followed and another, their fins pointing to the sky, and their powerful tails propelling them upward.

A soft sigh of pleasure escaped. Apparently it could.

"I see I'm not the only one who loves the ocean," said a voice behind me.

I turned my head, but even the sight of the crown prince wasn't enough to make me break the perfect moment with words. I remained in place, inviting him with a gesture of my head to take the place beside me.

He stepped up to join me, standing straight, his hands placed lightly on the railing. For a long moment of beautiful silence we watched the pod of dolphins frolic in our bow wave.

"I've always liked the sea," he said after some time, breaking our silence. "It's so constant and unchanging."

"Unchanging?" I thought of the sea as ever-changing. Each day a slightly different mood.

He gave me a rare smile. "It roars or whispers, but in the end, it remains here, unchanged. That's what I meant."

"Oh." I thought about it. I could see what he meant. The storms that raged across it always faded, and the sea remained behind as it had been before.

"It gives me comfort, I suppose." Another smile flashed across his face. "That I'm not nearly as important as I sometimes feel. That Lanover will still be here after I am long gone." He paused and eyed me sideways. "I'm sorry, I don't know why I said that. I think I must be feeling giddy from being on a ship again. It's been too long."

I hid a smile at the idea of this serious prince being giddy about anything.

His eyes watched me, and I wondered if he could read the thought on my face despite my effort to hide it.

"Or maybe it's just you," he said, unexpectedly. "You're easy to talk to, Evie."

"I am?"

He raised an eyebrow. "You sound surprised."

I bit my lip. "You have honored me with a confidence, so I will give you one in return. You are far more selfless than me. While you enjoy being reminded of your lack of importance, I have always longed to be more significant than I am."

I flushed immediately. What had possessed me to say such a thing? What was it about this man that made me throw caution to the wind and speak of such things? I had long ago learned to keep my emotions on a surface level—it was how I survived—so why was I acknowledging things to him that I didn't even like to acknowledge to myself?

Frederic's face showed surprise, although his voice was carefully level. "I would not have picked you as a person of great ambition. Although I suppose I should consider the remarkable things you have already achieved with your dressmaking in the short time you've been in the capital." He gave me a small half bow, but a shutter had dropped across his emotions, despite the compliment.

"Oh no," I rushed to say. "Not ambition. I don't want power, or to be important to the kingdom." I realized my mistake as soon as the words were out of my mouth, as soon as I saw the curiosity return to his face. My eagerness to reassure him had led me to reveal more of the truth than I had intended.

"One person would be enough for me," I finished in a whisper. "I just want to be important to one person." I looked away, humiliated, and not wanting him to see the tears swimming in my eyes.

Frederic said nothing, and I appreciated the opportunity to gather my emotions back under control. Did he sense my need for silence? Celine would have rushed to fill the void with reassurances, but I preferred Frederic's restraint, even if in truth it was merely that he had no reassurances to give.

When I drew a deep breath and gave a tremulous smile— although it was aimed at the dolphins and not the man beside me —he finally spoke. "We all deserve that, I think. It is a worthy ambition."

I was startled into looking up and meeting his eyes, and something passed between us that I couldn't name. His eyes seemed to truly see me, and an unfamiliar warmth settled somewhere in the vicinity of my heart.

"Dolphins! I love dolphins!" said a voice behind us, and I closed my eyes for a breath as the moment was broken.

Opening them again, I smiled at Celine. "Me too." I almost added that I had loved watching the dolphins in my years on

Catalie, but I stopped myself just in time. If I admitted I had once lived there, the princess would want to know why I no longer did so.

Celine leaned perilously far over the edge, stretching out her hand toward the beautiful creatures, before her brother tugged her firmly back down to the deck. She looked over her shoulder at him cheekily.

"Do you think if I fell in, the dolphins would rescue me?"

He looked at her blandly, his voice calm. "I think it is possible they might rescue you from the water, but they wouldn't be able to rescue you from me once we hauled you back on board."

Celine winked at me, looking entirely undaunted. "But just imagine getting to ride a dolphin! Celeste told me once that dolphins rescue people from the ocean."

"Did she now? Was it by any chance when she was playing stupid?" Frederic asked, referring to the curse that had forced his now-married sister to spend years pretending to be empty-headed.

Celine scrunched up her nose. "You're no fun, Frederic."

"You know, I have heard such stories. Of dolphins rescuing people," I said. They were popular stories in Catalie where the dolphins were beloved. "Not that I can completely vouch for them, though. I've never seen it myself."

A new light entered Celine's eyes as she gazed over the rail, and Frederic gave me a wry look. Oops. That might have been a mistake. I mouthed an apology at him, and he shook his head, although his eyes showed amusement.

"Now you can't possibly go overboard, Celine," he said gravely. "Because it would be clear the blame lay with Evie, and my wrath would come down on not only you, but her as well."

"Frederic!" gasped Celine. "You beast! You wouldn't!"

"Feel free to try me," he said with a straight face.

"Oh, ugh," said Celine, swinging around to lean her back against the railing. "You really are just like Mother."

He gave a small bow. "I take that as a compliment."

"You would," she said darkly, and I smothered a smile. The prince had played that one well. For all her talk of rebellion, Celine was too large hearted to get me into trouble. Then I remembered her plan for me to help find wives for the princes, and my amusement fell away. She might still lead me into strife yet.

The ship was now well underway, and most of the nobles had been coaxed back on deck. One in particular led the way, calling gruff encouragement to the others in a booming voice. When he spotted us, he waved a greeting to the royals, and remarked on the fine weather for a sail.

"That's the Earl of Serida," whispered Celine, while Frederic replied to him in kind. "He always treats me like an absolute child and says the most awful things to me, as if I were four. But he's as loyal to the crown as can be, and he grew up on the islands, so Father insisted he come. I just hope he doesn't ruin all our fun. I've been so looking forward to spending time on one of the isles. I've never spent more than a few nights there before."

"Which island are we to visit?" I asked, attempting to keep my voice casual.

"Well, we wouldn't all fit on Inverne," she said with a grin, naming the smallest inhabited island. "Some of us would have to sleep in the water. I think Viscount de Villa has invited us to stay with him. So that would be…"

"Catalie," I said softly when she stopped to think. "The viscount lives on Catalie."

"Oh, yes, of course." She looked at me curiously. "How did you know?"

I just shrugged and turned back toward the water. She regarded me for a moment, but let it drop.

So, we were going to Catalie just as I'd feared. I told myself there was no reason for the nobles on the island to even notice me among the hordes of servants and guards accompanying the

Tour, but I didn't really believe it. Then I told myself that maybe it was a good thing. Catalie was only the first of the painful places from my past that we might visit, and the royals were bound to drop me sooner or later. Surely it was better for it to be sooner—it would only hurt more later.

But I didn't really believe that, either.

CHAPTER 6

I had been assigned a hammock in one of the cabins below deck which had bunks lining the sides and hammocks hanging down the middle of the room. The other two girls sleeping in hammocks needed help working out how to climb in, but I slipped in without trouble after showing them the trick. I had been sure I would have nightmares given our destination, but the rocking of the ship proved soothing enough to grant me a good night's sleep.

I felt much less calm when I stood back in my spot on deck, watching the main harbor of Catalie grow from a distant speck into a bustling dock. Someone had obviously sighted the royal yacht some time ago because it looked like half the island had crowded down to the harbor to welcome us. Their clamor sounded clearly across the water, almost drowning out the birds who had once again joined us as we approached land.

Our approach had brought us in around the far side of the island, and the sight of its quiet beaches had brought an unexpected surge of excitement at the opportunity to revisit favorite places. The harbor, however, brought only bitterness. I still remembered how it had looked in the opposite direction, fading out from full-size to the barest pinprick on the horizon, my future before me as uncertain as it had ever been. I pushed the thought aside and decided I needed to find a spot to hide myself in case Celine decided to drag me off the ship at her side or something.

Part of me actually wanted to march down the gangplank next to the princess, proud and sure in a triumphant return. But I was too afraid the viscount would renounce me on the spot. So I instead lost myself in a group of servant women, keeping my head down as I shuffled off the ship and stepped once more onto the island that had been home less than two years ago.

A dock worker recognized me and nodded a greeting, and I replied with a tight-lipped smile. For all its size, the island was still too small a place for me to think I could remain lost in the crowds for our entire stay.

The royals and most of the nobles were being accommodated in the viscount's manor, with the rest of the Tour in tents stretching around his extensive property. As tempted as I was to get a glimpse of his family, I instead stayed out of their way. I had plenty of experience hiding myself in the gardens and woods around the house.

Since organizing a fitting with the princes would involve approaching the house, I decided to take up another project instead. I had long ago memorized Celine's measurements, so I was confident of my ability to produce a well-fitted garment even without chasing her down to model it for me. For the first time I felt thankful for the wide range of fabrics I had brought with me from my supplies in the capital.

But after the second day sewing in my tent, I had to admit I couldn't continue hiding forever. The island was calling to me, and I wanted a long ramble through my old familiar, secluded haunts. When I put in the last stitch, I stood and stretched, admitting to myself that I had run out of excuses to put it off.

Collecting a snack from one of the camp kitchens, I refused a friendly offer of company from a girl I had shared the cabin with on board ship. This was one trip I needed to make alone.

The woods around the manor seemed to welcome me, and I soon found my old stride, altered by so many months of walking through crowds in the capital. The air carried slightly more moisture than in Lanare, but a pleasant sea breeze had found its way in among the greenery, so the heat didn't feel oppressive. Birds called familiar greetings, and rustles in the surrounding undergrowth suggested small animals fled from my approach. I had soon passed through the thickest section of trees and was struggling up a tall hill on the other side. As my breath came more heavily, I chastised myself for losing some of my conditioning in city life. I needed to take more opportunities to exercise.

As I crested the hill and came down the other side, I picked up my pace. I loved the beaches on this side. The softest white sand sloped gently into the sparkling water. At these shallow levels, the water sometimes appeared green, sometimes blue, and sometimes so clear you could see translucent fish darting beneath the surface. And although it was only mid-afternoon, still a long way from twilight, I hoped I might see a turtle making his way up onto the sand.

A reef kept the waves lapping gently against the shore and also meant the beaches were of little use for boats. Subsequently, no one had bothered to build a road out to them, and they were used only for leisure by those willing to make the cross-country walk. It had always been one of their big appeals to me.

As soon as I arrived, I slipped off my shoes and wiggled my feet in the velvet soft sand. Tucking my slippers behind a rock to collect on my way back, I hurried down to the water to let the waves roll over my toes. Down here the wet sand was somehow, impossibly, even softer, and I wriggled my feet, letting them sink down until they were covered.

Unfortunately, it was right at that moment I heard voices. As I pulled my feet free and turned to flee, several figures came into view.

I sucked in a breath, churning filling my stomach. I recognized all of them. The viscount had three children, and there had been no love lost between me and my temporary foster siblings. A situation I should have been used to by the time I reached Catalie. And now, coming around a curve in the beach were Monique, the viscount's eldest, Shantelle, his youngest, and their friend, Carmel.

Carmel was the first to see me, her eyes widening as she nudged the other two. Both looked up, Monique gasping dramatically when she saw me. Immediately she stalked over in my direction, glaring as she came.

"I had heard you were on the island, Evangeline, but I didn't think you would dare show your face. Let alone follow us here." She shook her head. "I should have known better."

I sighed. "I didn't follow you, Monique. I didn't know you would be here today, or I certainly wouldn't have come."

"A likely story," she sneered. "If you were thinking we would be forced to acknowledge you and introduce you to the royals, you can think again. I wouldn't presume to introduce a thief and a liar to a prince or princess." She had reached me now, and her eyes narrowed as she leaned in close. "An orphan with no family and no name."

I sucked in a breath. I longed to snap back at her. To rage and scream that she was the liar. To tell her that I had no need of her services to introduce me to Celine or Frederic or Cassian. But I knew from experience that saying any such thing would only make her worse.

And I could now hear voices behind them on the beach. While they were still out of sight, her words had told me who I would find among them. The last thing I needed was for the royals to find me in a screaming match with the viscount's daughter. It was beneath my dignity, anyway. Whatever the noble girl might think, I did have some.

"I didn't expect to see you again, Evie," said Shantelle, diffidently.

I forced a weak smile in her direction. She had never tormented me of her own volition, like Monique had done, but she had never backed me up, either. The youngest of the viscount's children, she followed where her older sister led.

"I didn't expect to ever be back," I said.

"You should have stayed away. We don't want you here," said Carmel. She had always been a more enthusiastic follower of Monique than Shantelle. Perhaps because her parents were only wealthy merchants, and she valued her place in the inner circle of the noble girls. At least Marcus wasn't with them. Unlike the viscount's haughty son, Julian, who had seemed surprised by my presence on the few occasions he had ever noticed it, the viscount's nephew had been a worse harasser than Monique.

I had been fourteen when the viscount found me on a visit to the mainland and decided to take me in as a ward. I had been small for my age, used to being treated as a child. But I had grown up in my years on the island, and Marcus had seen me not as a homeless child but as a threat. At the beginning I had seen how he hung around the viscount's family—part of it and yet not —and I had thought it a commonality between us. But when I had attempted to reach out to him in friendship, he had made his feelings clear.

I was a usurper. Angling for a place on the island he thought should be his. After years striving to please his uncle, the viscount had chosen to take a nameless, homeless waif in as a ward, giving me the place in his family that Marcus had never quite been able to command. And all his years of pent up frustration and anger had been directed toward me.

I had longed many times to tell him that the viscount was

hardly likely to welcome him with anything warmer than obligation when the boy so clearly wished his older cousin gone and himself heir in Julian's place. But saying such things to Marcus would produce even worse results than speaking truth to Monique. After I turned sixteen, there had been a look in Marcus's eyes that told me I had better do everything in my power never to be alone with him. I had become so good at avoiding him entirely, that I had barely even seen him my entire seventeenth year. He had succeeded in his revenge, anyway, of course, gaining the outcome he had always most desired. My departure.

A revenge all too ably assisted by the girl in front of me. Monique had been incensed from the beginning at the idea that she should treat a nameless nobody as anything even approaching a sister. A small, vicious part of me felt glad to note her growth spurt. She wouldn't fit into any of the dresses I had made for her anymore, and the one she had on in their place was clearly inferior in quality. I tried to remind myself such thoughts were beneath me but didn't quite succeed.

A familiar voice I had hoped never to hear again rang out, and I blanched, all thought of Monique's gown driven from my mind. So Marcus was with them, after all. Another more measured tone sounded, and I sighed, some of my instinctive anger and fear lightening. Julian was here, too. He had no doubt come on account of the princes, Marcus trailing inevitably behind. Like his father, Julian was unlikely to notice the small jabs and pricks offered me by his sisters and cousin. But his presence was as effective as that of the viscount or their mother for protecting me from anything too outrageous.

Another voice sounded, and the band across my chest tightened for another reason. Their cruelty used to hurt me, but I now recognized my current fear came from a different source. I no longer feared their humiliations for my own sake, it was what they might say about me to Celine and the others that made me quake. That was the true reason I had been hiding since our arrival.

"You should leave. Now." Monique's hiss only seconded my own opinion. I couldn't leave fast enough as far as I was concerned. She took my arm and tried to shove me toward the trees, but we were too late. A small clump of young people wandered into view.

Monique still faced me, her back to them, but she saw me freeze, my eyes darting over her shoulder.

"You heard me," she whispered. "I won't besmirch their dignity by introducing you, so you might as well run along right now."

"Evie! There you are!" called Celine, and Monique stiffened, her eyes going wide.

I couldn't resist a small smirk in her direction as I pulled myself free of her grip and ducked around her. There was no escape now, so I meant to make the best of the situation.

"I've been busy on a project," I told the princess. "I think you're going to love it, too."

"Ooh." Celine abandoned Marcus who walked beside her and danced across the sand toward me. "A project! That sounds fun." She flashed me a broad grin, a bizarre counterpoint to the death glare I was receiving from Marcus behind her.

The expression only lasted a moment before he smoothed out his features, but I saw Frederic look quickly between us. The crown prince didn't miss much normally, but I wished him a little less perceptive on this occasion.

"What do you think of Catalie?" I asked, a wicked thought flashing through my head. "Do you like these beaches?"

"Oh, they're divine, of course," said Celine. "You'd have to be a monster not to love them. I even saw a turtle earlier."

"They're even nicer to swim in." I carefully kept my eyes away from Monique. "The water is so lovely and warm, and it's so refreshing after the hike over here."

"I want to swim!" said Celine immediately as I had known she would. The bright water was too alluring to resist.

"Why don't we all come back tomorrow?" I suggested. "For a swimming expedition. We could bring a picnic lunch and everything."

"Oh, yes, let's!" Celine was already gazing longingly at the water.

"I don't think…" Monique sounded slightly panicked.

"The reefs make it perfectly safe," I earnestly assured the royals before turning to the slightly older girl. "What's the matter, Monique? Don't tell me you've forgotten how to swim in the time I've been away?"

"Of course not," said Monique.

Celine cast a bemused look between us, but merely said, "Oh, excellent, it's settled then, I can't wait."

Monique coughed and sent me a glare I knew didn't bode well. "My issue is not with swimming, Princess Celine."

Liar, I thought.

"My issue is swimming with this girl. I'm afraid you've been deceived. This girl is a liar and thief, without family or position."

CHAPTER 7

A shocked silence settled on the group as if she had reached out her hand and slapped me. Marcus's look of satisfaction made me itch to give him a real slap, but the rest of the locals looked merely uncomfortable.

Celine's look of horror was almost comical, but the worst expressions were Frederic's and Cassian's. I couldn't read them at all. Was I about to be sent back to the capital when the Tour had barely started?

But as I gazed at Frederic, I remembered the spark of connection between us earlier on the boat, and a matching spark of defiance rose inside me. I was eighteen now, no longer a child. And I was done slinking away, running from others' hatred.

I forced a tinkling laugh from my tight throat. "Oh Monique, I love you, too."

I shook my head at the royals playfully. "You'll have to excuse Monique, we were foster sisters once, and she always did love to tease me." I rolled my eyes.

Walking over to Frederic, I placed my hand lightly on his arm. His muscle jumped under my touch, giving away that he wasn't quite as calm as his face suggested. "What do you think, Frederic? Shall we all come back for a swim tomorrow?"

A gasp of outrage sounded from Monique, and I wasn't sure what had enraged her more, the casual way I addressed the prince, or my dismissal of her insults. She had always liked to be the one in control of the situation.

My eyes pleaded up into the prince's, so close to mine now. *Play along, play along—please!*

He answered without taking his eyes from mine. "A swim would be most welcome, I must admit."

I breathed an inaudible sigh of relief and gave him a tiny smile.

"Excellent," said Cassian briskly. "I'm sure the viscount will excuse us when we are in such excellent company."

"Yes, indeed," said Julian, speaking for the first time since they had all appeared. "A dip can be an excellent refreshment on these warmer days. We are eager for Your Highnesses to enjoy all our humble island has to offer." He smiled. "And I daresay we will be more than ready to cool down after our sparring practice in the morning."

Frederic gave him an answering smile. "My brother and I are looking forward to it. I have heard something of your skill with a blade even in the capital, and we are both eager to try ourselves against you."

Julian looked pleased, nothing in his mannerisms suggesting he had even noticed the earlier altercation. Monique, her mouth hanging open, looked between her brother and the princes. Her lips slowly closed as she knit her brows. I had never seen her at such a loss.

Celine, looking back and forth between Monique and me, said, "But what about—"

"Don't worry, Celine," said Frederic, interrupting her. "We'll be finished sparring in plenty of time for your picnic and swim."

Her eyes snapped to him, and her look turned thoughtful. She didn't attempt to finish her thought, which had clearly not been about the swim, instead breaking into lively chatter about the plans for the next day.

I swallowed, grateful to all three of the royals, although I was aware the danger wasn't over yet. I wouldn't always be around to laugh off Monique's accusations, and I couldn't see her leaving it there.

But for now, she seemed to have accepted that the tide had turned against her. And when Celine slipped her arm into mine for the walk back to the manor, Monique dropped to the back of the group.

Celine made me promise I would bring my project up to her room for immediate perusal, so for the first time I found myself stepping once more into the viscount's house. The elegant building included many pillars and long open breezeways, built for the casual culture and warm climate of the islands. I had once loved the building almost as much as I loved the island's beaches. But it carried too many unpleasant associations now.

I flagged down a local servant who started and gave me a second look. "Miss Evie?" she asked. "I heard a rumor you were about somewhere."

"Yes, here I am," I said, forcing a smile. She had been a chambermaid when I had been here last but appeared to have moved up in the world.

She saw me looking at her dress and nodded. "That's right. I'm lady's maid to Miss Shantelle now." She grinned at me. "And I only wish I had the gowns you used to make to put her in. She'd be looking so good all the time, I'd have found myself a better position by now." She winked at me.

"What better position is there on Catalie?" I asked dryly. "Lady's maid to Monique?"

The girl shuddered. "Gracious me, the ideas you come up with."

I chuckled, and she joined in before abruptly sobering. "And who is it you're after, Miss Evie? The young people have all arrived back, and Miss Monique looked real fierce."

"I'm here to see Princess Celine, actually," I told her. When she hesitated, I added, "She's expecting me."

"Oh, well, that's all right and tight, then. They've put her in the rose room. I suppose you still remember the way?"

I nodded, wishing I didn't, and climbed the stairs to find Celine's room. It wasn't the nicest of the manor's guest rooms, but it was the most feminine. I supposed the nicest had gone to the princes, and possibly the Earl of Serida who I had a vague feeling was some sort of distant relative of the viscount. Islanders were funny about their own.

I blew out my breath as I mounted the last step. That had always been my problem, of course. I wasn't one of them. I tried to push the thought aside. My usual strategy of ignoring the past was harder to maintain in the face of so many memories.

Celine pulled me inside the room, almost slamming the door behind me. "Well? Did you bring it? I've been dying of curiosity over here. And that includes whatever was going on down at that beach. Why did Monique say those awful things? Were you really sisters once? And why do you want to go swimming? I saw your expression, you had something in mind."

I held up my hands, laughing in protest. "I can't possibly answer so many questions at once. How about we start with the most important one?" I walked over to her large, neatly-made bed, and unwrapped my parcel.

"I want us to go swimming because of this." Turning around I held out my latest creation for her to see.

Celine's eyes grew round. "Is that…?"

"A bathing costume, yes," I said.

"But that's…I mean…" She hurried over and examined it more closely. "We don't have any swimming beaches in Lanare, but I'm sure this isn't what we swam in last time we were on the islands."

"No, it wouldn't have been," I said. "It's my own design."

"I knew you were a genius, Evie," said Celine reverently. "Please tell me you made one for yourself as well."

I bit my lip and then nodded.

"It's going to be a triumph," Celine breathed. "Can I try it on?"

"Of course, that's why I'm here. We need to make sure it fits perfectly."

I knew exactly why Monique had not welcomed a swimming expedition with the young royals. Men on the islands happily stripped down to their underclothes to swim, many swimming bare chested. The women, however, were not so fortunate. Most of the local commoner women happily dove in wearing their clothing. They would pull the front of their skirts between their legs and tuck them securely under their waist sash at the back, creating the effect of giant, puffy drawers.

Lanover was the most relaxed of the kingdoms and the culture on the islands was even more relaxed than the mainland. Even young, unmarried girls were permitted to show their lower legs in such a way while swimming. But the noble girls were not as free. Since long before I arrived, the fashion was for noble girls to wear loose, full-length, full-sleeve swimming gowns in a chemise style but made of wool. They were hot and heavy and unattractive. Weights sewn into the hem kept the skirts modestly around the ankles but also proved a significant obstruction to floating or swimming. It was a ridiculous costume, more covering than the usual style of day clothes, and I had to admit it was a testament to Monique's swimming skills that she could swim at all in the ridiculous outfit.

To make the situation even worse, there was nowhere on the beach for them to change, so the poor girls had to wear the hideous costumes on the walk down. Early on in my time on Catalie, I hadn't ever visited the beach. But once I began to explore and observe the young people swimming, I quickly adopted the local style rather than the awkward imported style of the nobles.

But for some time, my mind had been working over an entirely different sort of design. I hadn't thought I would ever have use for it, and so had tucked the thought away into some distant part of my mind. But seeing the island again had brought it rushing back, and I had been working tirelessly over the two costumes since our arrival.

"Now that I'm here," said Celine while I helped her into the garment, "it seems obvious you must once have lived here. I can see several aspects of the islander gowns that you incorporated into a couple of my designs."

"I try to take inspiration from everything I see, and then mix it with something else to turn it into something of my own."

"You succeed marvelously which is why you're such a raging success, of course. I got all sorts of complaints from the other girls at court when they heard I was stealing you away for so long, you know."

I flushed with pleasure at the praise.

Once I had fastened the costume securely in place, I stepped back to get the full effect. A slow smile spread across my face. It was even more magnificent than I had hoped.

The inspiration for this design had come from the islanders' own fashion. Most wealthy women here wore dresses of light flowing material that draped elegantly across one or both shoulders, often gathered at each shoulder with some sort of elaborate clasp, and fell in soft folds to the ground. A wide band under the bust, usually in a contrasting color, gave it shape. The dresses generally had two or three layers and were worn without petticoats to combat the heat. I had always admired the elegant simplicity of the design, requiring so little sewing.

I had taken the concept and gone even further. Celine's bathing costume was crafted from the lightest silk, so fine as to be almost—but not quite—sheer. Three layers gave it a full, floating look, and the material broke from the usual pastel shades chosen for such gowns. The band below her bust was a deep orange-red, while the material itself started at her shoulders in an orange so deep as to be almost red, gradually lightening through several shades of orange and peach before finishing on a soft yellow at her feet. And it was her feet that were the real triumph of the design. The flowing material wasn't a true skirt, although it was full enough to look like one if she stood still. Instead, I had sewn the material into two separate legs which gathered around her ankles in solid yellow bands. She looked like a sunset, or like living flame, and she would be lighter and more mobile in the water than the local girls without ever revealing any part of her legs.

"And this is the best bit," I said, producing a final piece from my bag. The soft single layer of silk matched the color shades of the costume perfectly, and I showed Celine how to fit it around her torso, securing it under the fiery red band. Once it was in place, it covered the trouser legs completely so that she looked as if she simply wore a striking gown.

"That's for you to wear until we reach the beach."

Celine examined herself in a mirror and shook her head. "Whatever we pay you, I'm sure it's not enough. It feels like the most outrageous thing I've ever worn, but I can't see a single thing my mother could complain about." The reflection of her eyes took on a wicked twinkle. "And, of course, you could not have devised a more fitting revenge for the awful things Monique said. She's going to die when she sees us tomorrow. Which reminds me. You haven't told me what that was all about."

I sighed, the rush of excitement from seeing Celine in my design instantly disappearing. I decided to keep my story as simple as possible. "When I was fourteen years old, the viscount took me in as a ward, and I lived here on Catalie in this house. Monique and her cousin Marcus didn't appreciate my inclusion in their family, so when I was seventeen they accused me of stealing a piece of jewelry. A family heirloom owned by the viscountess but loaned to her eldest daughter for her coming out ball. Sure enough, it was found beneath my pillow. The viscount refused to listen to my pleas of innocence—as if I would be so stupid as to hide such a thing beneath my pillow—and immediately turned me out of his home and island."

"Evie, how awful," said Celine softly.

I shrugged, meeting her eyes in the mirror. "I traveled to the capital and was able to get work that left me enough time to take on extra dress commissions. It didn't take long after that for me to save enough to open my little shop. And without my shop, I would never have had the opportunity to dress royalty. So it all worked out for the best." I tried to keep my voice light, hoping she couldn't see the extra moisture in my eyes. My emotions had been far too near the surface ever since we'd stepped on board the royal yacht.

"Evie…" Celine said again, turning from my reflection to look directly at me. But something in my face made her pause and put on a smile. "You're right. Not meeting me would naturally have been a terrible fate."

"Of course, Your Highness," I said demurely, grinning when she stuck her tongue out at me. Sometimes when she was particularly sensitive and thoughtful, as she had been just now, I forgot she was still half child.

After I had helped her back into her regular gown, she took me by surprise with a quick hug. "Don't worry, Evie," she said, "we believe you."

Back in my tent that night, I lay awake for a long time feeling the weight of her arms around me and hearing her words again and again. Sometimes my mind wandered back further to the beach. The feel of Frederic's arm beneath my hand was still vivid, along with the intensity of my relief and gratitude when he backed me up, stark against the humiliation of the moments before. But I found I couldn't dwell on that moment for long, it awakened something in me that I wasn't ready to look in the face.

Do you really still think they'll drop you eventually, like children who grow tired of a new puppy? asked a small inner voice. But something else in me rebelled. I had been given many promises before, and I had grown too experienced to be taken in again.

CHAPTER 8

My hands trembled as I dressed myself in my own bathing costume the next day, glad the tent had already emptied of its other occupants. I didn't usually dress so lavishly, but the spark of defiance that had awoken on the beach gave me courage. I had sewn the costume for myself not really thinking I would get the chance to wear it—just creating it had felt like a small rebellion. But here I was about to face both my old tormentors and royalty, and I knew I needed to look my best.

The material I had brought with me had come from my personal stores, and I had reminded myself that the commissions I received for my creations were making me into something of a wealthy woman. Even after I had hired assistants some months ago, I had been left with no shortage of coin. It was time I dressed the part.

But still I gulped twice and had to stop to gather my courage before exiting the tent. My own costume had been made in shades of blue, green, and aqua, also starting dark and fading down to a pale pastel at my ankles. Bearing in mind the queen's orders, I had made Celine's costume to drape across her collarbone. I, on the other hand, wasn't fifteen. Mine gathered at each shoulder, the material coming down to cross at the bust. It gave me a v-shaped neckline only slightly higher than I might have crafted for a ball gown.

Moving through the tents, I heard a few whispers following me, but I held my head high and walked quickly to the front terrace of the manor house. Most of the rest of the group had gathered already, meaning I had missed the initial response to Celine's outfit. But from the satisfied look on the young princess's face, I suspected she had made a splash.

"Evie!" she called, waving to me. "We're to ride to the beach."

A group of horses along with several grooms—a couple carrying large, covered baskets—waited to one side of the terrace. I might have suspected Monique of trying to discomfort me, except she already knew I could ride well. A moment's further reflection suggested the truth. She wanted to limit the time she spent in her own less-than-comfortable costume.

Looking around, I realized we were only waiting for the princes. No sooner had the thought crossed my mind, than the two of them stepped through the front doors. They strode toward us, nodding greetings to the various members of the assembled group. They still wore their sparring clothes and looked comfortable and relaxed. Their matches against Julian had obviously gone well.

Frederic came to a sudden halt when his eyes fell on his sister. "Celine, what in the kingdoms are you wear..." His eyes traveled on to me, and his word trailed off, a dumb-struck look on his face.

Yes! I barely restrained a celebration. I didn't usually get to witness the effect of my creations at the various occasions they were crafted for, so it was satisfying to see the reaction for myself. To get such a response from the usually serious crown prince was even more of a triumph. Even the detached Cassian looked visibly shocked. Even with the covering skirts, the outfits looked impressive.

"We're to ride," I said, moving over to them. "So you'll have your cool dip, soon enough. Did you triumph in your matches?"

"Matches?" Frederic looked confused for half a moment before shaking his head. "Oh, against Julian."

"We had some success," said Cassian, helping him out. "Although Julian is a formidable opponent."

Julian, who had emerged just as I approached, nodded his acknowledgment of the praise. He had raised both eyebrows at sight of our costumes, which I considered a compliment coming from him.

We were all soon mounted and winding our way through the trees. The children of a local baron, ranging from Celine's age to older than me, had joined us, and one of the girls started up an island ditty. Other voices soon joined hers, and I surprised myself by singing along. I had never felt so free with this group of people before, and I wasn't sure if it was the time that had passed away from the island, my stunning costume, or the presence of the royals. But somehow my heart felt much lighter than I would have thought possible.

When we arrived, the grooms took the horses and began to set out the picnic, while the nobles made for the water, the boys shedding clothing as they went. Most of them even discarded their undershirts, diving bare chested into the cool water. The girls followed more slowly, their cumbersome outfits making the water less inviting. I noticed that the younger two of the baron's daughters had worn plain cotton dresses and secured them in the way used by the common islanders.

Celine wandered over to me, clearly happy to make a late and sensational entry to the water. I soon had both of our overlay skirts removed, and we walked down to the water together.

"Look at them," giggled Celine, "if they don't close their mouths, bugs will be flying in."

I smiled, even more pleased at the look on the girls' faces than she was. It was very obvious that if I could just convince Celine to organize an expedition to a swimming beach down the coast from Lanare once we got back, the orders would soon be pouring in. I could probably hire a new assistant just to sew swimming costumes.

The water, cool enough to be refreshing but warm enough not to bite, provided a welcome relief after the hot ride. I soon waded all the way in and was making lazy strokes through the water.

"This is incredible," said Celine, not far behind me. "It's so light and easy to move."

"You *look* incredible," said Delphine, swimming up beside us. "And so comfortable. How do I order one? I want one, and I don't even care if it costs me my whole season's dress budget."

I smiled at the baron's second youngest daughter. She had always been friendly toward me, although she had been painfully quiet when I was last here. Apparently she had gained some confidence in my absence.

"I made them. You can send an order to my shop in the capital, but I'm afraid I won't be back until after the Tour."

"Oh, of course, I should have guessed! I can't believe I nearly forgot your skill with a needle. Monique and Shantelle haven't been half so well dressed since you left." Her smile faltered, and I could almost see her full memory of the situation returning.

But I knew the words had been kindly meant, so I smiled at her reassuringly.

"I didn't mean...I mean..." She stopped and shook her head. "Some of us were sorry to see you go. Especially in such a way." She frowned and then muttered, "No one is stupid enough to hide such a valuable item beneath their own pillow."

I laughed in jubilation. "Thank you! That's what I said."

"It's only common sense," said Celine, now floating on her back. "But some people only see what they want to see."

"Or what they planted themselves," Delphine muttered again.

I bit the inside of my cheek. I had always assumed either

Monique or Marcus placed the jewelry beneath my pillow but had occasionally wondered if a true thief among the staff had stashed it there, happy to use me as a scapegoat if the thievery was discovered. I didn't like to think it of any of them, though. They had always treated me with respect, even if the noble family had not.

Celine righted herself and splashed us, and we both swam away, squealing and splashing back in her direction. I checked quickly that I wasn't inadvertently splashing in Monique's direction—a course of action sure to bring some sort of revenge—but she seemed to be sulking in the far corner of the cove. So I redirected my attention to Celine, who was pursuing us, chuckling evilly, and took off at a faster pace. Celine had soon pulled half the group into her splashing war, but I continued to duck between them, enjoying the chance for a proper swim. It had been far too long since I had been in the ocean.

I had never seen the two princes as relaxed as they were now, playing in the water as if they were ordinary young people. Celine, however, was her usual self, sending a wave of water into Cassian's face. For a split second I wondered if her antics might provoke some stronger reaction than his usual calm, but he merely shook his head, flicking several drops in her direction.

Frederic, on the other hand—although he looked equally undisturbed—responded by casually brushing his arm along the surface of the water, sending a mini tidal wave to engulf his sister. She disappeared under the water for a moment in a flash of orange and bubbles, and he smiled.

Unseen behind them, I ducked beneath the clear water, took a firm grip on both his ankles, and tugged. He went straight over with a huge splash and muffled yell. I surged out of the water, grinning in triumph, to applause from Celine.

Frederic reemerged, sending water spraying from his hair with a flick of his head. He came up just in front of me, and the air seemed harder to breathe all of a sudden as I tried to tear my eyes away from the muscles of his bare chest. His skin glistened in the sunlight, and I was suddenly conscious of the way my bathing costume clung to my curves despite its layers.

But unlike me, the prince didn't hesitate. Swooping toward me, he scooped me up, cradling me for a brief moment, before flinging me straight up into the sky. I gasped, only just having time to grip my nose closed as I flew through the air and back down to splash into the water. Flailing, I reemerged, making sure that everyone in my vicinity got splashed in the process.

Frederic laughed, a martial light in his eye. "No one dunks me and gets away with it."

My hand, which had been about to send a surge of water in his direction, paused, a grin spreading across my face. Hearing his deep laugh was even more satisfying than I had imagined. A rapid-fire barrage of water hit me from behind, jerking me out of my thoughts and back into the battle being waged across the calm cove.

Monique continued to hang back, well out of the way of any splashes, a look of haughty disdain on her face, and Carmel stood with her, clearly torn and wishing she could join the fun. Shantelle, however, to my surprise, joined in with a goodwill, ignoring her sister's glares.

When we found ourselves next to each other at one point, she said, "I can't imagine you would consider making me one of those costumes. And I can't say I blame you, either."

"You never know, I might be feeling generous." I swam away leaving her with a surprised look on her face.

My words had even surprised me, but the light-hearted feeling remained. And though it hadn't been an apology, it was closer to one than I had ever expected to get from anyone in their family.

I swam back toward Frederic, trying to position myself for a stealthy approach, but he was alerted to my tricks now. Instead of sending him sprawling into the water, I found a strong arm wrapped around my waist, and I was flung through the air, shrieking and flailing the entire way. I forgot to plug my nose this time and a rush of water shot up my nostrils and down the back of my throat.

I got my feet under me and began hacking and coughing, trying to blow out the remaining water. The sound of a swimmer approaching made me whirl around, suspicious, but Frederic made no attempt to attack, a concerned expression on his face.

"Are you all right?"

I smiled. "You clearly need to spend more time in the ocean if you think a little salt water up the nose is a problem. Here, I can help with that." I aimed a splash upward, directly toward his face, and he tried to scramble back so quickly that he fell backward into the water.

I laughed, my heart lightening even more, if possible. His trust in me the day before had been a beautiful gift, and I wanted to repay the favor. He had confided in me how heavily his responsibilities weighed on him—an admirable trait in a crown prince—but he needed to let off steam every now and then. Or else one day he would explode.

And for a reason I didn't understand, from the very first, something about Frederic of Lanover had made me want to see him laugh. So the sound of his low chuckles, and the sight of the smile on his face—shining from the glow of the sun against the droplets of water which lined his lashes and ran down his straight nose—made my heart sing.

Once we had all exhausted ourselves in the water, we scrambled back on shore to enjoy the picnic that had been spread out for us. The light breeze and the sun soon dried Celine's and my silk, although the other girls didn't fare as well. From the envious glances sent our way, I began to suspect I wouldn't even need to send Celine out on an expedition from the capital. At this rate, the island girls would have written to their friends and relatives in the capital by the time I got back.

Once all the delicious food had been consumed, the group broke up. Celine demanded that Julian find crabs for her in a rock pool they had passed the day before, and soon young people were spread all up and down the beach, most out of sight of our picnic spot although I could still hear their voices as they called to one another.

I had chosen to stay, finding a spot on the sand where an occasional adventurous wave rushed over my outstretched feet. But when I looked up and saw only one other person left, his angry eyes trained on me, I paled. The grooms must still be close by, but would they step in against Marcus if I needed them to? They had come from the manor not the Tour, so I couldn't be sure. If I got up now and tried to walk away, would he let me go?

CHAPTER 9

ut my heart rate had only begun to race when a shadow fell across me. Apparently we weren't alone after all. Frederic sat on the sand beside me, and I almost cried from the relief of his presence. Only the slightest flick of his eyes in the noble boy's direction gave any hint that he knew Marcus was there. Had he seen Marcus's expression and come to rescue me? For some reason, my heart rate sped back up.

After a moment of silence, I heard retreating footsteps and peeked across to see Marcus's disappearing back. I let out a breath.

"Tell me," said Frederic quietly.

I looked at him with a furrowed brow.

"Tell me what happened to you here on this island. And I don't mean how you came to leave. Celine already told me about that." His hand, which had been resting against the sand, clenched, squeezing a handful of sand tight in his fist.

I looked across the water, wondering where to start, wondering what he wanted to hear.

"The viscount was on a visit to the mainland," I said eventually. "And he found me in a small town on the edge of the jungle. I had run out of food while traveling through it and so had stopped to pay for my meals with work. He asked me who my family was, and I told him that I had none."

I paused, working down a lump in my throat, and Frederic waited patiently, asking no questions.

"He invited me to be his ward, and to return to Catalie with him. I was so grateful to him at first. Becoming the ward to a nobleman seemed like a literal fairy tale come true. I didn't realize then…It was only later…" I stopped again, working down a second lump.

"Did he…hurt you?" asked Frederic, his voice sounding strange.

I looked at him in surprise and nearly recoiled from the anger in his eyes, un-reflected in his otherwise strangely-still face.

"No, no," I assured him. "Not physically, anyway." I sighed. "I was so determined that this home would last. It didn't matter what Monique or Marcus said, I was determined not to let them drive me away. But then the weeks turned into months, and the viscount—my supposed foster father—never made any move to reprimand them or defend me. That's when I realized the truth."

I stopped again, and Frederic said, "Evie," in a voice so gentle I shook my head, my eyes focused back across the water. If he gave me any sympathy, I would break. And now that I had started, I wanted to get through this. I wanted someone to know.

"My lack of family had given the viscount the excuse he needed to make me his ward instead of his servant. But his purpose had never been generosity or any true intent to include me in his family. He had seen my skill—even then I could design a dress that stood out, and doubly so in that tiny village where he found me—and he had wished to secure my services. Services he didn't have to pay for, services that couldn't be stolen away from his family by someone willing to pay more."

Anger made me ball my hands into fists. "He never introduced me to anyone here as his ward. But my thankfulness blinded me.

I worked hard because I so longed to show my gratitude for being taken in and given a home. But eventually I noticed that they never took me with them when they left the house. They never introduced me to their friends at all. When I eventually started going out on my own, the people I met were surprised to learn of my existence. Though I crafted the dresses that the viscountess and her daughters wore to parties, I was never invited to attend myself."

"Such a man does not deserve a noble title," said Frederic quietly.

I didn't look at him since I didn't know if I could handle whatever I might see on his face. Instead, I shrugged. "My life actually changed for the better after I recognized my true situation—once I stopped looking for love from any of them. I sewed less after that and explored the island more. I figured if the viscount didn't want to pay me as a servant or hire my services as a dressmaker, he couldn't require me to work unceasingly, either."

Silence fell between us, and I began to regret my words. They were gone from me now, and I couldn't take them back. This prince, strong and sure of himself, knew some part of how pathetic and friendless I had been for most of my life. It wasn't the image that I wanted him to have of me. And his last words rang through my mind. Had I just sowed the seeds of trouble between Lanover's future king and one of his important nobles? If so, that hadn't been the action of a friend. I should have bitten my tongue, however nicely he asked.

I forced myself to look past my own hurt and consider the viscount as objectively as I could.

"You asked me earlier if the viscount ever hurt me. I never feared him in such a way. I often feared…" I paused. "…someone else. But, in truth, no one ever lifted a finger against me. And I think that's because everyone knows the viscount would not permit such behavior within his lands. I have heard the villagers talk often enough. They do not find him liberal with his wealth, or generous with his time and attention, but they all feel safe on his lands."

Frederic seemed to consider these words. "It is a relief to me to hear that he has some honor, at least—some sense of responsibility to his people, even if it is not what it should be."

A part of me hated to admit any strengths in the man I had once longed to look up to as a father, but the fair part of me admitted it was true. "And he has raised his son to think the same way."

"Yes, Julian seems to be a decent sort," said Frederic, with a strange sideways glance at me, "if a little blind on some things."

The statement was so exactly how I would have described him that I couldn't help a smile despite the emotional toll my confessions had taken. The warmth of the sun and my full stomach were making me sleepy, and I wished I could lie down and take a nap.

"Frederic!" Celine's yell brought us both to our feet, but when she appeared she looked happy. "Julian tells me he has the most cunning little catamaran. And he'll take us all out for a sail any day we like."

"Except tomorrow," said Julian. "Some of the officials from the surrounding islands are coming in for a day of meetings with the princes."

"The next day, then?" asked Celine.

Frederic weighed his sister's hopeful expression before glancing out to the horizon. Something on his face told me he liked the idea of a sail himself. "Certainly, if you would like it," was all he said, however.

That wasn't the end of the matter, of course. Much conversation ensued, especially once it had been established that the catamaran didn't have room for our whole group. I checked out of the conversation at that point since I obviously wouldn't be one of the sailors. Especially not given that Monique—who had been unusually silent up until that point—took direction of the sailing expedition.

Delphine told me she'd found a rare sea anemone that she wanted to show me, so we wandered away from the rest of the group to the rock pools located on the far end of the beach. Some time later, her younger sister came into view calling loudly for us to return. Half the group had already mounted up by the time we made it back, so we scrambled onto our horses and headed back to the manor house.

When we arrived, Celine drew me aside and asked if I would make some more bathing costumes so she could distribute a few as gifts on her departure. "Not as magnificent as ours, of course," she instructed with a wink. "But I think even a simpler version will do a lot to win good will toward the crown among some of the younger nobles.

I chuckled and agreed and spent the next day sewing, trying not to think about the possibility that I might be once again sewing for Monique and Shantelle. I reminded myself that while the previous dresses I had created for them had been done under false pretenses, the royals paid generously for my skills, and it wasn't for me to dictate what they did with the commissions I made for them.

Celine popped past my tent in the late afternoon, but when I tried to report on my progress, she waved my words away. "Oh, don't worry about that. I have no doubt you'll have them ready by the time we leave, and I don't need them before. I just came past because I wasn't sure if you knew what time we're leaving in the morning."

I knit my eyebrows. "Did you want me to come and see you off?"

"See us off?" Celine laughed. "You're coming with us, silly."

"Coming with you?" I blinked.

"Of course." She winked at me. "Don't forget our secret

mission. A couple of the girls here seem nice, but you're the one who really knows them. I need your insight."

I gulped. Oh dear. Still. I used to sail sometimes with some of the villagers, but I had never been on Julian's catamaran. And I had to admit I had always wanted to do so. It was a beautiful craft.

"Thank you—for convincing them to include me," I said, not wanting to seem reluctant or ungrateful.

Celine gave me a quizzical look. "I'm delighted to have you, of course, but it wasn't me who insisted on your presence. That was Frederic."

Frederic? I bit the inside of my cheek. Had he done it because of our conversation on the beach? Was he trying to force the viscount's family to do something to make up for their earlier neglect?

The next morning, I arrived early at the meeting point, not wishing to make the royals look bad after they had honored me with a place on the sail. Celine had informed me that she wanted to swim off the boat but didn't want to do so alone, so I was obediently wearing my new swimming costume.

I wasn't surprised, though, to see that the other girls had all come in attractive day gowns. However, surprise did hit me when I saw the rest of the group. Julian, Monique, and Shantelle were all present, of course. Along with Frederic, Cassian, and Celine. And I had expected to see Marcus as well. But Delphine and her oldest sister and brother were there instead of Carmel or any of Monique's other friends.

I greeted them with enthusiasm, even going so far as to smile at Shantelle, but I kept as much distance from Monique and Marcus as possible. They sent no insults my way and refrained from so much as glaring in my direction. Because the royals had shown me favor? Or was it possible they had actually let go of their former hatred?

A moment's reflection on their behavior so far made me reject that possibility. So I kept a close eye on them as we all loaded onto the sleek forty-foot catamaran. Its white hulls shone so brightly they looked as if they had been polished, the sails crisp and new. Julian was an experienced sailor, but a crew of two had joined us for the day so the noble would be free to host his guests.

Monique carefully positioned herself to ensure Frederic offered her his hand to help her on board. Celine rolled her eyes at this, clambering on alone before turning to help me. I grinned at her, but the expression fell away when I saw an odd look pass between Monique and Marcus. Her eyes seemed to question him, and the conspiratorial look he gave her in return, one of clear satisfaction, made me want to check if anything disgusting had made its way onto the back of my dress. It had been one of their favorite pranks in the past.

But Celine assured me nothing had gone awry with my costume, giving me a confused look along with the reassurance. So, I forced myself to smile and chat with Delphine's brother and sister as I accepted one of the drinks that were being passed around. The cool sweetness of the tropical fruit juice blend against my tongue made some of my muscles relax. And soon the added delight of full sails and a warm sun had me laughing along with the others.

A pod of dolphins arrived to form an honor guard around the boat, and we spread out across the deck, no one wanting to go below deck on such a beautiful day. The sun sparkled off the turquoise water, our catamaran gliding sleekly through the small swells. Mesmerized, I watched the white bubbles dissolve back into the smooth water.

"I always wanted a vessel like this," conceded Frederic's voice in my ear.

I turned my head to regard him. "You're the crown prince. If a viscount's son can afford one, surely you can."

He shook his head. "Of course, but I have little time or opportunity for leisure sails such as this. It would have been a waste of royal resources to keep such a boat unused."

"It's not like people think it is, is it?" I asked quietly. "Being a prince or princess."

"No," he said with a sigh, "not exactly. You don't get to choose your responsibilities or pass them on to someone else. They can never be laid down, either."

He took a breath and forced a more cheerful expression on his face. "But today is just the sort of day people imagine when they think of being a prince. And I for one intend to enjoy it."

I thought he was about to say something else, but Monique's voice called him from the other side of the deck, and he excused himself with a wry smile. I watched him walk away, raising my hand in farewell when he glanced back at me over his shoulder.

It had never occurred to me that I might find myself back here on Catalie, in such company. You would think I would have grown accustomed to the twists and turns life took by now, and yet it still took me by surprise.

Celine and Cassian each wandered in my direction at different times, standing beside me for a while, and Delphine called me to join her further down the rail at one point to observe two calves playing in the waves beside their sleek gray parents. Eventually we reached the other side of Catalie, and the crew threw down the anchor. We could see one of the other islands far in the hazy distance and, much closer, a stunning beach of white sand, surrounded on all sides by thick greenery.

This mini cove was a favorite destination of boats, virtually unreachable by land. On occasion I had even rowed out here from the nearest village in a large canoe with a group of the locals for a full-day excursion of pleasure. Memories like that kept ambushing me from forgotten recesses of my mind. It had been all too easy to forget my many happy memories of Catalie.

With the sails furled and the anchor down, the crew turned into serving men, producing a lavish lunch. When I had eaten my fill, I lay on the deck, shielding my eyes from the sun, too content to attempt conversation.

"Behold, Sleeping Beauty," said Frederic with a laugh in his voice.

"Perhaps she needs to be woken with a kiss?" suggested Celine's cheeky voice behind him.

I sat up fast, inducing a head rush, and glared at her. She just laughed and wandered away. Frederic gallantly offered me his hand to help me rise, but I couldn't meet his eyes as his fingers warmly clasped mine. Hurrying for the opposite end of the boat, I faced the unpleasant thought that I was becoming far too fond of the crown prince's presence. I had adjusted myself to so many different communities in the past, and here I was doing it again. Forgetting that, just like all the others, this community had no permanent place for me. How many times did I have to learn the same painful lessons?

The crew had packed away the remnants of our feast and raised the anchor. They fought now to bring the sails under control and turn us to the correct heading. I could hear the exclamations of the rest of the guests, who had gathered at the front of the boat to watch a swarm of bright fish pass by in the clear water, but I felt no desire to join them.

Something about the creased faces of the two crewmen as they conversed in an undertone caught my attention. A shiver of fear raced through me. I told myself I was giving way to a flight of fancy. But I had learned to trust my instincts over the years, and I could feel my heart thrumming in my chest.

I looked around for Julian—he would know what was going on—but he was nowhere in sight. I frowned. It seemed unusual for him to absent himself in such a way when he had been so assiduous in his duties as host to the royals during our visit thus far. But then, surely he would be with the crew if there were truly a problem?

I started down the few stairs into the small cabin area. I

would find Julian, and he would reassure me—with a look of astonishment at my existence, no doubt—that all was well.

But as I stepped down onto the polished boards of the cabin, the opposite certainty gripped me. Water sloshed around my feet as a terse command I couldn't quite understand sounded from back up on deck. The boat rocked unnaturally, throwing me against an attached table, as the water at my feet climbed higher.

A louder call from on deck rang out. "Abandon ship!"

CHAPTER 10

I cried out, nearly falling as I twisted back toward the stairs. The water already reached my knees. But as my grasping fingers found the smooth handrail, a sound from inside the cabin drew my attention backward. I paused.

A banging, which I now realized had been sounding ever since I descended inside, had erupted into a fury at the sound of my cry. I looked longingly up the stairs before wading through the rising water after the source of the noise. When a hoarse call sounded from inside a cabin, it confirmed my guess. Julian.

Reaching the door, I tried to twist the handle, but it didn't budge. The banging stopped, however, so I called through the solid wood panels. "It's Evie. It seems to be locked. Do you know where I could find a key?"

"Get one of the crew," he called back.

"There's no time," I shouted. "They're abandoning ship." I didn't mention that the water had now reached my thighs, since he must be experiencing the same thing.

He swore and then was silent for a moment.

"Julian?" I was starting to shake although the water wasn't

actually that cold. My mind was screaming at me to get out now while I still could, but I pushed it down. Julian might not be my favorite person, but that didn't mean he deserved to die. Perhaps one of his crew would come looking for him and absolve me of responsibility. They probably knew where to find a key, too.

"Try the table," Julian called at last. "There's a small hidden drawer on the underside. It's at one of the corners. If you run your fingers underneath, you should be able to feel a small mechanism to open it."

I growled and sloshed back toward the table. Why couldn't he have kept them on a nice obvious hook like everyone else? The water was starting to slide across the tabletop now, and I hoped the mechanism would work while submerged. Running both hands along beneath the table I shuffled along as fast as I could, pushing against the resistance of the water. Finally, on the third corner, I felt something out of place. Wiggling my fingers around, I felt it release, a small section of the table dropping down.

With a gasp, I squatted, submerging the rest of my body up to my neck in the water, as I felt around for a piece of metal. One of my fingertips hooked around a ring, and I triumphantly pulled out a small bunch of keys.

"I've got it!" I yelled, not sure if he could hear me from over here.

The boat lurched, and I slipped splashing into the water, before scrambling back to my feet. I was half swimming now, as I made it back to Julian's cabin.

"Which key?" I shouted, even as I tried shoving a random one into the keyhole, now below the waterline. I tried a second one, but as I maneuvered it around the ring into position, the whole bunch fell from my hands.

"The round one," called Julian.

I took a deep breath and plunged beneath the water. My

grasping hands quested wildly until my fingers hit the ring. Shooting back to the surface, I sucked in a deep breath and examined the keys.

Taking a firm hold on the round one, I thrust it into the lock and turned. I could feel a bolt drawing reluctantly back, and then the door swung forward. The resistance of the water slowed its progress, but Julian immediately lunged out of the cabin. A trail of red followed him.

It took me a moment to find its source in the swirling water. "Your foot!"

"There's no time for that. We need to get up those stairs."

I couldn't see the extent of his injury, but the water was high enough that he wouldn't be putting weight on it, at least. Moving through the red trail that followed him made my stomach turn, but my terror and claustrophobia drove me forward as fast as I could go.

By the time we reached the stairs, the water had reached his armpits and my shoulders, and my breaths were coming hard and fast, more from fear than exertion. Julian lurched up the stairs, hopping on his good foot, and had nearly reached the top when he cried out and fell.

I surged behind him, bracing myself on both handrails to hold us both up. He groaned, "My foot," and then his weight pulled away from me, and he was out on deck. He disappeared from view, and my world narrowed to getting up those stairs and across that deck as fast as I could go. So the reappearance of his hand, reaching down to assist me, took me by surprise.

I met Julian's grim eyes as he hauled me up on deck beside him, my feet merely skimming the final steps. We both took a moment to breathe now that water no longer pulled at us. But a gurgle from the stairway made me look down to see only water where the hole had once been.

I looked around and found the deck deserted. Rushing to the railing that faced toward the beach, I located a number of heads bobbing in the water part way toward land. Several voices called mostly unintelligible words.

"Look! There!" called one voice clearly, and a distant figure pointed in my direction. Looking down, I saw the water rushing up to meet me as the boat continued to sink. Soon it would swamp the deck.

"We need to get swimming as well," said Julian behind me. "I'm not exactly sure what will happen once she goes down completely, but I'd rather observe from a safe distance."

I nodded my head and was about to ask after his injury when he scooped me off my feet. Without further comment, he flung me through the air away from the boat. I hit the water hard and sank before twisting and propelling myself back to the surface. I reemerged in time to see him dive from the deck.

Still spluttering and wiping moisture from my eyes, I trod water while I waited for Julian to reach me. He didn't arrive. Looking back, I saw him bobbing next to the rapidly sinking boat, struggling to stay above water. I struck out toward him, glad for my light and mobile swimming costume.

When I reached him, I hesitated. "Don't pull me under."

He grimaced. "You need to be swimming away, not toward the boat."

"I know. That's what we're doing." I slipped under one of his arms and tried to take some of his weight. Instantly I began to sink. Dis-attaching myself, I frowned. "This isn't going to work."

He said nothing.

"Give me a minute."

I swam off around the sinking vessel looking for any useful flotsam. Thankfully, I found a piece of wood floating nearby. It had obviously come from the boat, but I couldn't tell what useful purpose it had once served. Draping myself across it, I rested for a second, relieved when it held my weight. Then I kicked back to Julian. Slipping off, I let him take my place.

"Kick with your good leg. I'll tug you along."

I grabbed the end of the piece of wood and struck off hard toward the shore. Slowly, inch by inch, we crept away from the boat. Within minutes I knew there was no way I could pull him all the way to shore. I paused for another rest, letting the wood hold me up as well.

A splashing caught my attention. Two swimmers powered through the water in our direction. I soon recognized Frederic and one of the crew members.

"Your Highness," the man said as soon as they stopped. "You need to swim to the beach."

"And I will," snapped Frederic, more angry than I had ever heard him. "When everyone is safe. You assured me…"

"Yes, Your Highness," said the man hurriedly. "I'll assist—" He looked over at us, and his brows creased. "Sir?" He addressed the question at Julian.

I looked down into the water and both of their eyes followed me. The man swore when he saw the red trail that still followed us. "You leave this to me, miss. I'll see him safe to shore." He looked back at the crown prince. "Perhaps His Highness can help you to shore ahead of us?"

I had already heard enough to know his concern wasn't for me, but I was so grateful to have someone else take responsibility for Julian, that I could have kissed him anyway. Nodding, I let go of the wood and floated for a moment before kicking away from them.

Frederic kept pace with me. "Are you all right?"

"Yes." I squeezed the word out between breaths.

"What happened, where were you?"

I shook my head, my eyes fixed on the beach, still a long way ahead of us. "I'll explain…on…shore."

He seemed to understand I couldn't swim and talk and said nothing more. Without another person to weigh me down, we made steady progress, although my arms and legs soon ached. With each stroke they seemed to grow heavier in the water. If the ocean here hadn't been so flat, I doubted I would have made it at all. I mentally kicked myself for not taking the time to scavenge for further wood.

For some reason, the closer we got to shore, the harder each stroke became until I felt as if we were making no progress at all. Looking up, I saw that Marcus and Delphine's brother had already made it and were climbing dripping out onto the sand. Cassian had also nearly reached dry land, assisting a clearly protesting Celine. I could well imagine she would reject the idea that she needed help.

But the other girls, weighted down by their dresses, still struggled in the water. Like Celine, Shantelle had outstripped the others, assisted by the second crew member. And Delphine's sister had somehow found a small piece of wood and was making extremely slow, but unlabored, progress toward the shore. Her sister, however, and Monique appeared weak, their forward progress almost entirely halted, and their heads sometimes slipping under the water.

My brows drew together in disgust as I looked again at the two young men already safe on the sand. I paused in my stroke. "They need our help," I said to Frederic.

He nodded silently and immediately took off for Delphine. I was too exhausted even to groan as I made my own slow way toward Monique. I paused next to her as I had beside her brother.

"I'm going to help you, but not if you try to drown me. Don't pull me under."

The sight of me seemed to have given her a tiny fresh burst of energy, fueled no doubt by her rage, but she reluctantly nodded. The silent action softened my heart a tiny bit. She must be full of fear to acquiesce so easily.

"I'll swim in front, and you can hold onto my shoulders. Help as much as you can by kicking."

I maneuvered into position, and she clasped her hands onto

my shoulders, immediately propelling me under the water. But the moment my head submerged, the pressure lightened, and I pushed myself upward.

"I didn't mean—" she panted out the words, stopping when I shook my head.

"I know."

Neither of us spoke again as we crawled toward the shore. I could only be thankful she had already made it so far. I couldn't have gone long in such a way. Cassian and the second crew member had deposited Celine and Shantelle in safety and were wading back in our direction when we paused our progress, and our questing feet found the sand. For a moment we both stood, letting the slight swell carry us up and back down, relishing in each connection of our feet with the bottom.

I was the first to move, but Monique wasn't far behind. Frederic and Delphine had made better progress and were stumbling forward ahead of us. I could see Monique glaring daggers at Delphine's back. Every now and then she would turn her anger-laden eyes sideways at me. I ignored her. I couldn't even blame her for wanting to be saved by the crown prince rather than her worst enemy.

Frederic helped Delphine all the way onto the sand, out of reach of the lapping waves, before turning back to us. Monique's expression immediately transformed, but he didn't seem to see her. Walking over to me, he slipped an arm around my back, and I guiltily let him take some of my weight.

"So…tired." I muttered. "Just…going to…have…a little…rest." I dropped to my knees on the beautiful, wonderful, delightful, blessed sand and flopped on to my back.

Celine crawled over to lie beside me. "I told Cassian he should help Monique instead of me."

"You're his sister," I said, when some of my breath had returned. "And he was coming back for her."

Celine propped herself up slightly to survey the others. "I don't think Monique appreciated being rescued by you of all people," she whispered.

I smiled weakly. Looking sideways I saw several others sprawled on the sand, while the rest of the group stood and watched the sea. Forcing myself to stand, I followed their gazes. The beautiful, still blue of the ocean no longer held any trace of the catamaran. The only disturbance to the serenity of the water was the two crew members now both involved in pulling Julian toward land.

Monique stood with her hands on her hips, trying to hide both fear for her brother and her unladylike attempts to regain her breath. I had long ago learned to easily read her emotions—the result of years spent in a state of constant wariness around her—so they presented no challenge to me now. The other faces varied between numb exhaustion and deep concern. And, to my astonishment, Marcus's face carried the gravest look of anxiety as his eyes tracked his cousin's progress.

I narrowed my eyes. I had spent more time avoiding Marcus than observing him in my stay on Catalie, but I knew enough of his psyche to anticipate glee at Julian's injury, not concern. Yet no hint of hope or pleasure showed in his countenance or posture.

Without discussion, Celine and I both drifted toward Frederic and Cassian. After a moment, I realized that without any stated intention, the three of us had formed a shield around Frederic. The thought had no sooner entered my mind than Cassian spoke in a lowered voice.

"Well, we have been waiting for trouble. It looks like it found us."

No one replied because no one needed to. In the frenzied moments in the cabin as I tried to free Julian, there had been no room for anything but terror. But in the seemingly endless swim to shore, one thought had dominated. I didn't need any expertise on catamarans to know that sinking had not been natural. Someone had just tried to murder Julian. And possibly the rest of us in the process.

CHAPTER 11

*N*one of us moved or spoke as Julian was finally dragged to shore, Delphine's brother and Marcus rushing forward to help once the swimmers were in close enough to walk. The pale noble, who hung limply between his crew, roused himself to push his cousin away. Frederic raised his eyebrows, but still none of us spoke.

Delphine's brother helped one of the exhausted crew members lay Julian on the sand, out of reach of the water, while the other crew member pulled out a small knife and cut away the cloth from around his injured ankle. The wet material of the man's shirt provided a bandage which was tightly wrapped around the jagged gash. Julian groaned once but otherwise lay on the sand, unresponsive. He had lost a lot of blood.

Monique and Shantelle kneeled on either side of him, although there was nothing they could do to help. The crew member who no longer had a shirt looked up and asked if anyone had located any water. Marcus started and announced he would find some, leading Delphine's siblings across the sand.

Still the three of us grouped around the crown prince remained in place. The two crew glanced our way and then began to talk in voices too low to hear. Finally, one of them peeled away and approached us.

"Your Highness's safety is our first priority."

Frederic nodded once, his eyes cold. "That much you have demonstrated." For some reason the man looked nervous at this response instead of pleased. He clearly knew he had displeased the prince in some way. "But can you say the same for the rest of the party?"

"Your Highness…" said the man uneasily before trailing off with a helpless shrug.

Cassian glanced across the sand at the others. "What happens now?"

The man shrugged. "We wait."

"I would prefer to start back toward the viscount's manor across land," said Frederic. "We have no way of knowing how long it will take someone to come looking for us. If they even know where to look."

The man instantly became animated, his distress obvious. "Your Highnesses must not attempt such a thing! The way is impassable! You might suffer any number of injuries far from assistance. Here we are safe. Here we know rescue will come."

Frederic moved restlessly. "But are we safe here? Can you guarantee such a thing?"

"With my life," said the man with an earnestness that made me uncomfortable. I didn't want anyone laying down their life for me.

Frederic examined him for a protracted moment and then relaxed, nodding his head. "Very well, we will await rescue here."

The man let out a deep breath and bowed several times before retreating back across the sand. I surveyed the small beach. How long were we likely to be here? I could have sworn no more than an hour had passed since lunch, and yet the sun already hung low in the sky.

A shout sounded from the edge of the green behind us, and

the searchers returned, each carrying handfuls of water cupped in large green leaves. The liquid burdens were all carefully tipped into Julian's mouth. When they started back toward the trees, most of the group followed them.

Frederic sighed. "We must drink."

Cassian nodded once. "We should check on Julian first, though."

We moved as a group toward the still prone injured man, but when we reached him the rest of us hung back as Frederic dropped to a knee beside him.

"Are you well?" he asked.

Julian opened his eyes and stirred as if attempting to sit up, but Frederic placed a firm hand on his shoulder.

"I believe I will live, Your Highness."

"What happened to you?" asked Cassian, behind Frederic's shoulder.

Julian shrugged. "I had the misfortune of injuring my cursed ankle on a protruding nail. I went below deck to wrap it up at what turned out to be the worst possible moment."

I frowned at him, waiting for him to say more, but he fell silent. His eyes, which had been focused on the princes, moved to me, and their message was clear. My frown deepened.

He had no more locked himself in that cabin than the catamaran had spontaneously sprung symmetrical leaks in both hulls causing it to sink rather than capsize. Someone had wanted it to sink, and that same person had wanted it to sink slowly enough to ensure their own escape. Why did he wish me to keep silent about it?

"I owe a debt of gratitude to Evie," he said, and I was almost surprised to find he knew my name.

I chewed on my cheek. I had no great love for the viscount's son, but he had aided me back there, just as I had aided him. He had even ordered me to swim for shore as he struggled to stay afloat. Perhaps I owed it to him to at least find out why he wished to keep the truth of the situation to himself.

"We will leave you to rest," said Frederic, signaling to the rest of us to follow him. Together we followed the rest of the group toward the stream Marcus had found.

"What happened on deck?" I asked as we walked. "Why did none of the crew come searching for Julian?"

Cassian's low voice was even. "It is exceedingly obvious that the viscount's orders to Julian's crew in the case of danger were to protect us at the expense of his own children."

I frowned, but the idea didn't particularly surprise me. As I had long ago discovered, the viscount was not a sentimental man. He would take his responsibility to the visiting royals seriously and expect his son to take care of himself.

Celine shook her head. "They basically threw the three of us into the water at the first hint of danger and commanded us to swim for shore. Frederic wasn't too happy about it and would have climbed back on board if they hadn't jumped in themselves to physically prevent him."

"They would have ended up drowning me along with themselves if I hadn't stopped resisting." Frederic scowled. "Infamous for us all to abandon ship when some of our group were unaccounted for." He glanced over at me.

I shrugged. "We all escaped in the end." I hesitated. "Do you really think this was connected to the fire in Medellan? To the rebellion?" I had seen the ashes of an entire town with my own eyes, more proof than I could ever need that the rumored rebellion was more than just talk. And yet, the idea that it could have reached its insidious tendrils all the way out here to Catalie seemed somehow fantastical.

"Surely you do not think that catamaran sank itself?" asked Cassian.

I frowned. "No, of course not…" My voice trailed away. A different theory had started to take shape in my mind, but I couldn't explain it without also explaining the truth of what I had found below decks. And I wanted more time to ponder it, to be certain before I accused anyone.

At least I now understood Frederic's faith in the words of the crewman earlier. Their actions on the boat and in the water had demonstrated they were trustworthy in the matter of the royals' safety, at least.

Plodding across the sand made my tired legs scream, but my thirst proved stronger than my exhaustion. We walked up the course of the small stream that trickled out onto the beach until we found a section clear enough to drink. Frederic gallantly stood aside for Delphine, who had obviously been left to drink last out of the previous group, offering her a large leaf he had just picked.

Something stirred in my stomach as she smiled at him gratefully. She had always been a kind girl, and in my absence, something had brought her out of her shell. Her features were attractive, and she belonged to the noble class. I remembered the way Frederic had rushed to support her in the water. Wasn't this what Celine had wanted me to keep an eye out for? Shouldn't I be telling Celine the good qualities of the other girl?

But I found I could not bring myself to do so. No more than I could bring myself to watch them laughing as they stooped to drink side by side. It seemed I had truly lost all sense of the appropriate.

I drank—blessed relief for my parched tongue—and stumbled back to the beach, unable to process anything more in my exhaustion. But as more time passed, I began to make mental preparations for a night on the beach. And then a sail was sighted.

Once more our small group formed up around Frederic, but the first person to hail us from the deck was the Earl of Serida, and I could feel both princes relax.

We were soon bundled in blankets, drinking from actual cups, and attempting to keep our eyes from the endless expanse of ocean as we sailed back to the manor with all speed. I wanted to curl up and sleep, but now that I had rested a little, my mind wouldn't let me relax. Someone had put us all in danger, and I was fairly certain that I was the only one—with the exception of Julian—who knew who it was.

PART II
THE JUNGLE AND THE DESERT

CHAPTER 12

The viscount met us at the dock with a contingent both from the Tour and the manor. Gasps arose from the small crowd when Julian was carried off on a stretcher, the doctor who had accompanied the earl hovering over him. Our group straggled off after them, dispersing among the family and friends waiting. Except for Frederic who strode straight to the viscount.

"I want a full investigation."

"It shall be done." The viscount gave him a full bow, deep concern etched in the lines of his face. Only once did his worried eyes stray to his son's face.

We were led up to the manor where I attempted to peel away from the crowd to slip into my tent. But a firm hand on my arm halted me. I looked up into Frederic's face.

"Not tonight. You should be up at the manor with us."

I opened my mouth to protest, but Celine spoke first, her words interrupted by a yawn. "You can sleep in my chamber. The servants can easily lay out a pallet for you."

I reluctantly closed my mouth and nodded.

But I awoke abruptly from my exhausted slumber after only a

few hours and could not return to sleep. Trying not to toss and turn in case I disturbed Celine only made it worse, so as soon as the palest hint of dawn appeared, I slipped silently out of bed, to pace the corridors instead.

A few of the servants were up, but the halls were otherwise deserted, and I wandered through them in a haze of memory. It had been less than two years since I had called this place home. And yet the me who had lived here felt distant and strange. But, as I paced up and down, my eyes alighting on familiar objects and rooms, I was forced to admit to myself that in some ways I was still the same person.

I examined my motivations of the day before. I had told myself I remained silent out of respect for Julian, but that wasn't the whole truth. Part of me had been gripped by fear. If I spoke up and told the truth and Julian did not back me, who would believe me over the son of a viscount? Especially when the story painted me in such a heroic light.

My steps quickened as my thoughts twirled. The royals had shown me nothing but kindness. They had included me where I had no right to be included, they had trusted me, and when I had told them of my past life here, they had believed me over Monique's lies.

So why did I hesitate now? *People have believed you before*, spoke up that voice inside. *For a while.*

I wrestled with myself. Surely my hesitation harmed no one. If my theories were correct, the royals had not been the target of the accident. And surely, now that he had arrived safely home, Julian would tell his father the whole truth, and a proper investigation would be conducted.

My steps slowed, and I drifted around a corner. The sight of two unwelcome figures made me draw swiftly back.

"What did you do?" hissed Monique to her companion.

"You can't blame me if your precious prince rushed to rescue somebody else," said a haughty voice that sounded somehow less confident than it had in the past.

"You told me I would have my chance to be thrown together with the prince, not that you meant to sink the boat—with Julian inside! I thought this would be like our trick with Evangeline and my necklace. Not murder!"

I gasped, and then clamped my hand over my mouth. Was this the confirmation of my theory, then, as well as the past wrong against me? Two confessions in one.

"Sink the boat? What are you talking about? So now I am to be blamed for Julian's catching his leg on a nail as well as the prince's desertion of you? It seems to me, he likes that little baron's brat better than you—not to mention the commoner."

I didn't have to see him to picture the smirk that no doubt accompanied his statement. But Monique, to her credit, would not be deterred.

"Do you think I care about that when Julian could have died!"

"So he has made it through the night, then?" Marcus tried to sound nonchalant and failed.

"No thanks to you," she snapped. "I'm telling my father everything you told me."

Did her voice sound closer? I drew further back.

"Wait, Monique," Marcus sounded a little desperate now. "You're misinterpreting everything."

Their voices seemed to have paused again, as if he had halted her progress somehow. I continued to inch back silently, however.

"Let go of me!" Monique's outraged cry was followed by running footsteps and then we were face to face. She halted for the briefest moment, her glassy eyes widening. Then she threw up her hands. "Oh, of course. *Of course!*" She almost cried the final words before taking off again.

I stood frozen in shock as Marcus also rounded the corner.

"You," he said, his voice icy, as he advanced toward me. In all the years I had known and feared him, I had never seen such an expression on his face. I abandoned any pretense of dignity and ran as fast as I could.

Several corridors over, I was still running headlong when I collided with a tall figure. My momentum nearly carried us both to the ground, but I managed to steady him at the last moment, stepping back to look up at Julian in surprise.

"Should you be out of bed?" I blurted out, the words the first to come to my lips.

"Perhaps not," he said, "but I needed to speak to my father."

I waited for him to say something else, but for a long moment he just regarded me, a confused look in his eyes. I remained silent. He was the one who owed me explanations, not the other way around.

"You risked your own life to rescue me," he said at last. "And then you held your silence. Why?"

I blinked at him. "Would you have rather I left you to die?"

"No, of course not. But it would not have surprised me if you had."

"A pretty idea you have of me," I said, shaking my head, knowing I must see the humor in the situation or I would cry from so much pent up emotion.

He shrugged. "I am aware you disputed your banishment. It would not be unnatural for some resentment to remain."

I stared at him, slowly shaking my head. Did he really think my only complaint against his family was my banishment? I considered pouring out all my grievances, throwing the many injustices into his face, but instead my shoulders slumped. What would be the point?

"I would not let someone die over such a thing," I said instead. "As for why I stayed silent, I have been busy asking myself the same question." I said no more. The inner workings of my mind were none of his business.

"Well, whatever your reasons, I thank you. I have told the whole story to my father, and he will see justice done."

I thought of my own experience with the viscount. He was certainly implacable once he perceived a crime had been committed. It seemed I could rest easy and put aside my internal struggle. But I couldn't help asking.

"It was Marcus, I suppose?"

Julian nodded, his expression difficult to read. "I cannot imagine why he felt our trip to be an appropriate time to dispose of me, but his jealousy is hardly a secret on the island. It was he who injured me, though he claimed it to be an accident. He accompanied me below deck and when I went into the cabin, he locked me inside. I can only imagine he then sabotaged the boat. If it had not been for your fortunate arrival, and the fact that I keep a second, hidden, set of keys, I would now be at the bottom of the ocean. He heard, as did I, my father charge my crew with the care of the three royal persons. I suppose he saw his opportunity." He shrugged. "Whatever motivated him, we shall now at last be rid of him."

I stared at him. Perhaps I should not be so surprised by the cold statement. His cousin *had* just tried to kill him. I opened my mouth and then closed it again. What more was there to say?

Moving slowly now—the route taking me far longer than it should have, lost as I was in my thoughts—I made my way back to Celine's chamber. I found the other girl already up and gone. Throwing off my dressing gown, I hurriedly prepared for the day. Perhaps I would find her in the breakfast hall.

But halfway there, a call of, "Evie!" interrupted me. Turning, I found Celine and both princes hurrying toward me.

"There you are!" the princess exclaimed, falling on my neck.

Frederic, who was still hurriedly buckling on his sword belt, slowed, his face relaxing. "Celine became concerned when she woke to find you gone."

"Oh, I'm sorry," I said. "It never occurred to me...I couldn't sleep and have been walking the halls." I drew a deep breath. "I hear the viscount has determined the boat was indeed sunk and has even discovered the culprit."

Cassian raised an eyebrow as Frederic said, "Already?"

"I just ran into Julian," I said. "But perhaps we will find them all in the breakfast hall. They should be the ones to tell the tale."

The three of them joined me, and we did indeed find the viscount calmly involved in consuming several slices of ham and toast. When he saw who had arrived, he stood and bowed.

"Your Highnesses."

Frederic indicated he should be seated, and we all took seats of our own, although none of us touched the food. Monique, who sat beside her father, looked nervously between us. Her mother and Shantelle were absent, as was Marcus. Julian had presumably returned to his sick room.

"We hear you have discovered the truth of yesterday's events," said Frederic, his eyes never leaving the viscount.

The man paused and placed his food back on his plate.

"It is more than regrettable, Your Highness. It is infamous beyond words that you should have been placed in such a situation, and I am merely grateful that you all escaped harm."

Frederic said nothing, his face grim.

The viscount sighed. "I regret to say that my brother has been dead for many years, and his son, my nephew, was encouraged to treat my manor here as a second home." He shook his head, and I barely refrained from shaking mine. He thought that was where he went wrong?

"You speak of Marcus," said Cassian.

"Indeed." A wave of some emotion passed over the viscount's face, and he looked suddenly older than he had before. "I am afraid my nephew has long envied my son's place as my heir. And it seems that yesterday he seized the opportunity to attempt to remove my son from the line of succession. Thankfully he was not successful."

"Thanks to Evie," said Celine, her eyes steady on his.

"Pardon me?" He looked confused by her words.

"It is thanks to Evie that he was unsuccessful. Or did your son leave that part out of his recounting?"

"He left nothing out," said the viscount stiffly. "And indeed, our gratitude lies with the young lady." He still hadn't looked at me, and the sting of his words took me by surprise. I had not thought this man had any capacity left to hurt me. "Even now arrangements are under way to provide her with a suitable reward."

I opened my mouth to protest, but Frederic placed a cautionary hand on mine where it rested on the table. "Gold, I assume?" he asked.

"Of course, Your Highness." The viscount gave a half bow from his seat.

I wanted to protest that I wanted none of his gold, but Celine's eyes were telling me not to be an idiot, so I held my tongue. And after a moment's reflection I had to agree with her. It was unlikely to be more than I had legitimately earned from three years of unpaid labor in his household. This wasn't a reward, it was my due.

"We will talk to Marcus ourselves, of course," said Cassian, not distracted from the primary question.

"I am afraid that will not be possible," said the viscount, his eyes hooded.

"Excuse me?" Frederic's voice was pure ice.

"I am most sorry, Your Highness. Such a crime against my house and the crown must be met with the swiftest justice. My nephew has already been sentenced to banishment and has left this island with nothing to his name."

Frederic stood up, his chair clattering loudly to the floor behind him. "Banished? Already? You did not think to consult us first?"

The viscount considered him with lidded eyes. "It is not

customary. It is my role to see justice served, and I wished to honor you with the speed of my actions."

"Fred," said Cassian quietly and a silent exchange took place between the brothers.

When Frederic turned back to the viscount, his fury had frozen to ice. "We will speak of this again."

The three of them stood in unison, me a beat behind as Celine prodded me to my feet.

We were going, it turned out, in search of the Earl of Serida. My fear that we would find him still abed turned out to be groundless. Instead we found him entering the manor, his face etched with lines of deep anxiety.

"Your Highness," he said on sight of Frederic, giving him a low bow. "I have come from the docks, and I have some unsettling tidings."

"As do we," said Frederic. "But perhaps they would better be discussed in my suite."

And so, for the first time since we had arrived, I saw the inside of the suite of rooms assigned to the crown prince. I had never had occasion to enter them when I lived here, but I knew them to be the grandest of the manor's guest rooms. Opulent red and gold proclaimed the viscount's wealth more loudly than it did his taste. It was the wrong decoration for an island home.

"It seems we have been betrayed," said Frederic as soon as the door was closed. His words snapped me back into the moment. Betrayed?

"It is certainly a matter of grave concern to see one of yesterday's party, the viscount's own nephew, shipped off in such a hasty manner," said the earl.

"The question," said Cassian, thoughtfully, "is whether he is really responsibly for the sinking, or whether the viscount just wants it to appear that way."

My eyes grew wide. What conspiracy did they suspect?

CHAPTER 13

The earl mopped his brow. "Very troubling indeed. You have spoken to the viscount, then?"

"We have," said Frederic. "He claims it was an attempted assassination of his son, and that his nephew has been banished in punishment."

"That is our custom, certainly," said the earl slowly. "Banishment, I mean. As it is your own family's." He eyed the princes somewhat warily as he spoke, but neither of them commented on his assertion. The royals had a special island, far in the south, for the banishment of traitors—and had used it even on their own family.

"However, this haste is unusual, and—dare I say it—unseemly," the earl added.

"It certainly appears clear that the viscount did not want us to talk to his nephew," said Cassian, his eyes grave. "Upon consideration, however, I am inclined to think Marcus did truly commit the crime. The obvious victim was Julian, and Marcus is certainly the one with the strongest motive against him."

"Julian himself has accused Marcus," I said. "I ran into him in the corridor." Everyone looked at me. I drew a deep breath. I had told myself that my silence harmed no one, but now I had seen that wasn't so. It was time I stopped thinking of myself. "I have a confession to make."

Celine snorted. "As long as you're not going to try to convince us *you* sank that boat." A chuckle rippled through the group, releasing some of the tension. I managed a weak smile.

"No, indeed. But I did not find Julian merely injured below decks. He was also locked in a cabin. It's why it took me so long to free him."

Celine gasped, and Frederic's face went white. I forced myself to meet their eyes and face their judgment.

"You're fortunate you weren't drowned with him," said Frederic tersely.

"You really are a heroine," said Celine. "I wish I'd found him instead. I've always fancied being a heroine."

Cassian rolled his eyes, as I glanced between them all. Were they…concerned for me? Not angry? My knees suddenly felt weak, and I wished I had a chair to sit on.

"So it was most definitely an attack on Julian, then. Surely the viscount himself wasn't party to an attempt to kill his only son!" exclaimed Celine.

"No…I cannot imagine it to be so," said Frederic thoughtfully. "But neither can I imagine that after so many years of such close companionship, it was coincidence that Marcus chose now to act."

"Whatever do you mean, Your Highness?" asked the earl. "It seems to me the matter has been most neatly resolved." He looked hopeful.

"Marcus is not unintelligent, that much is certain," said Cassian. "He must have known there was a chance his plan might fail. If Julian had gone down with the boat, Marcus would have found himself heir. But, if he didn't—as turned out to be the case—Marcus must have known he faced banishment without any resources. He doesn't strike me as the type to risk such a thing."

"Unless he knew he had somewhere to run," said Frederic. "Perhaps to those who instructed him to make such an attempt, for instance?"

I swallowed. What were they saying?

"Our first stop was marred by a tragedy. The type that strikes fear into the heart of every commoner," said Cassian, when the earl still looked confused. "What if our second stop had been marred by the type of tragedy feared by every noble? The death of their only son and heir."

"It is subtle, this attack," said Frederic, "with everything designed to look like an accident." He frowned at his brother. "We must write to Father."

This time I did stagger back into a chair. My fear and my mistrust had held my tongue, and now they would never have the chance to question Marcus and discover if he were an agent of this shadowy rebellion. My mind whirled as the talk continued to swirl around me.

"You think the viscount was protecting his nephew with his haste? Even after he attempted to kill Julian?" The earl frowned. "I find it hard to believe. I know I would never do such a thing."

"And if we had found Marcus to be guilty of not only attempted murder but treason?" asked Frederic. "Would that not be a far worse and more dangerous taint on the family?"

"It is hard to explain the speed of his judgment any other way," said Cassian. "He has willfully deprived us of information in an effort to protect his own name."

My head had begun to throb, but that didn't sound right. And while part of me wanted to let the viscount burn, the other part was still reeling from the consequences of holding on to my knowledge the day before.

I tried to speak, but the words came out so quietly no one heard. I stood and tried again.

"I don't...I don't think so," I said. For the second time the talk stopped as everyone stared at me. I straightened my spine. "As you know, I spent several years living on Catalie."

The earl looked at me curiously, but I pushed on. "The islands are loyal to the crown, but their culture differs from that of the mainland. They don't see things in quite the same way."

The earl was frowning now but also nodding. I focused my attention on Frederic.

"Here on Catalie, it is the viscount's role to maintain order. Any breach of order is seen as a personal stain on his honor. It's why he is so harsh against crime of any kind. The larger the breach, the faster he must act to restore the island's order, and thus his own honor. He can expect neither respect nor obedience from his people until he has acted. They are an insular community here, and far more concerned with honor than most mainlanders. An attack on his own son and three members of the royal family is so grave a breach of order that I am not in the least surprised to find that Marcus is already banished."

The earl rubbed his head. "The girl..." He looked at me blankly.

"The royal seamstress," I said, at the same moment as Celine said, "Evie."

He looked confused but shook the thought aside. "The girl, Evie, speaks truth, Your Highnesses. It has been many, many years since I lived here on the islands. So long, in fact, that I sometimes forget I was an islander born and bred." He chuckled. "Although it does the old bones good to be here once again, and it's amazing how it all floods back. In fact, I am a relative of the current viscount, and spent some of my youth with him before I unexpectedly inherited my title on the mainland. I would vouch he has not gone rogue against the crown. Indeed, by the customs of the islands, his swift action—where guilt was certain—is a sign of respect toward the victims."

Silence reigned for a moment as everyone digested his words.

I would have smiled at him in gratitude for backing me up if I hadn't feared he would consider it an impertinence.

"We must bow to your experience," said Frederic at last. "And be grateful to have you both with us. The last thing we want is to drive a wedge between loyal subjects and the crown."

"No, that's exactly what the rebels will be hoping for." Cassian sighed. "I do wish we had been given the chance to interview Marcus, however. And I cannot find myself easy at the choice of punishment."

"Banishment is a customary penalty on the islands," said the earl, and I nodded. It was a custom with which I had personal experience. "As it is customary with the royal family. It is considered a very grave punishment for an islander, few of who would willingly leave our beautiful shores under any circumstances, let alone leave without friends, family, or money."

"I no longer question the intent behind the act," said Frederic. "I concede to your wisdom as my father desired in such an instance. However, it does not change the fact that a potential agent of the rebellion is now loose on the mainland, free to wreak further damage."

I shivered as the truth of his words sank in. Somewhere in the back of my mind, I had been rejoicing to be once again free from Marcus. But the very opposite was true. I thought of the final expression on his face, and my insides clenched. Soon we, too, would leave Catalie and, when we did, I would have to go back to watching over my shoulder. But now it was not only me, but the whole kingdom that had something to fear.

CHAPTER 14

Frederic used the excuse of Julian's injury to leave the island early without impinging further on the viscount's honor. The noble seemed to understand the true motive but appeared grateful for the reason given, assuring the Tour that he was touched by their thoughtful consideration of his family at such a difficult time.

It still took us two days to organize our departure, during which time I managed to put the finishing touches on three bathing costumes. Celine apologized profusely when she told me that courtesy required her to gift two of them to Monique and Shantelle. I merely smiled knowingly and told her which ones I had made to my guess of their measurements. I had already made my peace with the destinations of my creations. And surprisingly, it didn't even sting. Something had changed in Monique since the boating accident and Marcus's departure. She hadn't actually done anything as shocking as apologize, but she had been subdued, avoiding me rather than seeking conflict. And Shantelle had done nothing but cry since Julian's injury.

Returning to the island had reminded me of the many things I had enjoyed about my life here, and my experience of island culture had even proved to be of use to my new friends. I found I now viewed my years here through a different prism, and I couldn't begrudge either girl the gift.

But Celine still seemed to want to make it up to me and suggested that I choose the destination of the final costume. I hesitated, ashamed of myself for finding this gift harder than the other two.

"Delphine," I forced myself to say at last. "You should give it to Delphine. She is sweet and kind and everything the viscount's children are not." I watched Celine's reaction. Would she understand the second meaning behind my words?

"She *is* a sweet little thing, isn't she?" said Celine, for all the world as if she weren't three years younger than Delphine herself. "It's a pity Cassian didn't take a liking to her. But then, she looks like the type to harbor secret, intense dreams of romance, so I can't imagine Cassian would be to her liking."

She looked at me to share the laugh, and it was far too easy to join in. It had not occurred to me Celine might think of the other girl for *Cassian*.

Stop being a fool! I told myself—but I didn't seem to be listening.

I boarded the royal yacht with some trepidation, drawing courage from the way the three royals strode on board without sign of hesitation or fear. I had been afraid my joy in sailing might be gone forever after three nights of dreams about being trapped in a small place while water slowly rose around me. But I found, to my relief, that the deck of the royal yacht—so much farther above the water than on the catamaran—seemed sturdy and secure by comparison. I even felt relaxed enough to smile at the pod of dolphins that soon found us.

In fact, with the sun beating down, its sting removed by the stiff breeze, and the foaming wake streaming behind us, I could even imagine that the whole sojourn on Catalie had been nothing more than a dream. But when I looked at my companions, my time there was not so easily dismissed.

Far too many new emotions filled me to be easily discredited: shame for remaining silent and gratitude at being neither judged nor disbelieved when I did speak up; a strange peace about my years on the island mixed with a lingering shame. I had admitted to them what I had seen in the cabin, but not that I had strongly suspected Marcus. If I had told them that at the time, they could have arrested him themselves the night we returned.

The needling memory of Medellan only made my mistake worse. There, too, I had hesitated to share vital knowledge with the royals. My unease about my welcome in their tents had led me to make what may have been a significant delay. And now I had done the same thing again: I had hesitated, not sure where to place my trust, and the consequences in this case had been definite. I didn't like making the same mistake twice.

And over it all, a giddy feeling that swirled in my stomach whenever I looked at Frederic and remembered his strong arm around my waist as he threw me playfully into the air. In some ways, that was the most troubling emotion of all, since I had no right to feel it.

For several days we made our leisurely way down the coast. We were to be deposited further south, although not as far south as Largo, to make our way from the coast into the jungle. Once we had visited a string of towns in the jungle, we would emerge on the eastern side of Lanover and visit one of the tribes of nomadic desert traders. From there we would travel to Largo and rejoin the royal yacht.

It wasn't lost on me that the Tour was retracing the steps of my life. And the memory brought with it a new anxiety. So far, the royals had shown me remarkable trust. But what would happen when they saw the same pattern repeated over and over —the only constant, me?

I hated that I still didn't trust them not to turn on me, but I could no more erase my fear than I could cease breathing. The more I allowed myself to relax around them, the more it would hurt when Celine, or Frederic, or even Cassian, looked at me with that shadow of doubt in their eyes. And the thought lingered that perhaps they would be right to do so. What sort of person couldn't fit into even a single community in a kingdom of this size?

But emotions like these were more than troubling—they were also exhausting. And as we sailed, I let them blow away on the breeze, choosing to relax and enjoy the sun and sea instead. This was how I had survived everything life had thrown at me so far, by refusing to give it space in my mind. I had one small perfect slice of life on this ship, and I refused to spend it alone and worrying.

Celine dared a young lieutenant, an old friend of hers apparently, to race her to the top of the mast, and she would have fallen to her death in her haste if he hadn't caught her. Entirely undaunted, she challenged him again the next day and was only stopped by Cassian stepping in and telling the boy, Tom, that he must on no account accept.

"Climb all you like," he told his sister, "but please desist with this racing business. I, for one, have no wish to inform our parents that their baby has broken her neck through her own foolishness."

Celine promised laughingly to leave a fish head in his bunk for spoiling her sport but otherwise accepted his criticism with unexpected cheerfulness. Tom looked more than relieved, and I felt a little sorry for the young man. That is, until I found the two of them the next day lowering themselves down the outside of the ship with ropes to let their feet dip into the water.

I was still goggling over the edge, trying to decide what, if anything, I should do, when Frederic strolled over to join me.

"What has you so fascinated…oh." He sighed. "She was a surprising help in the rebellion last year, but Celine doesn't do well with boredom."

I suppressed a laugh and looked at him through my lashes. I could hear in his voice how much the last rebellion still hurt him. He and his father had uncovered and dismantled it in the end, but not in time to prevent the rest of their family from hurtling into greater danger than he himself had faced. I knew him well enough already to know how that would sting. How he would feel he had failed.

"Shall we spoil their fun?" I asked.

Frederic looked at me and then shook his head. "I'm tempted to cut the ropes myself and let her swim to shore." The laugh in his eyes betrayed the words, and I remembered how satisfying his actual laugh had sounded.

"Come now," I said reprovingly. "You couldn't do that to poor Tom. You must know this is not his idea, and he faces discipline from a senior officer at any moment. You should rather grant him your clemency."

Frederic grinned. "Are you teasing me, Evie? You do know I'm a prince, do you not? We are far too important to be teased."

I leaned over the edge again, directing my eyes downward significantly as an unusually large wave splashed over Celine and sent her spinning on her ropes, laughing wildly. "Yes, I've observed the overbearing dignity of the royal family and immediately apologize for my impudence."

He chuckled this time, and my heart thrilled.

"Are we anything like you expected, Miss Seamstress?"

I bit my lip, not wanting to turn the conversation serious if he was still joking around. But something in his eyes encouraged me to answer honestly.

"Nothing at all, so far."

"So far," he said softly. "So we still need to prove ourselves to you."

I flushed at having so revealed myself. "Of course not!" I rushed to say, the lie heavy on my lips. How could I tell a prince that an orphaned commoner without name or family required more from him than he had already given?

An urgent need to tell him something at least of the truth overwhelmed me. "It's my fault that Marcus got away," I said in a rush before I could change my mind.

Frederic raised both eyebrows but waited in silence for me to gather my next thought. "I knew someone had acted against Julian. And I strongly suspected that Marcus had scuttled the boat in an attempt on his cousin's life. It never occurred to me he could have any deeper motive or that any harm could come of my silence. But that doesn't change the fact that I was wrong. And that if I had spoken, you would have been able to prevent Marcus's banishment before it happened."

Frederic sighed. "If we can be blamed for a failure to foresee the future, then I am as guilty as you and of greater crimes."

I bit my cheek. I hadn't intended to bring up his own regrets. When he looked at me, I looked away, unable to hold his gaze.

"Tell me Evie," he said quietly, "why did you hold back on your knowledge and your suspicions? You owed no loyalty to the viscount or his family. And to Marcus least of all."

I flushed again. So he had worked out who it was on the island who scared me, despite my earlier restraint in not naming him. And he was calling me out on my mistake. After all of my experiences with them, I should have trusted the royals above any member of the viscount's family. I shouldn't still be wondering when they, too, would let me down. And yet I was.

After a moment of silence, he sighed again. "No, don't answer that. You've already said why." He paused again before laying a hand on my arm.

I tried to ignore the thrill that raced through me at his touch.

"I do not know everything in your past, Evie, and I have no right to demand such knowledge from you. But I will show you that you can trust me. That much I can do."

I flushed again, still not meeting his eyes.

When I said nothing, he turned to leave before pausing and looking back at me.

"And I can protect you from Marcus, that much I can do. He will never touch you, Evie."

His words echoed in my head long after he was gone. That he was trustworthy I wanted to believe was true. That he would do his best to protect us all from Marcus I did not doubt. But over my past he had no protective power. Some things could not be changed, however much we willed them.

The next day we made landfall, and the day after that we slept in our first jungle village. The moist, heavy air and dense greenery bore down on me, a sticky web that I could not escape. The islands had proven to hold unexpected happy memories. The jungle brought back only misery.

hat night I dreamed the same dream that had gripped me my one night in the palace. Once again, a small woodshed contained me, my only protection from the taunts of the children who hammered on its walls. I woke up twisted in my thin coverlet, hoping I hadn't cried out in my sleep. A quick glance showed Celine sleeping peacefully.

Both princes had agreed that after two instances of violence, regardless of its direction, they didn't want their young sister sleeping alone. It had been Celine herself who insisted that she would much prefer me to any maid.

Some light was already seeping into the tent, so I sat up and resumed work on the dress I had been adjusting the day before. The fashion of the jungle-dwellers, or junglers as they called themselves, had changed little since I had been here over four years ago, but it differed significantly from the styles popular in the capital. With any luck our visit to the jungle would be short, and I would only need to modify a handful of outfits for the three royals.

I had almost finished my current project when Celine awoke.

"There's so much moisture in the air, I feel like I'm swimming instead of walking," she said, as she slipped into the light dress I had already adjusted for her. Sheer sleeves protected her arms, and her skirts were as light as modesty would allow. "Thank goodness I brought you along, I would look like a fool wearing my normal gowns next to all these junglers."

We walked together to breakfast which was served, like all the other meals, in a large communal hut without walls. The locals had initially offered for the royals to eat in one of their few fully-enclosed huts, but Frederic had elected to join the rest of the village and Tour for the communal meals, as all junglers did regardless of rank. Celine loved the look of the treetop houses preferred by most of the locals, but I was glad to be sleeping in a tent and eating on the ground.

I had arrived in the jungle, traumatized and alone, at twelve years old. My new foster siblings commemorated the occasion by holding me over the edge of their home until I broke down and cried. In my two years living in a treetop home I had overcome my subsequent fear of heights, but that didn't mean I ever wished to climb up to such a dwelling again.

"I would love to live in such a place," said Celine as we ate, having no idea of the source of my distaste. She scrunched up her face. "Well, without all these bugs, and as long as it wasn't so hot."

"So, in other words, not in the jungle," said Frederic, joining us. "How undiplomatic of you."

Celine merely rolled her eyes and kept eating.

"Don't worry," I said dryly. "You won't convince a jungler there's anything wrong with their beautiful jungle. Any criticism will be taken merely as a sign of the poor breeding of the speaker."

"Excellent," said Frederic, "how reassuring."

The twinkle in his eyes made me nearly choke on my star-fruit. I had come to the conclusion that he had more of a sense of humor than I had first suspected, I just needed to learn when his serious voice hid a less-than-serious sentiment. Celine had assured me he was just like their mother in that regard.

"Don't worry," she'd told me earlier, "you get used to it."

Much to my relief, she apparently hadn't noticed I was fast becoming a lot more than just used to it—at least in Frederic's case.

"It's not as if I hate the jungle, or anything," Celine told us as she peeled a banana. "Just look at all this fresh fruit. And the colors are indescribable. I think I saw a flower as big as my head back there."

"Just be careful," I said. "You'd be surprised how many things are poisonous here."

"Poisonous?" Her eyes grew large and thoughtful.

Frederic was watching her with misgiving. "Don't get yourself poisoned, Leeny."

"I'm not a child, Frederic."

"I know."

Several locals joined us. "How is the food?" one asked, and we all heaped praises on the fare. Even I had to admit that I had missed the fruit and some of the spices used in the local dishes.

"Oh, yes," one assured us, "our bananas are far superior to the western ones. Our rissoles, as well. You'll see this evening."

I hid a smile. I had lived in one of the western villages and heard for two years about how greatly superior the western fruit and cooking was to the eastern. Junglers had no time to worry about outsiders when they had such an intense rivalry going on among themselves.

The villagers had arranged a series of exhibitions for the Tour, including archery, climbing, and an intense game called Kurau which was played high in the trees using vines and a small, solid leather ball. Just watching the game, which had been much beloved by my jungler foster siblings, was enough to make me queasy, so I wandered away.

Following a natural trail through the trees, I found a passion fruit vine and stopped to admire the incredible purple flowers. They had always been my favorite, and I had incorporated aspects of their design into many of my creations.

Steps behind me made me flinch and spin around. Frederic appeared around a tree and froze.

"I'm sorry, I didn't mean to startle you."

I shook my head. "I'm all right."

"That's a beautiful flower," he said.

I smiled. "Yes, it's my favorite."

He shifted uncomfortably. "It probably isn't a good idea for any of us to be wandering off on our own." He must have seen the change in my face because he added, swiftly, "For our own protection."

I took a slow breath. "You don't need to worry about me." He could have no way of knowing that I had spent as much of my two years here alone in the jungle as I possibly could.

"You're familiar with the jungle, then?" He looked half concerned, half curious.

I licked my lips nervously and tried not to notice the way his eyes dropped to my lips and then quickly away. I would have preferred not to talk about my time among the junglers.

"I spent two years here," I said at last. "Before Catalie."

"You've lived in the jungle as well as the islands?" He seemed to weigh me with his eyes, and it took all my self-control not to squirm.

"I've lived in many places."

"Evidently."

A moment of quiet passed between us, as I plucked one of the flowers and spun it in my hand. Perhaps I was wrong. Perhaps it would help to unburden myself of the pain of the past.

"When I was twelve, I was taken in by a kind jungler woman, who found me on the eastern edge of the jungle."

"Ah, one of the easterners," he said with a rare smile, clearly attempting to lighten the air between us.

"Indeed," I said. "You may or may not be surprised to learn they are almost exactly like the westerners."

"How disappointing. I had conceived a strong desire to meet them and now fear I will find myself greatly disappointed."

I smiled back at him, surprising myself with an unexpected buoyancy. I had never found anyone so easy to talk to as I did this prince, whose conversation should have been forbidden me given my background.

"I confess I can taste no difference in the bananas," I admitted with a small smile of my own. But when I thought of my next words, it dropped away.

"Unfortunately my foster mother had not consulted her own children when she acquired a new one. They saw me as competition for her love, and the more kindness she lavished on me, the crueler they became. I came to dread her smiles and warm words."

I looked away. "And for all I tried, I could not fit in here. I was perpetually viewed as an outsider. No amount of work or knowledge made any of them see me as a true jungler. Perhaps I am a coward. But after two years, I simply could not bear it any longer. I left the jungle, intending to slowly work my way north toward Lanare. That's when the viscount happened upon me."

"Rejected in two homes," said Frederic. "Evie, I cannot imagine…" He stepped toward me, and my breath hitched in my throat. The sounds of the jungle seemed to go quiet around us, and this time it was me who could not tear my eyes from his lips. Neither of us moved to touch the other, but we stood a single breath apart. If I leaned forward, I would be in his arms.

Heat raced over me as my mind scrambled unsuccessfully to retrieve the thread of our conversation.

"Evie," he said again, so quietly I could barely hear the word despite our nearness. The sound of it broke my heart.

"Evie, I…"

For a desperate moment, I thought he would close the

distance between us and press his lips against mine, but instead he stepped abruptly backward, gave me a small bow and retreated the way he had come.

I stood alone and reeling, heat and cold chasing each other around my body. What had just happened? What had I done?

But I already knew what I had done. For all the warnings I had given myself, for all I had tried to hold back, I had become too entangled with the royals. And while it was their rejection I had feared, it was something far worse that had happened. I had fallen in love with the crown prince of Lanover. A person who would never in a hundred years consider wedding an orphan who could not find even a small corner of his vast kingdom that would accept her.

I wandered for hours without paying attention to my surroundings, only returning for the evening meal. Why was I always unable to play the appropriate role for my surroundings? I could not be a good islander, a good jungler, a good trader, even a good daughter. And now I could not be a good seamstress, one who knew her place and kept to it. No wonder I had never been accepted anywhere.

Celine took one look at my no doubt pale face and dragged me to bed early.

"Frederic mentioned you once lived here," she said once we were safely inside our tent. "Which made me realize how wise I was to recruit you for my secret mission. It seems you've been everywhere and know everyone."

I stared at her in confusion until horrified understanding broke over me. I could not talk to her of potential brides for Frederic on this of all days.

"Oh, no, I lived on the other side of the jungle," I said. "I know no one here."

She waved my words away. "But you know junglers. Have you spotted any likely candidates?"

She sat on her temporary bed and gave me her full attention. I collapsed on my pallet, feeling suddenly shaky.

"I…I can't…say that I have." My dry mouth made the words stick in my throat.

She narrowed her eyes. "Whatever is the matter, Evie?"

When I said nothing, she got up and came to sit beside me. "Whatever it is, you can tell me. Is it something to do with Frederic? I saw him follow you into the jungle, and he came back out looking as if he had stumbled on a python."

I flushed. What did that mean? Had he been horrified by what nearly happened between us?

Celine chuckled. "And now you look just the same. What? Did he try to kiss you or something?" She chortled again while I froze.

Her laugh slowly died away, and her eyes grew larger and larger.

"He did! Oh my goodness! He tried to kiss you! Or, wait, did he actually kiss you?" She gripped my arms in her excitement. "Frederic, of all people! I can't believe it!"

"No!" I cried, frantically shaking my head. "No, of course he did not. I didn't mean…I never said…"

Celine looked closely at my face. "Ha! I knew it! You're in love with him."

"Celine!" I stood up, but she pulled me back down.

"Oh, don't be silly. You can trust me. I knew it anyway." She looked smug. "Although I didn't suspect he'd do anything so dramatic."

"He did not, truly he did not." I chewed the inside of my cheek while my eyes pleaded with her to believe me.

"Oh, very well, he did not." She smiled. "But you *are* in love with him. And he's in love with you."

I shook my head, looking down into my lap. "No, he's not."

"Oh, poo." She scrunched up her nose. "He's a wet blanket that's for certain, but I think I know my own brother."

"I really don't think he is."

She looked at me with knit brows. "I see. So we need to get him to admit it, then. Maybe even to himself."

I looked up at her sharply. "Celine!"

She stood up and laughed again. "Don't look so concerned. I'll be ever so subtle, I promise."

Misgiving seized me. I should never have let her see my reaction to her earlier words. It had been a day of mistakes.

"Why do you think I asked for your help?" she went on, striding up and down the small tent. "Well, I do legitimately need your help for Cassian, of course. I still can't imagine who might fall in love with him. But I could see from that first day in your shop that Frederic was struck with you. I just thought the two of you might need a little help."

I shook my head in bewilderment.

"I'm very observant," she added with a mischievous twinkle in her eye.

"Celine, you shouldn't be talking this way. Your brother is a prince. The crown prince. And I am a seamstress. One without a family, remember?"

She shook her head, not in the least cast down. "Evie, surely you know that's not how these things work. You know the godmothers help princes and princesses find their *true loves*. Rank is unimportant. If a kingdom is to prosper, it must be ruled by true love. Those are the rules."

I raised an eyebrow at her, and she grinned back at me. "Besides, all three of my sisters and my other brother have all made eminently suitable noble and royal matches ensuring all sorts of excellent treaties for Lanover. There aren't even any more eligible princesses left. Which means, Frederic's only job as crown prince to ensure the well-being of his realm, is to marry his true love."

I shook my head again. "That isn't me, Celine. It couldn't possibly be." I actually laughed, although the sound held no humor. "I'm not princess material, let alone queen. And I'm not true love material, either."

"Don't be ridiculous," the younger girl said briskly. "Of course you are. And now I just need to get Frederic to see it."

"Celine, please." I tried one last time without much hope of being heeded.

She continued to stride up and down. "You know, you're even an orphan," she pointed out. "With a horrible, downtrodden life."

"Celine!"

She grinned. "Sorry. But my point is that you're just the type to have a godmother, too. Are you sure you don't?"

I stood up as well and faced her, my hands on my hips. "Of course I'm sure."

"Not even a godmother object?"

The objects of power dispensed by the godmothers were usually handed down from generation to generation as heirlooms, even long after their magic had been exhausted. Celine didn't know how humorous it was to suggest that I, the most homeless of orphans, might have such an item.

"No."

"Sorry," she said again, absently this time. "Perhaps they knew you didn't need one. That you'd be able to captivate Frederic all on your own."

I swallowed, trying to guard my mind and heart before I started believing her talk of my captivating Frederic. I had far too much bitter experience with false hope. Because despite what Celine said, even if Frederic did have some passing interest in me, surely it was only because we were traveling in such close proximity. That didn't make me his true love.

CHAPTER 16

$\mathcal{F}$rederic confirmed my reading of the situation when he wouldn't even meet my eyes the next day. The Tour packed up and traveled onward the day after that, taking the one road large enough for us all, running through the jungle east to west. Even with only the one major road—which intersected with a single large north-south road—the junglers struggled to keep the length of it clear from the ever-encroaching greenery. Whole teams of them were employed by the crown in the task, and we passed one such team before reaching the next village.

We stopped for one or two nights at every village we passed and were feasted and entertained with exhibitions and competitions. Frederic and Celine both laughed with me at our first eastern village.

"It's exactly the same as in the west," Celine whispered to me over the evening meal.

"It even tastes the same," Frederic agreed in an undertone.

I chuckled. "I did try to warn you."

After that they both took great delight in pointing out any

tiny difference they could spot between the eastern villagers and the western.

In reality our slow journey took only a matter of weeks, but still I began to fear we would never leave the jungle. It didn't help that all the time we crept closer and closer to my own old village near the eastern edge.

Frederic had regained his ease around me, but Celine watched us with an eagle eye that made me jumpy every time I saw it. I spent my time adjusting clothes and avoiding the locals. And dreaming of returning again to a place that didn't buzz with the constant hum of insects.

My nightmares intensified until sometimes my restlessness did wake Celine. She asked about them, but I refused to give her details. The dreams of the taunting jungler children now mingled with more horrifying visions. Ones that now, as I had feared, included a smell that sometimes woke me retching. Because we would only leave the jungle when we reached the desert.

When at long last the Tour rode into my old home, it turned out to be rather anti-climactic. The village looked just as it had when I had left it more than four years ago, and yet, somehow, it looked also smaller and only half-familiar, as if it were a place from a distant dream—as if I had grown past this place and the emotions it had once roused in me.

The locals had all gathered to welcome us, and I scanned their faces for any familiar ones. I wasn't sure who I dreaded seeing more—my old foster mother or her children.

One young man looked familiar, his own eyes widening in recognition as they met mine. Brandon. I rode next to Celine, only two rows back from the princes, and his eyes raced between me and the princess.

I gave him a cold inclination of my head.

I thought I had seen everyone by the time I dismounted, so the soft arms that enveloped me in a smothering hug took me by surprise. I pushed back, disentangling myself from the sudden attack.

"My little one! My lamb!" The older woman wiped tears from her eyes. "My dearest daughter! Just look at you. So big! So beautiful!"

I drew a deep breath as I felt a familiar someone come to stand behind me. I didn't look back, but I did draw strength from Frederic's silent presence. I straightened my spine and regarded the woman who I had once called Mother Nora.

"Nora. You look well."

"Never mind me," she said, still apparently overcome by my presence. "The missing daughter has returned! What a wonderful day."

What was Frederic thinking of her words? Did he question my tale of hardship in the face of such profusions? I stood firm.

"I'm not your daughter."

"Evie? What is this?" She looked shocked and hurt.

"You call me your little one, your lamb, your missing daughter. But I wasn't lost. I left. And you made no effort to stop me when I did so, although I was only fourteen, and had only a small handful of coins to my name."

She stumbled back a step, her face falling. "I didn't want you to leave, Evie, I assure you. But you remember how it was…so difficult…"

"I am sure my leaving brought more peace to your days." I looked her straight in the eyes. "And I remember how your children constantly harassed me." I paused, my face set. "And I remember how you never made any true attempt to stop them."

"Evie, please…" She sounded weak now, and I remembered that she had always been so, although I hadn't seen it at the beginning. Her desire for an easy life and peace had overridden the kind heart that had led her to take me in. She was the parent, but her children had been the ones to rule.

And I realized, also, that it no longer pained me as it once had.

"You housed me for two years, even though you didn't have to. And for that I thank you. And for the rest I forgive you. But I claim no kinship. I wish you well in life, but you have not earned the right to be a part of mine."

She gave me one last beseeching look, but when I said nothing she left. As soon as she was gone, I slumped, my strength and determination overridden by a sudden wave of exhaustion.

"Well done, Evie," said Frederic.

I turned to face him, looking up into his eyes. "You did not think me cruel?"

"Cruel? She was the one who was cruel to you. I would not have been so gentle toward her." A cold look filled his eyes, and I shivered though it wasn't aimed at me. It was hard in moments like this to remember to keep my distance.

He looked down at me. "I don't know how you do it, Evie."

"Do what?"

"Be so gracious and poised after everything you've been through."

I stared at him, too startled to speak. Me? Gracious and poised? Fear filled me. How long until he saw the mess of distrustful fear inside me? I had been right to put no stock in whatever fleeting emotion he now felt.

The town elder approached us and pulled Frederic away. I let the swirl of action move around and then pass me, making no effort to follow the group of leaders, both Tour and village, who now bore Frederic toward our welcome meal.

But when I at last thought I stood alone, a voice startled me. It sounded different, deeper, slower than I remembered, but it remained recognizable.

"Brandon," I said as I turned toward him.

"You've returned."

I nodded, eyeing him wordlessly, unsure what he wanted from me. An instinctive urge told me to run, but I wasn't a traumatized young girl anymore. I didn't have to run from jealous children.

You would—and have—run from Marcus, an internal voice reminded me. But I shook it away. Marcus had never been cruel with the petty jealousies of childhood—he had been cold with the icy rage of a man who had grown twisted instead of straight and true. He threatened not only me, but the whole kingdom. It was only sensible to be afraid of him.

"What do you want, Brandon?" I asked, the weariness from earlier returning.

"You seem to be friendly with the royals."

"And?"

He cleared his throat. "I just wanted to...to welcome you back."

I raised an eyebrow, and he shifted his weight from side to side. "I thought there might be some...misunderstanding about before."

Comprehension dawned. "You mean, you're afraid that now I'm the one in a position of power, I might attempt to wreak some sort of revenge on you." I looked at him for a moment before sighing. "I won't, although if you've been fearing it since my arrival, it's no more than you deserve after the constant fear you inflicted on me all those years ago."

He looked away uncomfortably. "I'm sure you don't believe I mean it, Evie, but I am sorry. We were heedless, and...well... mean. I can see that now."

"Good." I rubbed at my temples where a headache bloomed. "If you wish to repay me, make sure no child in this village—or any you may live in—is ever tormented in such a way again."

He said nothing.

"Where are the others?" I wished I felt no curiosity, but I could not deny having just a little.

He shrugged. "They moved on to other villages." He gave a short laugh. "Lela even moved to a westerner village."

"That must have pained Nora."

"As you can imagine." He smiled at me, and then the expression dropped away as he remembered we weren't old friends exchanging reminiscences. "Ah, I need to get back..."

"Go. You don't need to fear me."

He hesitated. "Thank you, Evie."

I shrugged, unable to muster any gracious words despite Frederic's belief in me.

He disappeared into the trees, and I wandered toward the meal, taking a circuitous route to visit a handful of the old places. Some had changed but surprisingly few. The jungle had encroached in new ways and been beaten back in others.

When I reached the communal eating hut, Celine pounced on me.

"There you are, Evie! Where have you been?" She didn't pause for me to reply. "I've discovered your secret!"

I blinked, my sluggish brain unable to work out which of my secrets she could mean.

"Everyone in the capital has been wondering where your vivid material comes from, and now I know!" She winked at me. "If you promise to keep making me amazing dresses, I promise I won't tell."

I relaxed. So Celine had found Josinna. I hadn't seen her with the other greeters, but she had already had limited mobility when I had been here, and years had passed since then. I would have to go and visit her sooner rather than later.

"They have an impressive operation," she continued. "You must be so proud."

I stared at her. "What do you mean?"

She grinned. "Don't tell me you don't know! She did say it was new. Oh, you have to come and look."

I protested that I hadn't eaten yet, but she dragged me away anyway.

Josinna had once been the head weaver in the region, but age had slowed her down. She preferred experimenting with incredible dyes and new weaves to producing quickly, and her work had come to be seen by the village as a beautiful curiosity rather than a practicality. She wasn't exactly a warm woman, but she had never turned me away from her small weaving hut when I needed somewhere to hide from the other youngsters. And after seeing my interest in her material and hearing me musing aloud about a possible dress design, she had gifted me a length, telling me she wanted to see what I could create.

When I had handed her the finished product, she had stared at it silently for a full two minutes. I had feared she disliked it, but when she at last spoke, she told me to leave. "A talent like yours is wasted here, youngling," she had told me. "There is nothing for you here. Make your way to the capital and let your skill shine."

I had been too afraid to run, then, but she had often repeated her advice. And one day I had come to her hut and told her that I was finally going to do it. I promised her I would leave and make a name for myself as long as she agreed to let me buy all my material from her. During my three years on Catalie, I had always felt a vague sense of guilt, that I was betraying Josinna by not starting my own shop. But when I finally did make it to the capital and sent her my first order, she had filled it without delay. And she had never let me down since.

The weaving hut was tucked on the far edge of the village, so I hadn't passed it in my earlier wanderings. My steps quickened as Celine led me in the right direction. I should have gone to visit Josinna first, but I hadn't wanted our meeting tainted by all my negative emotions.

But as I neared it, I slowed. This section of the village looked far from familiar. Where had all these open-air huts come from? Even with the welcome feast underway, people bustled to and fro, the air of activity a far cry from the quiet haven this corner used to be.

Where was Josinna? I ignored the greetings from the villagers and hurried to her hut.

"Evangeline!" she cried in her trembling voice.

My eyes swam with moisture as I rushed over to embrace her where she sat.

"You did it." She patted my hand and beamed at me. "I knew you would." She nodded toward Celine. "I see your hand in her gown easily enough."

I flushed. "All thanks to you, Josinna."

"Nonsense." She looked past me to Celine. "I was always telling her she was made for bigger things than this jungle."

"You were right, of course," said Celine. "You look like the sort of woman who's always right."

Josinna laughed, a rumbling cadence, at her obvious flattery. "I like you, girl."

"Everyone likes me," said Celine with a cheeky twinkle, and the old lady laughed again.

"But what is going on here?" I asked her. "Who are all these people?"

She looked smug. "I charge you a lot for my material, Evangeline. I took a gamble that you would pay it, and you do. I knew that once you combined my creations with your designs, you would be able to charge a great deal for your gowns. And, clearly, I was right since your demand for material keeps increasing. Together we have proven that luxury cloth can be worth as much to the village as the more practical weaves. All the local villages send me their most promising weavers now. They work for me and, in exchange, I teach them my new techniques. Did you not wonder how I managed to keep up with your orders?"

"I did." I looked around. "But I was picturing you having taken on an assistant or two."

My emotions swung up and down as I looked around her expanding empire. She deserved to have her skills recognized and valued. It was only right. And I owed her a lot for being the first to believe in my designs and encourage me in them. But clearly her production was already starting to outstrip my demand. I couldn't hold on to my exclusive source any longer. Especially now that the Tour had visited the village—word would inevitably get out. But I could not begrudge her the success. I would simply have to work harder to ensure my designs stood out even without exceptional material.

Nora and Brandon avoided me after that, but I visited with Josinna whenever I could, admiring her new set up and discussing materials and designs with her. Both princes toured the set of weaving huts, full of compliments for the skill of the junglers. In fact, the villagers were so pleased with their reaction that they outdid themselves in demonstrations and activities for the royals.

Their efforts included showing off the beauties of the jungle, and several villagers insisted the royals must be shown the village's pride and joy—a beautiful waterfall hidden nearby. When Celine asked me about it, I did have to admit that it was an exquisite spot. Cassian decided to catch up on some paperwork, but Frederic and Celine expressed interest in going and insisted I come along as well—since I was, in Celine's words, "practically a local."

Two of the village's most experienced guides were given the task of leading us to the spot, for which I was grateful. I didn't remember the route well enough to trust myself to the task.

But just as we were about to set out, Celine groaned and doubled over.

"Celine? What's wrong?" Frederic steadied her.

"My stomach," she gasped and groaned again. "Horrible cramps. You'll have to go without me."

"No, no, we'll wait—"

She cut him off, shaking her head. "Don't be silly. We leave tomorrow. There's no need for you to miss your chance to go because I'm feeling poorly." She groaned again.

He frowned at her and then glanced at me and the guides. I could see in his eyes that he would rather stay with Celine, but he didn't want to offend the locals by canceling the trip altogether.

Cassian emerged from his tent to see what the fuss was about and promised to take Celine under his care.

Frederic nodded with some reluctance. "Very well, then." He gestured for the guides to lead us out and began striding after them.

I paused for a second longer, my concerned gaze on Celine. She looked toward Frederic's retreating back, and then winked at me before doubling over in a particularly loud groan.

I gasped, but Frederic was already calling for me to hurry. Reluctantly I followed him, sending silent insults back in Celine's direction. So this was her idea of subtly influencing her brother. With her absence, the tone of our expedition would be vastly different. Just as she had intended.

I sighed and plunged into the jungle.

CHAPTER 17

*W*alking through the jungle wasn't like strolling through the garden paths around the palace. The plethora of bright blooms was greater and more pungent, but no smooth gravel unfolded before our feet. Soon we were entirely enveloped in a cocoon of green, vines curling above our heads and snaking across the ground ready to trip us.

The jungle hummed with life, the calls of birds and distant monkeys mingling with the ever-present buzz of insects. I had forgotten how alive it felt here, how vibrant.

Frederic tripped on a vine and nearly fell, catching himself just in time.

"Careful," I said. "The jungle doesn't care too much about your dignity."

He smiled at me. "I've noticed that. Highly disrespectful."

I grinned back. "Why do you think even our nobles join our communal meals? It's hard to stand on ceremony in a jungle."

"Listen to you. Talking like a local."

I went back over my words in my head and frowned. He was right.

He glanced at me with concern. "That wasn't a criticism. There's nothing wrong with being a jungler, you know."

"Except I'm not one. I never truly fit in here. The person who was kindest to me in that village told me to run and not stop until I'd left the jungle behind. And she kept advising me to do so every day until I found the courage to escape. I was never a jungler."

He weighed me with his eyes. "Perhaps not. But the jungle is still a part of you. It provides the material for your dresses, and you understand it in a way that I do not. That is something to value."

I looked down at my feet, to give myself a moment to think. Was it true? Did I see each stage of my life as a burden that held me back rather than an integral part of who I was? It was an overwhelming thought.

The sound of rushing water had been growing stronger the nearer we came to the waterfall, until we broke free of the trees and stopped before the torrent. A small pool spread before us, constantly rippling from the disruption of the thundering water which poured down from rocky heights.

The waterfall looked graceful and delicate, like the softest lace, and yet strong and powerful at the same time. The water of the pool looked cool and inviting.

"Do the locals swim here?" asked Frederic.

One of the guides immediately shook his head.

"Only boys looking to impress one another," I said. "There's a strong current that will drag you under the fall and down. I'll show you where they do swim, though."

"Watch your step," called the second guide, as I led Frederic down the rocky lip of the waterway. The cool liquid from the waterfall's pool poured over a lip in the rock, looking like smooth, mobile glass. It filled a second, lower pool, this one's surface calm, dotted only with a few leaves. Leading him further,

I pointed to where the water flowed into a third pool before trickling away as a creek.

"The middle pool is the best for swimming. It's deep enough for a proper dip, but without the danger of the one above." I looked at it longingly. I should have worn my bathing costume.

"We should have come dressed for a dip," said Frederic, mirroring my thought. "The walk here was hot work. But I can see why the locals love the spot so much. It's breathtaking." He looked across the pool. "I wish I had such a haven within easy reach of the palace."

"Why? Do you often feel the need to escape?" The question popped from my mouth unbidden, the intimate setting promoting a sense of ease between us.

Frederic looked over at me, his brow creased. "Does it sound terrible of me? After all you've been through, what could I possibly have to run from in my life of ease?" He sighed. "No one has ever mistreated me, and I love my family. But sometimes I feel I shall be crushed under the weight of my responsibilities. Sometimes I fear I cannot bear the weight of a kingdom."

It was a different kind of burden he bore to the burden of my past, but it was a heavy load all the same. Except he, at least, was much more fitted to bear it than me.

"Our experiences have been so different," I said softly, "how can I hope to advise you? But I can say this—I have never met someone so suited to bear a responsibility he was born into. I have no doubt you will make a great king."

His face remained drawn, but warmth filled his eyes. "It means much to me that you would say so. I just wish I could have the same trust in myself. I've made grievous errors of judgment before—about even my own family. I made no protest when my sister was sent away to a marriage alliance with a prince who turned out not to be worthy even to look on her. And I never suspected…"

His voice trailed away, but the haunted look in his eye told me he referred to the rebellion the year before. He had never seen the betrayal coming, and it weighed on him, more heavily than all the rest.

"You told me not so long ago that we cannot be responsible for failing to foresee the future. If that is true for me, it's also true for you. You're not king yet, and Lanover is not yet your sole responsibility to bear. And it will never truly be yours alone. Didn't your sister see and foil the rebellion? You can trust in your family to help you."

"My sister Celeste, yes." He shook his head ruefully. "With her, too, I was blind."

I forced a cheerful note into my voice. "Well, console yourself with this. With so many failures behind you, you must be growing eminently wise by this point. When the distant day comes for you to be crowned king, everyone will marvel at your insight and discernment."

Frederic chuckled. "That's why I need you around, Evie. You make me laugh at myself whenever I start to take myself too seriously. I don't know how you do it, considering the life you've lived."

"It's an absolute requirement of such a history, I assure you, as it takes far less energy than constant weeping. And since you've so kindly confided your troubles in me, I daresay I can teach you the trick of it. But I should warn you that it takes a great deal of skill to learn, and you may not ever approach my level of brilliance." I winked at him.

He chuckled again and moved toward me before suddenly pausing. His head whipped up, his brow lowering. "Did you hear something?"

I looked back the way we had come. The lush foliage blocked our view of the higher pool's edge, and we couldn't see the two guides. I ran the last few moments back through my mind.

"Maybe?" I took a step in their direction, but Frederic blocked my passage with his arm.

"Let me go first," he said, his voice quiet.

I swallowed and nodded. What did he think he'd heard?

Careful of my footfalls, I trod silently behind Frederic. As we stepped up and around the greenery, he swore and dashed forward. I hurried behind him, not immediately seeing what had roused him.

But as he dropped to a knee, he revealed the prone figure of one of the guides. I gasped and would have knelt, too, but Frederic gestured for me to stay standing.

"Watch the trees. Let me know if you hear or see anything at all."

I tore my eyes away from the arrows that peppered the man's body, my fright holding back my tears as his blood ran over the mossy rocks. Where was the other guide?

Frederic stood beside me. "He's dead." His grim voice gave no hint of fear or grief, his focus on the danger confronting us.

I spared a quick look at the man. "He was an experienced jungler. And yet he had not time to call a warning to us. Who could have done this?"

"We need to find the other guide." Frederic looked hopelessly at the trees around us.

I followed his gaze, forcing my sickened mind to focus and concentrate. "There." I pointed to one side. "Someone has passed through there recently."

Frederic drew his sword, and together we trod carefully into the trees. The broken leaves and scuffed ground suggested someone had rushed through this way—and recently. After some minutes, voices ahead made us freeze. Frederic gestured silently for me to drop behind him as he crept forward, sword outstretched.

I followed behind, wishing the sword made me feel safer. But, unfortunately, I couldn't see how it would do us much good against bows and arrows. I shook my head, angry with myself. The Tour's journey had been so quiet since we entered the jungle that I hadn't even thought of the potential danger of an expedition such as this without any guards.

I halted at Frederic's signal, and we peered into a small, open space ahead of us. It contained three men with a body on the ground beside them. Our second guide stirred feebly, and one of the other men grunted. "We should keep moving."

He bent as if to pick the guide up when Frederic yelled loudly and charged out of the trees. All three men whirled around, took one look at the blade bearing down on them, and then ran for the trees. Their bows and quivers remained on the ground, along with a couple of bags.

As soon as they had disappeared, Frederic stopped, dropping down beside the guide. Stripping off his gag, he worked efficiently, tearing off the man's shirt to reveal several long gashes on his torso. Ripping the garment into strips, he began to bandage him. I rushed forward to help.

The man stirred several times, murmuring quietly, but he didn't seem fully conscious.

"What's he saying?" Frederic asked as he tied off the last of the makeshift bandages.

I leaned down to place my ear near his mouth. The man murmured again, his eyes still closed. Rocking back onto my heels I looked over at the prince uneasily.

"It sounded like 'west'."

Frederic frowned, his eyes raking the trees. "We've heard plenty of rivalry between the east and the west, does that include armed attacks?"

I bit my lip. "Not that I've ever heard of."

He looked down at the man on the ground and then stood. "There is nothing more I can do for him. If he is to have any hope of living, we need to return to the village and send proper help."

He looked at me expectantly, and I felt the blood drain from my face. We had no guides left. If we were to find our way back to safety, I would have to lead us.

Frederic gathered up the attackers' abandoned weapons and packs, distributing them between us. "We will send someone for you," he told the guide, although I doubted the man could hear or understand him. Had there been poison on the attackers' blades? Why had they fled, abandoning everything, when faced with a single armed man? And would they return for the guide as soon as we left?

I put the questions aside. For now it didn't matter. Four of us would die in the jungle if I couldn't find our way back to the village. Once we were back with the Tour, we could work out what had happened.

Trying to project more confidence than I really felt, I led the way back toward the waterfall. This part, at least, was easy, the path as clear on the way back as it had been on the way in. When we arrived back at the falls, I turned my face from the body still lying there, my shock having abated enough to allow a couple of tears to slip out and course down my cheeks.

Frederic removed his waistcoat, laying it over the man's face. Turning back to me, he nodded. "Let's go."

I swallowed. "I...I don't actually know the way. It's been a long time."

His face softened in sympathy. "Well, you have a better chance of finding the way than me." He stepped toward me, stopping at arm's reach. "I believe in you, Evie."

I took a deep breath, looking into his eyes. I needed to believe in myself, too. I nodded. "Let's go."

The local junglers meandered to the waterfall by different routes which, coupled with the speed of growth of the jungle itself, meant no true path had ever formed. They denied it, but I had always suspected the villagers did it on purpose, keeping the waterfall's location secret. Taking the royals there would have been granting an honor in their eyes.

I led Frederic slowly despite a constant beating drum in the back of my mind counting down the remaining minutes of the poor guide's life. But I knew it would do him no good for us to move quickly and end up hopelessly lost. I looked for small landmarks: strangely shaped vines, clumps of flowers, unusual trees—anything I could remember from our walk over.

And slowly, step by step, we made our way forward. The unexpected exertion, combined with the fear and anxiety, meant we had both drained our water skins long before we should have done so. But I didn't dare risk taking us off track to look for another source of water. We would simply have to go on with dry mouths.

"Do you think he'll live?" I asked at one point when we stopped for a brief rest.

Frederic considered. "I don't know. The wounds didn't seem deep enough for him to be so unaware. I'm afraid there may have been poison involved. In which case I can't even guess without knowing what the poison is. They were taking him somewhere, so perhaps they didn't mean him to die." He shrugged. "Or perhaps they merely wanted to dispose of his body somewhere far enough away to sow confusion."

I considered his words and shivered, looking warily around as if the attackers might spring out of the surrounding trees. Many more questions filled my mind, but we didn't have time to stop and talk, and I needed to focus on the task at hand.

But as I turned to lead the way again, my eyes fell on Frederic, raising a handful of purple berries toward his mouth. I lunged forward, knocking them from his hand.

"What's wrong?" he asked, as I looked around frantically for something to wipe his skin.

Choosing a large glossy leaf, wet from some sort of dripping moisture above it, I ripped it off and thrust it at him. "Wipe your hands on this and then leave it in the undergrowth. And never touch those berries again."

"What do you mean?" he asked, obediently wiping his hands. "What's wrong with them?"

I put my hand on my rapidly beating heart, taking a moment to close my eyes and take a deep breath. "They're poisonous. Horribly, horribly poisonous. If you'd eaten any, you would have been dead within minutes."

He swallowed audibly and scrubbed his hands a little harder. "But they look just like blueberries!"

I shook my head, pointing at a couple still on the bush near him. "There are lots of differences, although they're all small. They're more purple in color for one. And they don't have the star-shaped lip around the top. Plus, they're more completely round than a blueberry which generally has that slightly flattened shape."

He squinted at them. "Oh, yes, I see. Why has no one mentioned it before?"

I shrugged. "All your food has been served to you, you haven't been scavenging for your own. And locals may not have thought to mention it. Even very small jungler toddlers know not to touch a caracos berry."

"Well, it's a good thing I have you with me, then," he said, his smile a little lopsided.

I nodded, still trembling slightly from the shot of pure terror added to the constant state of fear already coursing through me. "Let's get moving again." I paused. "Try not to touch anything."

He managed a watery chuckle, and I grinned weakly back.

Thirty long minutes later with several pauses for backtracking, we found an area I recognized properly and picked up our pace, eventually stumbling wearily back into the village. A crowd immediately gathered around us, cries going up as we gasped out the important points of our tale.

Within minutes an armed expedition had formed. Frederic tried to send some guards along, but the junglers refused. "They'll just slow us down," explained the village elder, before pausing and meeting Frederic's eyes. "And I'd feel safer if they remained here with you. At least until we understand the nature of this threat."

Frederic nodded reluctant agreement before his own servants bore him off to be examined by the Tour doctor. Celine, miraculously restored to health, insisted I see the doctor as well, although I told her there was nothing wrong with me but for an intense dose of fear and some thirst.

Despite our exhaustion, Frederic and I waited with the same anxious energy as the others who had remained in the village. Wild rumors circulated as to the identity of the attackers, but no one seemed to have any sensible suggestions.

Frederic remained silent about the word I had thought I heard from the injured guide, and I followed his lead. We didn't want to whip up rage against their neighbors when I might have misheard or misunderstood him.

Every time I thought of the injured man who we had abandoned, I was driven to my feet to start pacing again despite my fatigue. Had I taken too long finding our way back? Had I ruined any hope he had for survival?

CHAPTER 18

When someone called that the expedition had returned, many voices taking up the cry, I rushed toward them. First came a group bearing a stretcher—the body on it covered in a black sheet. He hadn't made it, then.

My knees began to shake until I saw a second group following behind with a second stretcher. The man on this one had been properly bandaged with crisp white linen, a green paste oozing out the sides. He appeared to be sleeping, his chest rising and falling with regular breaths. They had made it in time, after all. I closed my eyes, thankfulness overwhelming me. And the evidence of the paste suggested we had been right, and a poison had been used.

My relief faded, however, as the villagers surged around the black draped stretcher which had now been laid on the ground. A wailing dirge rose up, growing louder and louder as more voices joined it. I closed my eyes and for a moment the years fell away, and I still lived with Mother Nora. In this moment, none of us were individuals, but instead one entity, united in our grief, and I was one with the village.

I couldn't have said how much time passed before the sound

began to die down, voice after voice falling away into silence. We would bury him tomorrow, but already we had begun the process of incorporating his death into the fabric of village life.

I opened my eyes and met Frederic's before he quickly looked away. His earlier words came back to me, and I knew he was right. There was no shame associated with my connection with the jungle. But it was yet another barrier between me and the prince, part of the ocean that separated us.

We stayed the next day for the burial and so Frederic could consult with the village leaders. Nothing in the attackers' belongings indicated their origins, although the second guide had recovered enough to answer questions. He and the other guide had been ambushed, and he had been grabbed and gagged before he even realized his companion was dead.

"They were westerners," he said, "they must have been. They were dressed like junglers, but they weren't ours. They must have hoped to turn the royals against us easterners. If they'd escaped with me, you might easily have thought *I* killed my companion and abandoned you to the jungle in an attempt to sabotage the Tour."

Frederic had said nothing to the injured man, but I could see from his face that he wasn't convinced. When he came out of consultation with the village council, he looked weary.

"I've talked them down from any immediate action," he told us. "I've told them we will send for proper investigators, ones who know the jungle. We cannot have a jungler civil war breaking out."

I nodded. It would be a disaster if the long-standing rivalry turned to violence.

The next day we left the village. I exchanged a fond farewell with Josinna, aware that it would in all likelihood be the last time

I saw her. Our visit had reminded me that when I remembered the jungle, it should be with as much gratitude for Josinna's support as hurt at my foster family's lack of care.

The members of the Tour, both commoners and nobles, were nervous now, their eyes constantly straying to the surrounding trees. At least we had a straight trip to the edge of the jungle from here. We had visited our last village.

The guards who had been chosen for the Tour came from all parts of the kingdom. Every time we made camp, even just to eat a meal, the ones from a jungler background were sent to scout the surrounding trees. We had nearly made it out of the jungle altogether when we stopped for a midday meal, and the scouts came racing back to the main column.

When Frederic had heard their report, he headed back into the trees with them and an extra contingent. As he stepped off the road, he paused and looked back, signaling to me to join him. I abandoned my food and followed, curious. Surely he wouldn't want me if they'd found something dangerous.

He looked grim but not afraid. "They've found some bodies close by. Looks like they were following the road among the trees. And they want to know if we recognize them."

The three bodies lay sprawled around the remains of a camp, as if they just keeled over while eating their evening meal one night. They had no visible wounds.

"That's them," said Frederic. He looked over at me. "Evie?"

I nodded slowly. "I think so." I shrugged. "I didn't get a good look."

Reluctantly I approached for a closer examination, covering my nose. Several of the guards had already begun digging a joint grave, and I didn't know where to look without making myself sick to my stomach.

"They are dressed like junglers," said one of the guards uncertainly.

My heart sank. It wasn't the answer we had hoped for, but I

could see nothing that truly identified them one way or the other. I looked helplessly at Frederic when a splash of purple caught my eye.

I knelt down beside one of the bodies.

"Frederic," I called. "Look at this."

He joined me, pulling back when he got a good look. "Aren't those…"

I nodded, looking up to meet his eyes. "Caracos berries in their hands. Yes. I think we know how they died." I stood up. "And we know they're not junglers. Junglers would never be dining on caracos."

Several of the guards nodded.

"Even the easterners know to avoid caracos," said one of them.

Frederic nodded. "We'll send messengers back to the village with the news. And we'll keep these belongings for the investigators. Although no one touch those berries. With any luck, the experts will find some sign of where they came from."

I smiled tremulously, but I suspected his words were meant for the morale of his men. How could investigators possibly determine such a thing?

Back with the Tour, he filled Cassian and Celine in on my discovery.

"Ugh, how horrible," said Celine, her usually mobile face downcast.

"At least we know they're not easterners," said Frederic. He looked at his brother. "But I'm afraid that means they must have been…"

"Rebels," agreed Cassian. "Yet another disaster following the Tour."

"I'm almost surprised Father hasn't called us back," said Celine.

Both of her brothers shook their heads.

"That would be a disaster," said Frederic. "A clear way to

signal to the rebels—and the rest of the kingdom—that we're weak and losing control. The kingdom is already recovering from the last rebellion. And these new rebels have shown themselves to be ruthless and willing to accept civilian casualties. If we lose control now, who knows what chaos and violence might descend?"

I agreed and told myself to be brave, but as my eyes fastened on Frederic, all I could think was who might be killed next time?

~

The next day, we left the jungle behind, and with it the last of my woodshed nightmares. It turns out I had only needed to face that fear to discover I had outgrown it. My foster family were not monsters in the night, and my experiences in the jungle had not been all bad. Josinna was the proof of that.

It helped that I had faced my past with my new friends beside me. Everything was easier when you weren't alone.

We rode upward, the ground becoming increasingly barren as the moisture leached from the air. We didn't feel high until we stopped ascending and gazed down the steep drop to the dry desert below us. The sand stretched out before us in waves and dunes, some of it blowing on the wind. My skin itched as a dry, hot gust blew up to meet us. I shivered, although not from the cold. Not all of my nightmares had disappeared.

A small group of people already toiled up the slope toward us, their forms entirely swathed in the voluminous robes favored by the desert traders. The coverings left only their eyes exposed, and they were still too far away for me to make any of those out. I wondered uneasily if I would know any of them.

Further in the distance we could see the camel caravan that waited for us. The familiar shapes against the yellow sand made me shudder again. But a moment later I picked out other, incongruous elements. The tents were too few, the human silhouettes vastly outnumbered by the animals. I had been expecting it, but still it stood out, an error in an otherwise standard scene.

Cassian had explained the crown's arrangements with this caravan to Celine and me. We were to travel with them south, and then west again to Largo. To make room for us, they had already left their young, their elderly, and those who cared for them in an accommodating village not far from the southern city.

Naturally they had been compensated for all of this. They were traders and did nothing for free.

Several of the older nobles reluctantly began to emerge from their carriages. The remaining nobles, all of the grooms and drivers, and a number of the servants were to take the carriages, wagons, and horses back through the jungle. When they hit the intersection with the north-south jungle road, they would head north back to Lanare. The rest of the Tour would travel by foot and camel south and then west again. In Largo, the royal yacht would be waiting to take us back to the harbor at Lanare.

The arrangement had been made long ago, and I understood that to have broken it now would have sent a clear message that the crown did not wish to send. But still, I wished we could all turn back—surprise the rebels by veering off course. It was too easy to lay ambushes on a path so well mapped.

As we waited for the approaching party to arrive, the Tour sorted its copious baggage, unloading what would be taken on by camel. We would all need to assist in carrying these supplies down to the caravan.

At last those who were to turn back had themselves in order, and Frederic wished them an official farewell. A moment later the desert traders reached us.

One of them unwrapped his head covering, revealing his face, and threw his arms wide. "Welcome friends, to the Sea of Sand."

CHAPTER 19

$\mathcal{T}$he contingent of desert traders had brought large pieces of sturdy canvas with them which they set up as sleds to drag our supplies down to the rest of the caravan. They made short work of the task, and we had all soon entered the desert proper. The royals hadn't seemed sure when I had suggested making them full wraps like the traders wore, but I noticed each of them wincing at the bite of the sun against their exposed skin. I suspected I would soon receive three orders for wraps.

I had spent my spare moments over the last few days making myself one from the lightest silk Josinna had been able to sell me. The length of material had seemed so cheap bought directly from the source without the cut usually taken by the traders for hauling it across the kingdom. I had bought several bolts in different colors under the assumption that the royals would want wraps of their own soon enough.

As the packs were redistributed from the sleds to the camels, I found my own garment and twisted it around myself. I had yet to wind it around my head when a boisterous voice yelled out, "Evie!"

I turned in time to leap into the arms held out for me, only to be spun around and around in circles.

"Evie! You're here! And look how grown up you are! And so elegant." The laughing young man winked at me.

I laughed straight back. "Ofie! I didn't know we were to travel with your caravan."

"But of course." He assumed an offended expression. "As if I would allow anyone else to transport my beautiful Evie."

I shoved him. "Don't try to fool me with your glib tongue. The arrangements for this trip were made long before I joined the Tour."

"I have a sense for such things," he said, his grave expression breaking down as he spun me around again. "You must come and see my camels."

He placed my feet back on the ground, but his arms were still around me, when I noticed Celine watching on in astonishment. Frederic, a step behind her, had a strange, almost dangerous expression on his face, his eyes glittering. I fought down a flush. There was no reason I couldn't greet an old friend in any way I chose.

Offar, or Ofie, as we had always called him as children, led me through the noisy, smelly mass of camels, talking the whole way. The other children in my own caravan might not have allowed the foolish city girl to join their games, but on the occasions when our caravans had crossed paths, Ofie had always cheerfully included me in whatever mischief he currently had planned. I had worshiped him as a result, despite his infuriating tendency to get us both into trouble. And I had spent many hours regretting that desert caravans seldom found themselves in the same place and rarely stayed long when they did. If my time as a trader had been spent in Ofie's caravan, it would have been different indeed.

"Two whole strings," he said when we arrived at a place near the back of the caravan, gesturing proudly. A young boy looked up from his place on the sand and waved at us cheerfully.

"That's my young cousin," said Ofie. "He leads my second string. An ungrateful scamp if ever I saw one."

"Reminds me of someone else I once knew," I said.

The young camel-puller chortled loudly. When his amusement died down he looked me up and down unashamedly. "So you're Evie. I imagined you taller."

I raised both eyebrows, turning to Ofie. "What terrible tales have you been telling about me?"

"None, I assure you," he protested, turning suddenly serious. "I only expanded to the second string this last year, and it's all thanks to you. You've kept me busy carting material between Josinna and the capital."

I smiled, glad to think my success had also brought success to my old friends. I just wished he had been able to bring his wares directly to the capital himself instead of offloading them not far from the desert to a regular traveling merchant caravan with wagons and horses. It would have been nice to see a familiar face in Lanare.

I shook my head as I surveyed his animals. When he was getting into mischief as a child, I would never have predicted he would be successful enough to own two whole strings of camels within Caravan Adira. He must have worked hard in the years between my leaving the desert and contacting him about transporting my material.

"Evie." Frederic sounded stiff and disapproving. Had he followed us through the caravan? "You're needed."

I shrugged apologetically at Ofie.

"Don't worry." He grinned at me. "I can see you're far too important now for the likes of me."

I rolled my eyes in response to his wink and followed the silent Frederic back toward the Tour.

When we had passed out of hearing range of the other two, he spoke. "Who was that?"

"An old friend." I shrugged. "Not everyone in the entire kingdom hates me," I added tartly, out of sorts at his judgment.

He glanced at me sideways. "I didn't mean…"

I shrugged again.

He cleared his throat and made another attempt. "So, you've lived among the traders as well, I take it?"

"Caravan Osmira took me in when I was nine years old."

A camel-puller within earshot looked up at my words and slapped his flat palm to his heart in a desert trader gesture. Frederic glanced between us, but I kept my eyes firmly ahead, refusing to answer the question in his.

Could he see the tears I was struggling to hold back? It had been many years since I had spoken the name of my old caravan aloud, and I hadn't expected it to hit me so hard. If only he would leave me alone before I embarrassed myself. I tried to think of something I could say without emotion.

"They trained me to be a camel-puller, and I led a full string by the time I was eleven."

"So how did you end up in the jungle?"

I increased my pace, still looking straight ahead. So many questions. "The trader family who had taken me in lost a number of camels over the course of a few months when I was twelve. They consolidated their strings and found they no longer had need of me."

Frederic lengthened his stride to stay beside me. "Evie." His voice sounded softer than before. But his sympathy was worse than questions.

When I didn't respond, he grasped my arm, pulling me to a halt. He looked into my eyes. "Evie, I'm sorry. I shouldn't have pried, it's none of my business."

I ripped my arm from his grip, tears welling in my eyes. Too late. Now he had made me lose my remaining composure. The emotion spilled out of me, completely out of control.

"No, it isn't any of your business. Just like my friends are none of your business, either. I have been nothing but helpful and obedient this entire trip, while you and your sister adopted me and paraded me around like your pet. Why can't you just let me be?"

I took off running, hating myself already for my words. I didn't look back because I didn't want to see the confusion and disgust that no doubt filled his face as he watched me flee.

Celine called to me in the distance, but I ignored her, running until I had lost myself in the crowd of animals. When I found a suitably abandoned spot, I curled up and cried until I had no more tears left.

When they at last dried, I remained where I was, still lost in misery. What had I done? I should never have agreed to come here. Despite the joy of seeing my old friend, the feel of the oppressive sun, the smell of the camels—even the sounds they made—brought far too much flooding back. I would have nightmares for months now, and I had just exploded and driven away my new friends.

Tears I hadn't thought still left in me squeezed out when I thought of how I had yelled at Frederic and what he would think of me now. I had known that my broken past would drive them away eventually. But for all my foreknowledge, I hadn't managed to protect my heart. It hurt just as much as I had feared it would.

We were to camp here for the night before moving on, so I had no reason to re-emerge. But eventually my rumbling stomach, combined with the odd looks I was getting from passing camel-pullers, made me shake myself off and stand.

I was here now, and it was too late to turn back. I must find a way to push it aside as I always did and pretend the coming rejection didn't sting. I took a few moments to arrange my features accordingly, scrubbing away as much evidence of my tears as possible.

As I walked back in search of the rest of the Tour, I took a more considered look around. This caravan, Caravan Adira, had always been one of the larger ones, but in the years of my absence, it had grown bigger than any caravan I had ever seen. There must be at least twenty strings of camels, each string with between ten and fifteen enormous two-humped animals. Most of them were owned by the larger trader families in the caravan, which made Ofie's achievement in attaining two whole strings all the more remarkable.

More tents, familiar ones this time, had sprung up while I was hiding. Dejectedly I found the steward and asked him where I was assigned to sleep.

"With the princess, of course." He looked at me as if I were mad. "I would have thought you knew the princes well enough by now to know the happenings in the jungle were hardly designed to ease their minds. "

"Yes, but…" I frowned. So they hadn't spoken to him yet. I chewed the inside of my cheek. I would have to wait until one of them did.

Wandering on, I caught sight of the three royals standing together and froze, a flash of heat racing through my body. I reminded myself I would have to face them eventually and tried to calm my face.

"I can't find her anywhere," said Celine, sounding upset. "And everyone just looks at me blankly when I ask if they've seen her."

"This isn't your fault, Celine," said Frederic, running his hand through his hair, "it's mine." His eyes looked tight and worried.

Were they talking about me? I took a step forward, and Cassian looked up.

"Evie." I couldn't pick the emotion in his voice, although he sounded slightly less calm than usual.

"Evie?" Celine spun around and dashed toward me, throwing her arms around my neck. "There you are! I've been so worried! I thought you might have run off into the desert and died!"

"Um…I haven't been gone that long." I patted the younger girl's back awkwardly.

"I told her you knew the desert. That you wouldn't do something so dangerous." Frederic's quiet voice sounded strained.

Celine suddenly pulled herself away and glared at me. "How could you do that to me? I was terrified."

"I…" I swallowed. I had been so absorbed in my past and my imagined pain at losing them, that it had never occurred to me I might be causing pain to any of them.

I looked up and met Frederic's eyes. He was the one I had most wronged when he had merely attempted to offer sympathy. Something in his expression told me that there was no question of my being cast off, and shame filled me. I insulted them when I continued to imagine the worst. A worst that never seemed to eventuate, no matter what I did or what they learned.

"I'm sorry," I said to Celine, meeting both of the princes' eyes to extend the apology to them. "It was thoughtless of me."

Celine grinned. "I forgive you. I pretty much have to since my family is always telling me I'm terribly thoughtless." She sounded cheerful again already. "Can we go inside one of the tents now? I'm dying out here! And I thought it was hot at home. I think I'm going to need one of those wraps, after all, Evie. Even if I do hate the idea of being surrounded by so much fabric when it's so hot."

She led the way with me trailing behind. Frederic fell into step next to me.

"I am also sorry, Evie," he said. "And I'm glad you're all right."

I sighed. "No, you have nothing to apologize for. I'm truly sorry for behaving so inexcusably, Your Highness. You did not deserve my outburst."

"Your Highness?" He frowned at me. "What happened to Frederic?"

I looked down at the ground, afraid he would read the emotion in my eyes. I forced light humor into my voice. "You're right, how foolish of me, I can't imagine what I was thinking. It's not as if you're a prince, or anything."

He chuckled softly. "There's my Evie." He said it so quietly I almost didn't hear the words. His hand reached up and touched my cheek in the lightest of caresses before he turned abruptly and strode away. I froze and watched him disappear. When I turned back to Celine, she had also stopped and was regarding me with narrowed eyes.

"In my tent. Now."

I grimaced and followed her, afraid of what she might have to say this time.

"That was brilliant!" she announced triumphantly as soon as we were alone. "I couldn't have planned it better myself."

I blinked at her.

"Except for the bit where you had me worried, of course. But blowing up at Frederic? Running away like that? I wish you could have seen how guilty and worried he was! We'll have him declaring his love in no time."

I sighed. "Celine, I didn't plan anything." But the heat from his touch still lingered on my face, and my admonishment held less conviction than usual. I had wronged him. Perhaps I had wronged them all when I assumed they were just the same as those who had made promises to me in the past.

The excess of emotions had left me exhausted, however, and I couldn't process the thought without a good sleep. Except that sleep would have to wait, at least until Celine had abandoned whatever plan she was currently concocting to throw together with her brother. Because if she thought what had just happened was brilliant, I trembled to think what situation she might thrust me into next.

CHAPTER 20

*C*eline must have read the rebellion in my face because she refused to confide any of her grand schemes in me. If she hadn't been a princess, I would have wrung it out of her, but even I had my limits in terms of how far I could push my position.

The next morning the remaining Tour guards and servants packed our tents and belongings and then stood back to watch the desert traders at work. I offered to help Ofie, but he turned me away with a grin.

"How many years has it been?" he asked. "Six? You're out of practice, city girl."

I glared at him. He knew how I had hated it when the children of Caravan Osmira called me that. But his laugh and wink took away any sting, and I couldn't stay mad at him. His cousin proved to be adept with the animals and skilled with the loading despite his small stature, and I could see why he hadn't been left behind with the rest of the children outside Largo.

"I earn my wage like a grown man." The lad puffed out his chest.

My respect for Ofie increased. Most children among the

desert traders helped with the work, but they did it to learn, and to increase their family's strings and standing within the caravan. It was kind of Ofie to pay his cousin in coin.

The groaning and bellowing of the camels continued throughout the loading process, stopping only once all the provisions and tents were stowed and the loads complete. Most of the traders would walk, but some camels had been fitted with saddles for the royals and the nobles still accompanying the Tour.

Some of the older ones looked dismayed at the idea, but Celine and the princes clambered effortlessly onto the backs of the kneeling animals. The two princes shared a beast, and I was ushered up behind Celine on hers. I had expected to walk but secretly felt a little relieved. It had been far too long since I'd spent a day walking beside a camel string, and I wasn't entirely sure I would still be able to do it. At least not for a full day.

Our camel was led directly by an older camel-puller, as was the one ridden by Frederic and Cassian. A line of camels stretched behind both animals, each secured to the one in front with a rope.

"Woah," said Celine as our camel stood to its feet, rocking us in the process. She peered sideways and down. "We're a long way up."

I had managed to put together a very basic wrap for all three royals the night before. They would stay on at least, even if they weren't as elegant as they would be once I put some more work into them. Celine looked over at the camel which carried her brothers, examining the bright material that draped over the saddle.

"I've seen camels before, of course," she said. "Even if they rarely come into Lanare, they're common enough in Largo. But somehow it's different from up here. When I was a child I couldn't understand why the desert traders were different from the regular traveling merchants, but it's obvious really."

"The camels used to scare me a little when I first arrived with the traders," I admitted. "But I got used to them soon enough. You will too."

She nodded, peering over the edge with fascination again.

The nomadic desert traders were an off shoot of sorts from the traveling merchants. They were much more restricted in their area of operation and differed in many of their customs, but they were still bound by the rules and treaties of the merchant council. I had thought this unfair when I first arrived since the desert traders only ever sent a couple of representatives north when a council of caravans was called.

But the traders had soon explained to me that the protections provided by the binding were worth the restrictions. "Without them we would be vulnerable," the older camel-pullers had explained to us youngsters around the fire.

The traveling merchants operated apart from the laws of any individual kingdom. Their own complicated set of laws were administered by the caravan leader or, if necessary, a council comprised of the merchants' most senior leaders. The treaty between the merchants and the kingdoms was one of the oldest in existence. It provided the caravans with freedom of movement and protection from persecution, among other things. Any violation of the treaty could result in a merchant ban against an entire kingdom, an event of which any sane ruler lived in fear. The merchant council would deal swiftly with any caravan greedy enough to enter a kingdom under a ban.

The camel caravans worked closely with the ordinary merchant caravans, the horses and wagons taking the goods on to the places the camels couldn't go. Thanks to the desert traders, the merchants didn't have to fight their way through the jungle down to southern Largo or take ships and risk the treacherous reefs along the coast. Instead they collected the goods closer to Lanare and distributed them to the capital and up to the northern kingdoms.

It was an arrangement that benefited everyone. And the

protection provided by the merchant treaty was doubly needed by the desert traders who were geographically tied to Lanover and the Great Desert that ran along its eastern border. It meant they weren't true subjects of the Lanoverian crown, but given their inability to move to another kingdom as the merchants could, they had long ago sworn a limited fealty to respect Lanoverian laws alongside merchant ones in exchange for protection and favor from the crown.

The desert traders treated the royals with all due respect, and slowly the Tour participants became somewhat inured to the burning heat of the desert sun. Celine never seemed to adjust fully to the dry heat, but she developed a strange affection for the grumpy camels that often made me laugh.

She marveled at their many uses, drinking the camel milk that sustained us all with delight and laughing every time she saw a camel-puller who had run out yarn for his knitting reach back to pull some hair from one of the animals. She made me explain to her how they could spin the hair into yarn on the move and even show her how to knit something herself.

But she was soon distracted from the camels by a far more fascinating situation.

"Evie," she murmured quietly to me one day as we sat upon our camel for hour after plodding hour. "Have you noticed that beautiful girl?" She pointed to a young desert trader who rode a string ahead of us.

"Yes, of course," I said. "How could anyone not notice Tillara?" I remembered Tillie from my days with the traders as a child. The few days I had spent with Caravan Adira in my childhood had been mostly spent with Ofie. But all the children knew Tillie. Even then she had been set apart.

The daughter of the leader of Caravan Adira, she had been trained as a leader, not a camel-puller, and had often directed our haphazard games. We had deferred to her naturally and would have done so no doubt despite her excessive beauty which stood out even in childhood. She simply had an air about her that made others wish to be near her and to listen to what she had to say.

"Well, it's not really notice *her* I mean." She paused and glanced sideways at her brothers, lowering her voice again. "Have you noticed anything strange about Cassian?"

"Ooohhhh." I considered her question, looking between the prince and the girl up ahead of us. "He *has* seemed even more reserved and detached than usual, possibly." I knit my brows. "Do you think that means something?"

Celine nodded enthusiastically. "Yes, mmhmm, absolutely. He stares at her all the time, and I don't think he's spoken in her presence even once. He's in love with her."

I felt a twinge of unease. Was that really enough evidence to draw such a conclusion? There were probably plenty of people who Cassian had never spoken to. I expressed my doubt.

"Oh, no," said Celine. "It's not just that he's never spoken to her, it's that he doesn't speak *at all* when she's around. I know he's reserved, but he's also usually self-assured. He doesn't really get nervous, precisely. Well, not before now."

I considered her words. She was right. Maybe?

"Well, what if he is in love with her?" I said. "It's none of our business. She might not be a traditional choice, but you said yourself the alliances with other kingdoms are all taken care of by your other siblings. A closer link with the merchants and traders wouldn't be a bad thing for Lanover."

"But exactly," said Celine.

"Why do I have a sinking feeling in my stomach?" I asked.

"Because you know I'm right," said Celine promptly. "You know I'm right, and you know we have a hard job before us."

"We do?"

"Yes. Because he clearly needs all the help he can get."

I narrowed my eyes and wondered if I should just push Celine off the camel right now. For poor Cassian's sake. But then I looked between the prince and the trader girl. She would make a wonderful princess, and it did seem like Cassian might need some help…

That evening Celine cornered Frederic.

"Frederic," she said without preamble, "Cassian needs our help."

"He does?" Frederic looked back and forth between the two of us before settling his eyes on me. "Why do I suddenly feel afraid?"

"I know exactly the feeling," I said, "but don't look at me. She's not *my* sister."

Frederic groaned. "What has poor Cassian done now?"

"The question," said Celine, not in the least abashed, "is not what he's done but rather what he hasn't done. And what he hasn't done is talk to Tillara. Or around Tillara. Not even once."

A dawning look of shock passed over Frederic's face. "Are you saying you think…"

Celine put her hands on her hips. "Just think about it for a minute, Frederic. You know him better than any of us."

Frederic frowned, clearly deep in thought. "You know, now that you mention it…"

"So, as I said, he needs our help."

Frederic looked uneasy. "Now hold on just a second, Celine. I'm sure the last thing Cassian wants is any of us getting involved."

Celine raised an eyebrow. "That's all very well, Frederic, but what exactly do you think is going to happen if we leave him to sort it out for himself?" She didn't wait for her brother to answer. "Nothing. Nothing is what's going to happen."

Frederic looked at me, and I held up both hands.

"Don't look at me, I didn't notice anything until she pointed it out."

"I have to admit it's true," said Celine sadly. "While Evie is a more than satisfactory friend and seamstress, she's been a highly unsatisfactory partner in crime."

Frederic threw me a look full of such admiration that I actually blushed. "That's high praise indeed. I hope you feel honored, Evie."

I grinned back at him, filled with a warm glow that he still wished to joke with me after everything that had passed between us, and that I now knew him well enough to be confident when his serious manner hid a jest.

"Oh, absolutely," I said, grinning back. "I have rarely received such an accolade."

"You are both highly disappointing," said Celine. "But I will not be distracted. The first step, I think, is to get close to this Tillara." She turned her bright gaze on me. "Do you know her, Evie? From when you used to live here?"

"Yeesss," I said, drawing the word out with reluctance.

"Excellent." Celine clapped her hands together. "Let's go find her, and you can use your old ties to reminisce and get close to her."

"I can what?" I said, just as Frederic said, "Right now?"

Celine ignored us both. "Let's go." She got several steps before looking back at us. We hadn't moved. "Well? Come on!"

I stepped forward, a little reluctantly. I hadn't spent much time with Caravan Adira, and Tillie and I had never been friends, exactly. Although she had never done anything to ostracize me, either. I just didn't know if she would even remember me, let alone put any value on our past connection.

Frederic looked like he wasn't going to come until Celine fixed him with a withering stare. "You wouldn't leave Evie to face this alone, would you, Frederic?"

He fell into line after that.

"Only three more years," he muttered to me under his breath as we trailed behind Celine.

I looked at him with a question in my eyes.

"Only three more years until she's eighteen, and I can ship her off to make a marriage alliance somewhere. I keep telling myself it's not that long, but…"

I stifled a laugh, knowing he didn't really mean it. "You'd miss her if she was gone, admit it."

He looked at me and grinned, the full smile I didn't get to see often enough. "You'll have to take pity on me and keep me company when that day comes, Evie."

My lips twitched, but I kept my eyes on the sand ahead of me, hoping he couldn't see the warmth in my cheeks. What did he mean?

A quiet intake of breath made my eyes fly back to his face. His gaze was fixed on my lips. I flushed again.

"I found her," called Celine, distracting us both. She flew back and pulled me forward by the hand, pointing to where the other girl sat beside a newly-lit campfire. Sighing, I walked forward out of the gloom of twilight and into the cheery circle cast by the dancing flames.

To my relief, the other girl leaped to her feet at the sight of me and circled the fire in my direction.

"Tillie." I reached to embrace her.

"Evie!" She placed a kiss on each of my cheeks. "Ofie told me you were here, I should have come to find you earlier." Her voice sounded just as musical as I remembered.

I shook my head. "You have many responsibilities, I hear." I let some teasing seep into my voice.

Tillie laughed, the sound like tinkling bells, and nodded. "Oh, so boring, is it not? Would that we were carefree children again."

"Except we had Ofie, so I'm not sure I'd consider it carefree." I grinned at her.

"Oh, Ofie." She sighed. "No, I suppose you are right."

I remembered the reason for my presence here and gestured toward the other two. "You've met Princess Celine and Prince Frederic, of course."

"Certainly," she said with a small curtsy. "We are honored to host them in Caravan Adira."

"As we are honored to be here." Frederic gave a half bow.

"Yes," said Celine, jumping in. "So honored that we would like to invite you to eat the evening meal with us tomorrow."

"How kind," she said, looking between us with curiosity.

I forced a smile. "You'll have to fill me in on all the news."

"But of course," she said with a smile of her own. "It has been so many years."

"Yes, indeed," said Frederic. "I would love to hear some stories about Caravan Adira and Caravan Osmira when the two of you were children."

A noticeable hush fell over the group around the fire. Several of Tillie's companions placed their palms to their chests as the camel-puller had done earlier. Tillie herself gripped both my arms and rested her forehead against mine.

"We grieve together." She said the rote words quietly.

"And together we find the strength to go on." I struggled to get the traditional reply from my suddenly tight throat.

Celine and Frederic watched us with questions on their faces that no one attempted to answer.

CHAPTER 21

*C*eline allowed us all to retreat after that, but she soon fell behind Frederic and me, getting further and further back until she disappeared into the darkness between campfires. I sighed silently. I shouldn't have been surprised, not when she had matchmaking so firmly on her mind.

We walked silently through the murmur of voices and the occasional grumble of a camel. When we neared our own section of tents, Frederic paused and gestured toward the edge of the camp where the sand dunes stretched away in almost complete darkness.

"It's a perfect night to view the stars."

I murmured a soft agreement and let him lead the way out onto the closest dune. The camp stretched out on one side of us, the darkness on the other. Tilting my head, I gazed up into the endless night sky. How many times had I gazed at it thus? And yet my skin had never tingled so at the awareness of someone beside me in the night.

"I feel as if I'm fumbling in the dark," said Frederic, breaking the stillness with soft words.

I bit my lip on a return quip. This time his serious tone reflected a serious mood.

"Why does everyone react so when I mention Caravan Osmira?"

I turned to look at him but could make out only the dim outline of his face. "You truly do not know?"

"Obviously not."

I opened my mouth, closed it, and then opened it again. "I thought you must know. It was six years ago now, but still, I thought…You're a prince…"

He turned to face me, his eyes reflecting light from the camp behind us. "So it does not just involve you, then? Tillara was not offering you condolences for being abandoned."

I shook my head. "She does not—" I cleared my throat and tried again. "She likely does not even know of it."

He sucked in a breath. "How is that possible? She knows you left the caravan."

I shook my head again. "No." The word was such a quiet whisper I forced myself to speak more loudly. "No, she knows my caravan was taken from me."

"Taken…?"

I swallowed. "They consolidated the strings and had no more string for me to lead. Some argued that I should stay, that they would grow their camel numbers again. But others said I would be just another mouth to feed until then. I was no kin of theirs, and they had younglings growing who would soon enough be ready for strings of their own."

I swayed, and he placed a hand beneath my elbow, steadying me.

"Someone said one of the jungler women had offered for them to leave me with her. They agreed they would do so the next time we stopped at the village." I paused to take a deep breath. "It's so near the eastern border of the jungle that the caravans will send a single laden string to the village if they have goods to sell or receive. But that means it is also near enough that a determined girl may walk the path out alone."

His hand on my elbow tightened.

"For three years I learned the trader ways. I had come so close to being accepted. I could not bear to throw it all away. So I followed them back to the desert." My voice dropped to a whisper. "I have wished sometimes since, in my darkest moments, that they had never left me. That I had still been with them when death came calling."

"Death?"

Silent tears tracked down my face as I struggled to keep my voice steady. "Those who hadn't been taken by the arrows or the sword had been burned. All of them. Everything. The goods, the tents, the camels, the men and women, the elders—" My voice cracked. "Even the children. Everything. When I at last stumbled into the desert there was nothing but their blackened remains. I counted them…"

My voice gave out, and I paused before continuing my tale. "I counted them all. I hoped…I hoped perhaps some had escaped, had already ridden on for help. But they were all there. Every last one of them. Every camel."

My knees nearly buckled, and he caught me beneath my other elbow.

"Evie, I don't…I don't know what to say. What…what did you do?"

"I stayed there, and I mourned them in the trader way, as best as I could on my own. Until I became almost crazed from thirst. That's when Caravan Golura arrived. I told them I had been late returning from the jungle, and they never questioned it more closely. They had far bigger concerns. Urgent messengers were sent to the other caravans on their fastest camels. They all stopped trading immediately and took up defensive positions as best they might. Many retreated to their secret oases."

"Secret oases?"

"There are a string of oases known to all the caravans and used throughout the north-south journey. But each caravan has one or two oases whose location they carefully guard. It is why certain caravans favor certain routes—it gives them a competitive advantage over the others."

I wiped at my tears. "Urgent messengers went to the capital, and all trade halted until the crown searched out and destroyed the group of bandits who committed the atrocity. They had attacked while the caravan was near the edge of the desert and taken all the gold and the smaller valuables. But they could not handle the camels, so in spite and to hide all traces of their identity, they had burned everything and everyone who remained."

"This was six years ago?" Frederic sounded thoughtful and troubled. "We were negotiating the Northelm-Lanover trade treaty then. Or rather the Duchess of Sessily was negotiating on our behalf. Father sent Cassian and me along because he thought it would be a good learning experience. Northhelm gets snowed in during the winter so we were gone for many months. I must have missed the whole thing."

"To the crown's credit, they acted swiftly and decisively," I said. "They upheld their end of the bargain between Lanover and the traders. Some of the respect you see now is because of your father's actions then."

"And you were only twelve." He drew me closer in an instinctual protective gesture. "And Caravan Golura then just abandoned you?"

I shook my head. "They would have taken me in, but I could not bear it. Those days alone with the burned caravan…" I shivered. "I could not bear to remain in the desert, so I returned to Mother Nora."

Frederic sighed. "And then we brought you back here."

Silence fell between us.

"Evie."

I looked up to find him staring down at me intensely, the

darkness hiding his exact expression. I had felt angry at him earlier—for bringing me here, for asking me questions, for making me lose control. But now that I had told my story, I felt nothing but an unexpected relief. With each step we took of our journey, this prince learned more of the story of me. And not once had he turned away from the mess and ugliness of my past.

He had given me a gift I had not thought to receive. He had looked at me—all of me—and had valued me. And in return I had given him my heart. I realized in that moment it wasn't a gift I could ever take back.

Warmth spread up my arms from where he still gripped my elbows. Without thinking, I tilted toward him, my face still raised to his. He stiffened for a moment and then pulled me close against him. A soft, dry breeze sent sand curling around our legs as I rested in his arms, my heart beating so fast I feared it would burst.

"Evie," he said, my name more a moan than a word. He lowered his head toward mine, and my heart stopped altogether.

Less than a breath separated us when the loud bray of a camel shattered the stillness. Frederic jerked and pulled back, letting go so abruptly that I stumbled and nearly fell. Cold rushed around me to fill the place where he had been, and I rubbed my suddenly empty arms.

"Evie, I…I'm sorry."

I waited for a further explanation, but it never came. Instead he turned and fled across the sand back to camp.

If Frederic felt something for me, he was fighting it. And although my heart wanted to, my head couldn't blame him. I forced myself to hold that head high when I saw him the next day, to laugh and joke as if nothing had happened. He seemed grateful for it, responding in kind, although every now and then I found him watching me with a confused look in his eyes.

I could only assume in the absence of probing questions that Celine hadn't picked up on it. Perhaps because she was so preoccupied with helping along Cassian's currently non-existent romance. Cassian himself was still unaware of this mission since Celine had decided that surprise was her best weapon on this occasion.

When Tillie arrived to share our meal, I watched Cassian over her shoulder as we exchanged cheek kisses. Somewhat to my astonishment, his face turned red and then deathly pale. Someone handed him a bowl of food, and he took it without looking, his eyes fixed on the trader girl instead. After standing immobile for a moment, he attempted to sit without checking beneath him first and nearly toppled over on the uneven ground. Anyone would have thought him a mere youth, and not a man grown.

My eyes widened as Tillie moved on to greet Frederic. Celine was giving me a knowing look, and I had to give her credit. Staid, calm, reserved Cassian certainly seemed to have strong feelings of some sort for my old friend.

But to my increasing dismay, Cassian proceeded not to open his mouth for the rest of the evening. The other four of us laughed and talked easily, and Frederic made several attempts to bring his brother into the conversation. But Cassian merely shook his head or nodded, no matter how inappropriate such a response was to the question.

I caught Tillie several times during the meal throwing him odd, almost concerned looks. Did she think there was something wrong with him? If she had heard he was destined to be his brother's Chief Advisor one day, she was probably experiencing some strong concerns. The whole situation was so humorous, I found myself fighting not to laugh on several occasions, despite my own personal heartbreak.

To my surprise, Celine made no attempt to praise Cassian to Tillie or to bring him into the conversation. She seemed content to let him sit there like a lump. It didn't seem the soundest strategy at first glance, but I had no doubt she had a devious plan in play.

It was easy enough to see that Tillie had charmed all three royals by the end of her visit, just as she had charmed all of us all those years ago. She was intelligent and well-educated, funny and graceful. She seemed to know everyone in every caravan, and she had even traveled for a year of her youth with one of the larger merchant caravans. In short, she was everything a princess should be. I had no doubt Frederic and Celine would approve the match and could not be surprised at Cassian's being captivated by her. Unfortunately, given the careful, sympathetic way she bid him goodnight, I also saw little hope for his suit.

As soon as she was gone from view and hearing, Celine collapsed onto the beautiful rug beneath us. "Can't…breathe," she wheezed between giggles. She sat up and looked at her brother. "Poor Cassian, I believe she thinks you feeble minded." She went off into a fresh wave of giggles. "She is most likely feeling sorry for us all and wondering how the royal family managed to hush it up for so many years."

"Be quiet, Celine." Cassian looked glumly into his now-empty bowl.

Celine instantly stopped laughing and fixed him with an intense stare. "Admit it, Cassian. There's no point trying to hide it after that dismal performance. You're attracted to Tillara."

Her strategy now made sense. It had been aimed at him, not at her, designed to make him confess everything to us. Still, I was surprised by his response.

"Attracted to her? Every man with sense must feel some attraction toward her. She is perfection itself. I'm not attracted to her—I'm in love with her." The words seemed wrenched from him, and when he had finished the impassioned declaration, he went back to staring dejectedly into his bowl.

We all looked at one another, shock keeping us silent.

He shrugged. "It does not matter, however. She would never look at me when I cannot even open my mouth in her presence."

Celine sat beside him and patted his shoulder. "Don't worry, Cassian, we'll help you." Her serious reassurance and motherly approach looked comical given she was both years younger and more than a head shorter than her brother.

"Cassian, what's happened to you?" asked Frederic with concern. "I've never seen you like this."

Cassian put his hands to his head, distraught fingers making havoc with his hair. "I've never felt like this before—could never have imagined such a feeling! I have always found girls nice enough, their company pleasant, but not gripping enough to divert my focus from my training and the kingdom. But now... now! I can't sleep, I can barely eat." He threw his bowl on the ground. "I can't seem to think of anything but her and how we shall soon leave the caravan, and I'll never see her again. She is like the moon and the stars—beautiful, but, oh, so achingly distant."

He subsided once more into moody silence. I knew my mouth was hanging open, but I couldn't seem to close it. Never would I have imagined that love would hit Cassian in such a way. He had never before showed even the faintest stirrings of a romantic, and Celine had assured me this had always been the case. And yet now he talked like a poet, comparing his unbearable love to the moon and losing all capacity for basic function.

Celine, fortunately, seemed undaunted. "We must make a plan," she declared.

While the rest of us remained silent—Cassian apparently from the pain of unrequited love, and Frederic and me from shock—she outlined her course of attack. And as day after day plodded on through the desert, she set it into motion.

She decided that familiarity might wear down Cassian's awkwardness and invited Tillie to join us more and more frequently. This did produce some progress, but since Cassian could still only stutter out a few words here or there, I feared we would need at least a year in the desert before we saw any improvement worthy of hope.

Celine's next step, of which I highly disapproved, was to inform Tillie of her brother's love. Tillie actually laughed—a far from promising sign—and assured Celine it could not be so.

"I have much experience in the matter," she confided with a grin. "Why, he doesn't even speak to me."

"He is overwhelmed by the depth of his feelings," Celine replied gravely. But even I had a hard time keeping a straight face at this. Tillie seemed unconvinced, and it was quite clear that if she could be convinced she would feel only sympathy for his heartbreak.

"That went well," Celine told me later.

I stared at her in confusion.

"He acts like someone without a brain, manners, or common sense of any type," said Celine. "Could you respect a girl who would be interested in him anyway because he's rich and a prince? No! Which means she has given just the response I wanted to hear. Now we just have to show her what he's really like."

This third part of her campaign was carried out in stealth and often required two of us to pull it off. We dragged a reluctant Tillie with us to all sorts of odd places around the caravan, positioning ourselves where we could—in essence—spy on Cassian. Often one of us accompanied her while the other engaged him in conversation. Other times we surreptitiously observed his conversations with Frederic, or the steward, or Tillie's father, the caravan master.

I reminded Celine frequently that it was impolite to eavesdrop, but she told me such concerns must be brushed aside in pursuit of the noble cause of love.

"Besides," she said. "It's not as if we're listening to them talk about *us*. In fact, they're usually saying the most boring things. The important thing is that Cassian sounds perfectly sensible. Intelligent even."

After a week of this, Tillie no longer laughed at Celine's claims that Cassian was desperately in love with her and that this love was the cause of his apparent stupidity. And I noticed a strange expression in her eyes when she watched him. Still, I didn't see how Cassian had any hope of winning her if he could not bring himself to woo her.

He could find no flowers to take her in the desert, and she had no need of expensive trinkets. As a caravan master's daughter, she had always received such things and valued them little.

The southern coast grew ever closer, and we would turn off for Largo before we reached it. His time was running out. My mind was occupied with this thought when the caravan arrived at the last oasis before the turn off to Largo.

Shouts of horror and wails from the front of the caravan soon distracted me, and I clutched at Celine. What new danger was this? Should I act now to protect the princess in some way?

But when members of the caravan ran back past us, none seemed injured, despite the fear on their faces. "The oasis," they shouted. "The oasis has been filled in." None of them mentioned what this meant. They didn't need to, not when we'd all spent so long traveling through the desolate sand dunes of the desert.

The reality of the situation sank in, and I began to tremble. Caravans always traveled deep in the desert to protect themselves from bandits. Only now we had no water. Time, it seemed, was running out for more than Cassian.

CHAPTER 22

*I*n the confusion that followed, it took a couple of minutes to get our camel kneeling so that Celine and I could tumble off. The princes were already gone at that point, off to consult with the caravan master. Celine and I raced after them.

We found a huddle of the senior Tour and caravan members in the midst of the hubbub. As we approached, the caravan master was addressing the princes, his face ashen.

"You must take our fastest camels, what youngsters we still have with us, and all the remaining water supplies and make for the edge of the desert."

"Absolutely not!" said Frederic.

"But, Your Highness, there is no hope for us all to make it. This route has already pushed us longer than ideal between oasis stops. The camels cannot go on forever, and we have only a small amount of drinking water left for the humans."

"I will not leave more than half our number out here to die. If we leave you no water, you will have not the smallest chance of survival."

"Is there no hope of digging down to the water?" asked Cassian. "Surely they cannot have completely blocked the source." I noticed that his serious gaze didn't stray to Tillie, although she stood near her father. Apparently a crisis was enough to break through his love haze.

Celine thrust herself into the midst of the group. "What has happened?" she asked breathlessly. "How could someone block an oasis?"

"We did not think such a thing possible," said the caravan master. He had unwrapped his head covering and now mopped at his forehead. "There must be magic involved, it's the only way." He looked helplessly at the princes. "If our unknown adversary has twisted a godmother object to achieve this nefarious deed, I do not see what hope we have to undo it. Unless…"

"Unless?" Cassian looked at him with narrowed eyes.

"Unless one of you who are royal would care to call on your own godmother? Perhaps she would be willing to reverse what has been done here."

"It doesn't work quite like that," said Celine, sounding frustrated. "They don't necessarily come when we call. They have a reasoning behind their actions, I'm sure, but it's not one that makes much sense to us."

Frederic looked at her, and she spread her hands wide and shrugged. "I already tried to call her."

"Which means they expect us to solve this one for ourselves." Frederic's expression grew thoughtful. "That means there must be a way. There must be a way to save everyone."

I lingered on the edge of the group, unwilling to push through as Celine had done. But when no one spoke in response to Frederic, I could not stay silent.

"Surely we should not be standing here! We must move at once for the next oasis—as fast as we can go without taxing the animals to the point of death."

Everyone turned to look at me, and I took a half step backward. "Should we not?"

The caravan master, who clearly didn't recognize me and

considered me one of the Tour members, shook his head sadly. "I'm afraid this is the last oasis before Largo. We could head back for the previous one, but it would be just as long a journey as pushing on for the city, and we would not make it. Our camels can go ten days between drinks, and some could perhaps be pushed further. But it has been so long since our last stop. We do not have enough days left to make it to another source of water."

I frowned, looking around me as if I could pull map coordinates from the sky. Without even thinking I had fallen into old habits on this journey, tracking our passage against the map of the desert that I kept in my mind.

"But that's not right. You're forgetting we have a good chance of reaching the…" I trailed off as sudden realization exploded in my mind.

They did not know of the Osmira Oasis. No one left in the entire kingdom knew of it but me. I paled as I realized that if we were all to be spared destruction, I must lead us to safety. And if I got the way wrong, the consequences would be catastrophic.

If I said nothing, at least the royals and a small group with them could have some hope of getting out of the desert.

The caravan master had turned back to his people, dismissing me, but Frederic still watched me with creased brow. He believed in me. I went over the route in my head. Everyone in the caravan as soon as they were old enough to talk were drilled in the locations of all the oases, public and secret. I could do this. I had to do this.

I cleared my throat, but the caravan master didn't look back in my direction. I raised my voice. "We still have some hope of reaching the Osmira Oasis. We have a good chance, in fact."

Immediate silence fell. The caravan master whirled to face me, his eyes narrowed. "The location of that oasis has been lost. Everyone knows that. There are none now living with that information."

"None but me," I said, putting every bit of strength I could muster into my voice. "I am the sole survivor of Caravan Osmira."

"It's true, Father," said Tillie beside him, her eyes wide. "Don't you remember Evie? She was in the jungle when the attack happened and only found it two days later. Caravan Golura found her mourning in the wreckage."

The man's face slowly lost its accusing cast, as he examined me carefully. "You are her? You are the youngling who survived the massacre?"

I drew a deep breath. "It is true I was not there. I missed the massacre rather than survived it. But that's not what is important. The important thing is that there is still time to save us all. The Osmira Oasis is near." I knelt to draw a rough sketch in the sand beneath our feet. "It allowed our caravan to cut a shorter route to Largo."

Several of the traders knelt beside me, examining the markings I had made. They pointed at several aspects, murmuring questions. At last they stood back to their feet, me with them.

"You are sure?" The caravan master pierced me with a stare. "You are sure you have the distances correct? You are sure you can find the way? All our lives would be depending on you."

I nodded my head and felt Frederic step up to stand behind me.

"I trust Evie," he said. "If she says she can do it, she can."

Celine nodded her agreement.

"Well, then. We must move out immediately." The caravan master clapped his hands loudly, and the caravan exploded into movement. All up and down the strings, camel-pullers called the news to each other. There was another oasis. We all had a chance to live.

Our camels had more water still inside them than we had in our water skins, so the caravan master declared that everyone who possibly could was to ride. The camel-pullers must still lead their strings, but they would be swapped out as often as possible.

Celine and I now rode at the front of the caravan. I had shown the others the way on my rough map, but they still wanted me to do the actual leading. I calculated the distance and the correct path over and over again in my head. It helped immensely that we were leaving a public oasis. Although Caravan Osmira had rarely stopped at this particular one, it had still been one of the locations drilled into us.

Our camp that night was rough and we stayed for as short a time as possible. Only the need to rest the camels had us stopping at all. We pushed on all through the next day, a headache building behind my eyes from the tension.

"We are getting near," I eventually told the caravan master. "But I don't think we can make it this evening. We will have to stop again."

He nodded his understanding, but I could see the distaste in his eyes. We had run out of water supplies, and it had been a particularly hot day. I suspected he would push us on for as long as he could now, so we would have as little as possible to traverse the next day with dry mouths and weakening bodies.

Finding the route and keeping to it had so fully taken my focus that I failed to notice anything else. Thankfully, however, others weren't so distracted.

"Dust!" went up the cry, to be taken and repeated by many lips. "Dust! Dust!"

"What do they mean?" asked Celine, sounding more fearful than I had ever heard her. "Do they mean a dust storm is coming?"

I twisted and scanned the horizon in every direction, looking for what had raised the alarm. I spotted it, and my mouth set into a grim line. "Worse. Bandits. I would have thought we were still too far out for them."

"Form up!" yelled the caravan master in the loudest voice I had yet heard. A flurry of movement surrounded us as the traders launched into well-practiced movement. Full-scale bandit attacks were rare, but everyone was drilled for them. I could only imagine the training had increased since Caravan Osmira.

I slid down from my camel, and for a moment I swayed, dizziness sweeping over me and nearly causing my legs to collapse. With my eyes closed I could imagine it was my old caravan moving in such a way. That it was old, familiar voices calling out the warnings and orders. Was this what it had been like for them before the end? Or had they had no warning, taken completely by surprise?

A steadying hand gripped my waist, and I swallowed, pulling myself together as I looked up into Frederic's face. He nodded once, calmly, and I nodded back, stepping forward on my own legs.

"This way," he said, pulling Celine along behind him.

The bandits must be coming fast to raise such a dust cloud around them—they would have to move fast to limit their time in the desert. But even with the speed of their passage, we had fair warning. The signs of their presence could be seen far on a clear, hot day such as this.

The camels were formed into tight circles, many camels deep. The royals, nobles, and few children—such as Ofie's cousin—were placed in the center of all the rings and told to keep themselves low to the ground. Celine and I lay almost flat, Tillie beside us, her face pale. The traders trained in combat and the guards were dispersed among the rings of camels, the majority of them on the outer ring where the largest of the packs had been placed as an outer barrier before the first of the camels. An overturned wagon would have been a better shield, but this was the best we could do.

Frederic and Cassian both crouched beside us, their drawn swords in their hands.

"Aren't you going to fight?" asked Celine. "Out there I mean?" She waved toward the outer rings.

"Celine!" gasped Tillie. "They are royalty. They cannot be risked."

Cassian shook his head. "It's not ourselves we're concerned for." He eyed his sister. "We promised Mother we'd bring you home safely."

"I promise you," said Frederic, sounding more grim than I had ever heard him. "We'll see fighting. We're your last line of defense."

I swallowed and wished I had some sort of weapon of my own. Once, many, many years ago, in my first life, I had possessed some little skill with a knife. But none of my lives since then had needed such a skill, and I had long ago lost it. Still, I would have liked a blade in my hand.

I looked over at Celine, and she must have read the look in my eye, because she reached into her boot and drew out a short dagger, handing it to me. I noticed that she had a second one in her own hand. When I raised my eyebrows at her, she merely shrugged and returned her attention to the outer ring of camels.

All of our archers had been placed on the external defenses. As the attacking party neared, they slowed, pulling their horses to ride in a tight ring around us. They hollered and yelled, but the defenders remained calm, shooting into their midst. Several men screamed and went down, trampled by the galloping horses behind them.

"Frederic," I said above the noise. "They don't look like bandits. Are those…?"

Frederic and Cassian exchanged a glance. "They're bandits all right. They must be. But you're right, they don't look much like it."

White-faced we all looked at one another. Our attackers were dressed as Royal Lanoverian Guards. They even carried a royal flag.

We weren't the only ones to notice. "Royals." The murmur

went around our circles, rippling in and then out again. Frederic risked standing straight, giving others a sight of him.

"Do not be fooled!" he bellowed above the initial sounds of battle. "These are not royal guards. These are bandits dressed in stolen uniforms. And when we have vanquished them, we shall bring them to justice."

The murmur died down, and Celine tugged him back toward the ground.

"Very heroic," she said dryly. He ignored her.

"There will be hand-to-hand fighting, for sure," said Cassian quietly. Frederic nodded, seeming to understand him, and they both moved, still at a crouch, to opposite edges of the circle. Whatever message they were sending rippled out through the ranks of the defenders. I soon saw the actual royal guard attached to the Tour stripping off any identifying marks that weren't actually part of their protective covering. Enlightenment dawned. When it came to hand-to-hand combat among the camels, we needed to be able to tell friend from foe. Or, more importantly, we needed the traders to be able to tell friend from foe.

No sooner was the job done, than the remaining attackers charged. The archers let off a final volley and then dropped their bows to bring up spears and swords. The clash of the two lines was almost defeating. The camels groaned and bellowed, many attempting to stand and run. Those of us who were not trained to fight had our hands full restraining them.

The screams and cries of the injured sounded above the clash of metal against metal, and I lost track of the progress of the battle as I turned my attention to the animals around me. When a royal guard leaped in front of me, I forgot for a precious half-second that our men had stripped off their uniforms. By the time I thought to bring up my own dagger, an almost useless weapon in the situation anyway, it was far too late. As death fell toward me, another blade appeared, ringing against the first and halting its downward motion. I scrambled backward to get behind Frederic. With a swift parry and thrust he dispatched the man.

"Stay behind me," he said, his eyes roving between the camels. "And keep Celine with you."

I forced my frozen body into action, swinging around and managing to catch at the princess as she attempted to throw herself into the fray.

"Evie! Let me go!" she panted, but I shook my head and held on tighter. "You only have a dagger Celine. They have spears and swords. Frederic gave me orders, and I'm not letting you be killed."

"I won't cower while others die," Celine said with a hiss. "I want to fight."

"And you can fight," I agreed. My hand tightened. "When you have the right tools and training."

I looked around but could now see no sign of most of the traders who had joined us in the center of the ring. Ofie's cousin still cowered near me, but Tillie was no longer in sight. The older nobles, however, had surprised me. They stood in a united block with finely crafted blades shimmering before them. Thanks to them, our inner circle still held, although everywhere else chaos seemed to reign. Cassian, however, had disappeared. I could only hope he was still alive and unharmed. Frederic, at least, seemed unconcerned about him, his whole focus on us.

Two more attackers appeared with ferocious yells, and Frederic lunged forward to engage them both, his sword flashing so quickly my eyes could barely follow it. Even with two, he was holding them off.

Then a third appeared. Frederic faltered for less than half a second, adjusting his rhythm to hold off the newcomer, but even with his superior skill, the strain was starting to show.

"Now, will you let go of me?" Celine asked with a significant look.

I nodded but didn't release my tight grip. I adjusted the

dagger in my other hand. "Both of us," I said as quietly as I could. "You crawl to the left, I'll go to the one on the right. Don't try to get fancy, just go for his foot. We just need to distract him for Frederic."

She nodded once, and I let go, shimmying immediately to my right. Giving a wide arc around Frederic, not wanting to risk tripping him up, I crawled unseen to the right-most attacker. As soon as I reached him, I heard a yell from the man to the left. Without waiting to check what had happened with Celine, I plunged my dagger into the foot of the man in front of me.

CHAPTER 23

$\mathcal{H}$e screamed and cursed, staggering and nearly falling as I scooted quickly back out of the way. A moment later, he fell and didn't rise again. With two of his attackers injured and distracted, Frederic made quick work of them all.

When his blade dropped, his breath coming ragged, he nodded at us both. I had half expected a reprimand, but his reaction indicated how much danger we had been in. Celine, looking paler than I expected, crawled quickly back to meet me behind her brother.

"I…I didn't think it would feel like that," she whispered in my ear.

I patted her shoulder. "If you need to vomit, try to hold it at least until the fighting has finished."

And the fighting did seem to be dying down, the battle decreasing in both scope and severity. No other attackers made it through to us, and soon the sound of fighting had entirely ceased. We had prevailed.

Frederic turned to look back at us, his eyes skimming over Celine, who was already pushing herself to her feet, to land on me. He dropped to one knee beside me, his hand cradling my cheek.

"Are you hurt?"

I shook my head mutely.

"That was very brave."

I managed a shaky laugh. "Hardly. Not compared to what you and so many others did."

He shrugged. "I have spent many years training to use a blade."

I swallowed. "Your leadership will be needed now. I'm unharmed."

He nodded, almost reluctantly, and then stood. "Take as many prisoners as you can," he called across the circles of camels, striding away from us.

I looked around at the aftermath, trying to see our toll for myself. "Where's Cassian? I saw him fighting over in that direction, but he disappeared from sight."

"There," said Celine, and something in her tone of voice made me turn quickly. My eyes widened at the sight of Cassian striding toward us, Tillie cradled protectively in his arms, her hands around his neck, and her face tucked against his chest.

"Is that...and..."

"Yes," said Celine. "I can't believe it." I couldn't tell if the shock on her face was from the battle we had just lived through or the sight of the two of them in such a lover-like pose.

Not far from us, Cassian gently placed Tillie's feet on the ground, ringing her in his arms and pressing his lips firmly down over hers. She returned the embrace enthusiastically while Celine and I watched with wide eyes.

When he let her go, he looked regretful. "I must attend to the wounded."

"Yes." Tillie's voice shook. "I know where to find the medical supplies. I will be with you as soon as I can."

After one last second of gazing into each other's eyes, they separated, Cassian to kneel beside the closest wounded trader, his steady hands assessing his wounds, and Tillie to frantically tear at a pack located near us.

After a brief exchange of glances, we joined her. Between the three of us, we managed to get the fastenings undone, searching through the bags and pockets inside for the necessary bandages and medications.

"What…what happened?" I asked as we worked, our hurried fingers slipping and sliding in our haste. I didn't even quite know how to frame the question.

"He saved me," Tillie said breathlessly. "He nearly died doing it. He was so brave." She cast a lightning quick look at us. "And he looked so handsome. I knew immediately he was everything I wanted in a man."

Celine paused for the briefest moment before quickly resuming her task. "I suppose it helps that he appears to be able to talk to you now."

"He's been fine ever since the crisis began," I pointed out. "I guess he just needed to be shocked out of it."

"He told me he's written poetry for me," said Tillie, sounding shy for the first time since I'd known her.

Celine choked. "Poetry? Cassian?"

"Here!" I said triumphantly, upending a bag filled with armfuls of clean bandage rolls. "Quickly now."

All three of us scooped up as many as we could carry and ran in opposite directions. I tried to shut my nose and ears as I picked my way among the wounded. To my relief, we seemed to have more whole than wounded, and everywhere I stopped there was someone ready to receive a roll of bandage. The trader life was rough, and everyone had some basic level medical training.

The Tour doctor, who had been protected in the middle of the nobles' circle—a sensible move of which I highly approved— worked frantically, moving between the worst of the wounded.

Night fell as we labored on to stem any bleeding and assess the damage.

Many of the camels had been lost, and I saw Ofie's young cousin weeping over three of theirs. To my relief, my friend stood behind him, comforting him despite the white bandage wrapped around his arm. When he saw me, he waved, shrugging off the wound as a graze.

Others had not been so fortunate, and the row of still bodies, while smaller than I had feared, still brought tears and a wrenching pain in my gut. Among the unfamiliar faces, I recognized a palace servant and three genuine guards, plus one trader who I had played with as a child. Fresh tears poured down my face.

Many times, when I faced another trader, I placed my palm against my heart, letting my action replace the words I could not find. Or I grasped their arms and rested my forehead against theirs, letting centuries of trader culture give me the words I couldn't form on my own.

"Does it work?" asked Celine in a subdued voice, at one point. "Does it bring you comfort?"

I considered her words. "All I know is this: I once mourned a bandit attack alone, this day I mourn one with others. I feel stronger now than I did then, as the words say."

She nodded once, her eyes shadowed. Someone had explained to her the fate of Caravan Osmira.

"Evie, Evie, there you are." Someone I didn't recognize gripped my arm and began to tug me away. "The caravan master is looking for you."

Celine trailed behind me, as the trader girl led me through the makeshift camp that had sprung up. When we found the caravan master, he stood beside a saddled camel, one who had been unharmed in the fighting.

"Oh, good, there you are." Without waiting for explanations, he grabbed my arm and pushed me on to its back.

"What's going on?" I asked.

Frederic appeared from somewhere, looking dirty and tired. "We desperately need water. The wounded, especially. We've stripped the fastest, strongest camels of their loads, and we're sending a team to ride ahead for water and bring it back. We need you to lead them to the oasis."

I nodded as the camel stood to its feet. A sudden memory of the last words I had heard Frederic say sprang to my mind.

"Where are the prisoners?" I called down to him.

He shook his head, his face haunted. "None survived. They fought to the last man, and despite our efforts, we could not save any of their wounded."

My camel moved off to join a small waiting crowd, and I looked back at him over my shoulder. His expression confirmed the sinking feeling in my gut. This had been no ordinary group of bandits.

My own throat felt parched and dry during that desperate nighttime ride. Thankfully a clear night had followed the hot day, and the stars kept us on course. When we reached the oasis at last, I would have cried if I had any moisture left to leak.

One of my travel companions helped me down from my camel, respect in his eyes. "I admit, I wasn't sure, but…"

I could feel no resentment at his doubt. I had doubted myself. I tried to reassure him, but my dry throat could barely form words. I managed to muster a small smile before stumbling the last few steps and thrusting my whole face into the water, just as the animal beside me did.

As soon as the humans had drunk our fill, we began to fill the skins we had brought, loading them carefully onto the replenished camels' backs. When we had loaded them all, we wearily remounted and began the ride back.

The camels seemed ready to drop by the time the camp came back into sight, and many people ran forward to relieve them of their loads. I tried to help, but Frederic caught me as I swayed and almost fell.

"Steady there," he said in my ear. "You've done your part tonight." Scooping me into his arms, he cradled me against his chest, the rocking motion of his walk and the warmth of his chest against my face soothing me into a half doze. Someone else had been carried like this today, I remembered, but I could not force my brain to form proper thoughts.

I was laid gently on a bed and thought I felt lips press against my hair. But that part might have been a dream.

The next morning, I led the rest of the camels to the oasis. The animals that had worked so hard the night before still rested, along with most of the camp. The remaining camels could easily bring enough water back for all the humans, leaving no need to attempt to move the wounded yet.

All three royals accompanied me, along with half the remaining guard and Tillie, who had barely left Cassian's side since the attack. Cassian, a proud and somewhat dumbfounded expression perpetually on his face, had regained his confidence. He made no secret of their engagement, and the poor caravan master had been swept along with the plan with a look of utter confusion. He could hardly refuse his permission for his daughter to wed a Lanoverian prince. I wished their betrothal could have come under happier circumstances, but at least Tillie seemed to find great solace for her grief in Cassian's steady presence.

The oasis looked different in the light of day, the water sparkling and blue against the yellow sand around it. Several palm trees grew on the fringe, along with some hardy desert grass, and the green and yellow along with the brilliant blue of the sky created a striking picture. Many of those who had accompanied us plunged fully clothed into the water and swam through the softly burbling pool.

A quick look passed between Celine and me, and then we were running for the water ourselves. The feeling of the cool water and the weightlessness as I floated seemed to lift off my pressures in some impossible way. I had done it. I had found the oasis, I had led everyone to the water we so desperately needed.

Tears welled, washed away before they could even fall. I just wished we could have done it without the heavy price.

But when I mentioned the thought to Frederic, who had joined us, he shook his head. Glancing around to see who was in earshot, he spoke quietly to Celine and me.

"Bandits don't dress as royal guards, and they don't come this far into the desert. They must have been rebels, it's the only explanation. We think they meant to destroy the caravan, as Caravan Osmira was once destroyed, but this time the fallen attackers left behind with the trader dead would have appeared to be crown men."

I had to admit the thought had occurred to me, and I had even forced myself to walk the line of enemy dead, looking for a single familiar face. The looming dread that hung over me due to Marcus's freedom had faded in the jungle, a place that had no connection with him. But with the attack, the old fear had come rushing back. But I had seen no sign of him.

"But what of us?" asked Celine. "What reason could they give for the royal guard attacking us?"

Frederic shrugged. "I suspect the plan was to keep us alive and take us as hostages. It was a bold concept, and no doubt concocted to sow fear and confusion on both sides, as Father would no doubt question if the traders themselves had taken us."

He looked over at me. "And their plan would likely have worked if not for you, Evie."

"Me?"

"Yes, you. It must have been them who filled in the oasis. They hoped to drive us hard for Largo, and no doubt had an ambush set up just before the edge of the desert, planning to attack when we were at our weakest. But instead we turned this way. They had to ride hard to catch us, and they had to attack sooner than they had planned. And in so doing, they lost the element of surprise. Their force wasn't strong enough to take a full caravan in a defensive position."

I let myself fall back into the water as I processed his words. So much more had been riding on my head than even I realized.

"Instead of disaster and a kingdom plunged into chaos, this attack has actually left us in a stronger position."

"Stronger?" asked Celine.

"The merchants and traders, instead of turning against the crown, now stand with us against the rebels. It is the rebels who have violated the ancient treaty, not us. It was a bold gamble on their part, and it hasn't paid off."

I thought of the row of motionless bodies and shivered. How many had to pay the price for future peace? I supposed it was always so in times of war. And it was increasingly clear that war was exactly was this was—even if it was a strange, guerrilla kind.

When we returned to the camp, plans were made to move on as soon as the worst of the wounded could be moved. Messengers had already been sent out to the other camel caravans and to the merchant caravans currently in Lanover. Any of the smaller ones who doubted their capacity to protect themselves would go to ground. The others would be ready for any attack. I didn't think the rebels would try that strategy again, however.

No one asked me for my opinion, but I announced that I would be publicly declaring the location of the Osmira Oasis to the other caravans. The caravan master made no protest, although he gave me a rather crestfallen look.

"A gift from Caravan Osmira to all the traders," I said. "In exchange for the oasis that has been lost."

Frederic approved my actions and said he would have a

formal announcement and map drawn up to be distributed to each of the caravans.

Two days later we rode out. The night before, Frederic, Cassian, Celine and I gathered as we generally did. Only this time our small group was enlarged by the presence of Tillie. The caravan master's daughter would be riding on with the Tour along with a small contingent of traders, her handmaidens of a sort. I knew her father had wanted her to stay with them to travel to Lanare, but she had refused to be parted from Cassian.

"This rebellion must be stopped, and soon," said Cassian, his voice hard, but his arm gentle around his betrothed's shoulder.

Frederic nodded. "Everywhere we've gone, they've attempted to wreak chaos and destruction, undermining the crown's control. And always they've striven to make someone else appear the villain. But none of the communities we've visited have been responsible. No, the center of all this still lies ahead."

"Largo." I said, and it wasn't a question. Somehow I had always known—from the moment I had agreed to this trip and long before I heard the itinerary. I was returning to where it had all begun.

PART III
LARGO AND HOME

CHAPTER 24

The traders brought their full caravan to the town east of Largo where they had left the rest of their people. Many times on our journey I heard the murmured words of relief that the most vulnerable among the traders had not been present for the attack. But our arrival at the town that hosted them drained us all, our grief resurfacing as we broke the terrible news to those waiting and expecting a joyful reunion with their caravan.

The entire caravan would have accompanied us on to Largo, but Frederic refused the gesture. "Stay here, grieve, care for your wounded. We need only two strings to carry our baggage."

And so we were a greatly reduced group when we reached the gates of Largo, the great jungle city of the south. Largo perched like a jewel between the desert, the jungle, and the sea, the one large city where the caravans would go. Built on Largo Bay with its deep-water port, the trading hub had become the center of the south. It was here I had been born.

Many people loved the diverse community that called Largo home, but I had always been more interested in the varied styles of clothing they brought with them. Every design known in the kingdoms seemed to walk these streets, a beautiful counterpoint to the bright colors of the northern jungle which still flourished here, giving a vibrant edge to even the most mundane aspects of life. It had been a shock to me when I eventually discovered that it was only in Largo, alone in Lanover, that pale-skinned northerners were almost as common a sight as the darker-skinned locals and that desert traders mixed freely with city-dwellers. Apparently its remote position at almost the southern-most tip of the Four Kingdoms suggested adventure and freedom to many. But I had not found freedom here.

Riding through the eastern gates felt more like a homecoming than any other arrival of our journey. And yet the city looked unfamiliar, too. I had grown accustomed, it turned out, to the lower level of moisture in the air in Lanare and to the constant sight of reddish sandstone that dominated the capital. Lanare had an almost dusty feeling that Largo lacked, but the air didn't attempt to stifle me with every breath.

The royals had been provided camels to ride as well as the animals carrying the baggage, but everyone had elected to enter the city on foot. I suspected they wished to avoid a spectacle after all the trouble with the rebels. My eyes roamed restlessly around the streets as we walked, sub-consciously looking for familiar faces as I spied familiar streets and buildings. But I had left Largo at the age of nine. The faces I had known best then had likely changed beyond recognition by now, their owners grown to adulthood, as had I.

We made straight for the governor's mansion at the center of the city, a building I had never before entered. Being ushered through its double doors alongside royalty felt so intensely surreal that for a moment I wondered if the last months had truly been only a dream, and I would wake to find myself back in my bed in Lanare.

But no such awakening occurred. Instead I was treated to a

welcome feast, and the seemingly endless ramblings of the governor who expressed over and over again his shock at the recent attack and his assurance that the princes' messages to their father would be delivered with the swiftest haste. It came back to me with blinding clarity that the man had always been unsuited for his role. A bureaucrat when a true leader was needed to hold sway over such a large and diverse populace. He had no doubt received the role because his father had held it before him and his father before that. And the earls of Largo had always been unswervingly loyal to the crown. So while their noble position didn't necessitate their receiving the role of governor, it seemed it had always been so.

I sighed and pushed my food away. It frightened me how quickly I slipped into the mindset of a Largoan, laughing at the inadequacies of the governor and seeing the crown as something distant and foreign. Here, perhaps more than anywhere else, I would have to watch my step.

Frederic and Cassian would have filled the next day with meetings, but Celine insisted we all needed to visit the market.

"We spent a few hours there last year when I came here with Rafe and Celeste," she said, naming her third brother and middle sister. "But we hardly had any time in Largo. It was incredible, though!" She rounded on me. "Tell them, Evie!"

I smiled. "It's true that even locals love the markets." The governor's mansion might be the geographical center of the city, but its true heart was the nearby marketplace, bigger than any other I had seen since.

"These meetings are important," Cassian reminded his sister. I suspected his reluctance might have something to do with Tillie who was occupied at the mansion for the day with the small number of Traders who had accompanied us and who would leave the next day to escort the two strings of camels back to the rest of the caravan.

She put her hands on her hips. "And the markets aren't? You

heard what Evie said of them. You should be thinking more like Celeste."

An expression of consternation crossed his face at the mention of their sister who had been gifted with exceptional intelligence and used it to develop an expertise in spy craft, among other things. He glanced at Frederic.

"Perhaps she's right," said Frederic. "We might learn more among the people than we will among the governor and his men."

When I rolled my eyes without thinking at the mention of the governor, he looked at me thoughtfully. "Yes, I think we had best visit the markets after all."

I insisted we go at the time of the midday meal since the food stalls sold as broad a range of delicacies as were represented by Largo's people. My favorites, however, were the succulent skewers of meat cooked with a blend of local spices. That stall had always been the most popular at the market.

Relief filled me to see it was still there, and no one protested when I suggested we eat first and nose around after. And with the smells of my chosen stall filling the surrounding area, no one protested my choice of food, either.

When every last piece of our meat had been devoured, we moved aimlessly among the seemingly endless stalls. How many countless hours of my childhood had I spent here? I picked out several familiar faces among the stallholders, but no one appeared to recognize me. And I did not expect them to. They no doubt saw an elegant noble girl whose clothes rivaled those worn by the royalty beside her. Who would connect me with the orphan girl, half street urchin, who had once dashed between the stalls without even shoes?

I flushed and glanced at my companions. Would they see me differently if they knew? The well-off citizens of Largo had always thought it mattered, and being here brought it all rushing back. But I reminded myself of the desert. I had wronged them by believing the royals were the same. And no matter how hard it went against my instincts, I wanted to continue to choose to trust them.

I plastered a smile on my face and reminded myself I wasn't the same girl who had started on this Tour. I had outgrown her. Yet the past still weighed heavy on my mind as my eyes wandered from stall to stall.

For that reason, I didn't at first believe my eyes when I spotted a familiar face that stood out from the others. A familiar face that didn't belong here in Largo. I almost stumbled to a halt, gripping the arm of whoever walked nearest me, which turned out to be Frederic.

"Frederic," I breathed, the word so faint he probably couldn't hear me above the normal hubbub of the market. I forced air into my lungs to make the next word louder. "Marcus."

Frederic, who had instantly stopped at my grip, followed my gaze. "Cassian, over here."

The other two turned and hurried back to us. I still hadn't moved, my eyes locked across a vast distance of marketplace with my old nemesis. He had clearly seen us as well.

"Guards!" called Frederic, and the small contingent that had been trailing behind us trotted to catch up the few steps that separated us. He pointed at one of them. "You, stay to guard the girls. The rest of you, with us."

He didn't stop to give Celine a chance to complain but took off running through the market, shoving people aside as necessary, his brother at his side and the rest of the guards on his heels. Marcus, his eyes finally breaking from mine, turned and fled.

"Typical," said Celine. "No one ever wants to include me in the action." But she made no attempt to follow them, for which I was more than grateful. I would have felt honor bound to follow and attempt to stop her, and I had no desire to get closer to Marcus.

"I think I should escort you back to the governor's mansion," said the remaining guard, looking around the crowded market uneasily.

Apparently this was a line too far for Celine, however, who instantly entered into an argument with him. I tuned her out and looked around, wondering what the market would make of the disturbance. But already people were moving again, talking as if nothing had happened. The crowd jostled me on several sides, and I decided to lend my hearty support to the guard.

But when I turned to do so, I found myself alone. My breaths came hard and fast as I looked around for Celine's familiar face. Where could she have gone? She had been here just a moment ago. I told myself how easy it was to get separated in a crush such as this, but I couldn't rein in the fear that she had been abducted from under my nose.

But my heartbeat finally calmed when I got a distant glimpse of her. The grim-looking guard was hauling her forcibly back toward the mansion. She had either angered him enough that he decided to take the risk of manhandling a princess, or he had decided that any penalty he received would be far lighter than the one he might get for failing in his duty to keep her safe.

I hurried after them.

But as I took a shortcut between two stalls, skirting the edges of the public garden that bordered the marketplace, strong arms lifted me from my feet. I screamed and thrashed, but the man quickly clamped a hand over my mouth. The sound of my struggles was easily lost in the noise around us. I kicked backward but couldn't gain enough leverage to do any real damage.

And then the prick of a blade dug into my ribs. I instantly stilled.

"That's right, be a good girl, now," said a voice from my nightmares. True fear flooded me. Somehow he had eluded them and circled around. I was all alone, at his mercy, and no one knew it.

CHAPTER 25

*M*arcus dragged me backward away from the marketplace and the garden and into a deserted alleyway. He spun me around to face him.

"I was hoping we would meet again," he said.

I spat at him.

"Uh uh uh, none of that now." He grinned a lazy grin that sent ice down my spine. "I knew you would all find your way here eventually, all I had to do was bide my time."

He already gripped one arm, his dagger pricking into my other side, but he leaned forward as he said the words, bringing his face even closer to mine. "With the others it's just business, but with you, my dear Evangeline, with you it's personal. If it hadn't been for my old-fashioned uncle, I would have taught you to mind your betters on Catalie. But I had to get rid of you instead. And then you returned, only to go and rescue my dear cousin, ruining everything in the process. I'm going to enjoy having my revenge on you, Evangeline."

I turned my face away, leaning my head as far back as I could without moving my body. He merely laughed and drew back a fraction. The band around my chest eased, and I could breathe again.

I cast a subtle look around the alley, but no one else was in sight. My eyes caught on an untidy pile of old crates. Something tugged at my memory, but the blade pressing into my side made it hard to focus.

I looked back at Marcus who watched over my shoulder as if waiting for something or someone. Perhaps he had back up coming. The thought sent my mind frantically wheeling as I tried to conceive of some means of escape or rescue. I should never have left Lanare.

But I gave my head the slightest shake, as if to dislodge the idea. All my life, as I had moved from place to place, I had tried to put the past behind me. Whenever the memories resurfaced, I pushed them away. Only at night in my dreams were they able to roam free.

I had thought revisiting the scenes of my past life would cripple me, and yet this trip had only made me stronger. I had needed to remind myself of the parts of my journey that had been good, and to visit the sources of my fear now that I was no longer a frightened child. I had needed to give myself space to grieve. I had needed to face my past to conquer it.

Which meant it was time for me to stop running from myself; it was time for me to embrace my past.

The thought brought my eyes snapping back to the crates and the crumbling brick wall behind them. They *were* familiar. I knew this place from the days when I ran with the street urchins of Largo.

Confidence and certainty filled me as I looked back at Marcus's distracted face. He was one part of my past I would have gladly left behind for good. But since he was apparently determined to seek me out, I would show him that I wasn't a weak and passive victim. I didn't know if I could defeat him, but I knew I had to fight.

As fast as I could, I whipped my hand up, smashing my flat palm into his nose. In the same moment, I stomped with all my strength onto one of his feet. He gasped and fell back a step, hopping and blinking hard. The moment the tip of the dagger left my skin, I ducked around him and ran for the back of the alley.

Reeling and surprised by the direction of my attempted escape, it took him several precious moments to pursue me. I spun around the crates, dropped to my knees and wriggled through the hole in the bottom corner of the brick wall. For a heart-stopping moment, I thought I wouldn't fit, but with a tear of fabric I squeezed through into the street beyond.

Rough hands grabbed at my left ankle, halting my forward momentum. I let him draw me several inches backward until I was close enough to kick backward with my right foot. It collided with something that felt like a face, and a scream split the alley. The anchor on my other foot dropped away, and I was on my feet and running.

I didn't even think as my feet took me down familiar roads and alleys, ducking between buildings and clambering over fences as necessary. I had barely fit through the hole, he would never be able to do so. By the time he made it over the top or around to the other side of the wall, I had every intention of being long gone.

So many hours spent with a needle in hand had decreased my fitness for such activities, and I was soon short of breath. A short distance after that, I had to stop, bending over and gulping deep breaths of air. Between gasps I looked around, getting my bearings.

Good sense suggested I should have run for the governor's mansion—Marcus wouldn't dare touch me there. But instinct had led me to a very different part of the city. And I found I couldn't regret my feet's decision. Something was happening on the streets of Largo, and I needed to talk to the people who knew those streets better than anyone.

Orienting myself, I took off again, moving more slowly and cautiously now. I saw no sign of Marcus but kept careful watch just in case. The streets emptied, and I entered a small pocket on the outskirts of the city full of crumbling buildings, most long ago abandoned. My eyes searched for a familiar sight, something to tell me I hadn't come on a fool's errand.

There. I quickly crossed the street and slipped into a tiny alleyway. I strode halfway up it, marveling at how few steps it now took me to reach the boarded window at street height. I assessed it with my eyes. Would I fit through? I thought so—just.

Feeling along the gap behind one corner of the boards with my littlest finger, I unhooked a series of clasps and swung the boards wide, revealing an empty window behind them. Taking a deep breath, I swung myself into the darkness beyond, feet first.

My shoulders squeezed through with another ripping sound. I sighed. This dress was undoubtedly ruined by my day's adventures.

I had barely regained my balance in the dim space below ground when a small shape hit my chest hard and sent me hurtling backward. I landed with a solid thump and struggled to draw breath given the heavy weight now settled on my chest.

"Someone get a light," said a small voice off to one side and then a single spot of flame flared. It quickly spawned several more until a rosy glow filled the large room.

I managed to wheeze several breaths in and out, before choking out, "Gerroff me."

"She sounds like one of us," said the first voice, which turned out to belong to a grinning girl of indeterminate age. I doubted she was more than eight, however.

"Look at 'er, though," said another, his voice dripping with scorn. "She's a full-sizer, she can't be one of us."

"Check 'er for weapons so's I can get up," said the one sitting on my chest.

The girl with the grin came forward and ran light hands over me. "She's clean."

The youngster on my chest bounded off, springing off my ribcage. "Ooof," I groaned, rolling over and pushing myself onto all fours. I took several full breaths before pushing myself up to standing.

Looking around at the short statures around me, I reversed course and sat down. They all regarded me with eyes ranging from curious to suspicious to hostile. I counted seven children in the large den, ranging in age from what looked like four to almost teenagers. I knew from experience that more than seven likely lived here—the others must be out on the streets. I wished I'd brought some food as a peace offering, but I'd hardly had the time or opportunity to stop for some.

The room, the large open basement of a long-abandoned shop, had all of its windows boarded. Grubby cushions formed a number of nests around the edges of the rooms, and several slightly broken shelves held a variety of treasures. Someone had attempted to hang brightly-colored pieces of material from the walls, presumably to brighten the place. It was a nice touch that hadn't been here in my day.

"What are you doing here, and how did you find us?" asked the scornful one when I didn't say anything.

I sighed and considered my answer. I hadn't thought this far ahead.

"I needed somewhere to hide. And I wanted to talk to you."

The boy who had knocked me to the ground raised an eyebrow. "Talk to us? Nobody wants to talk to us."

"Well, more fools them, then. You rule the streets," I said.

The girl laughed. "See, I told you she was one of ours."

A fourth child, a slightly older girl, approached me for a closer look. "I ain't never seen one of us dressed in clothes like that."

"But you heard her, she said our line. We rule the streets. She may look all fancy and stuff, but how would a noble girl know to say that?"

"Maybe she got one of our old lot slaving away for her," said the scornful boy with narrowed eyes.

Now I was the one to raise my eyebrows. "One of you slaving away for a noble? Pull another one."

The cheerful girl chortled again. "If she's not one o' us, she knows us well enough. Ain't we all here 'cause we didn't want to slave for no one?"

The boy who looked to be the oldest stood and walked toward me. He had been silent so far, examining me with searching eyes. He approached to within a foot of me and then leaned his head forward, squinting his eyes.

"She weren't ever one o' us, exac'ly," he said after a moment's contemplation of my face. "But she most good as were." He stepped back and looked around at the rest of them. "I never forget a face."

Even the scornful one seemed to accept this utterance, wandering away as if he had lost interest, although I noticed him casting surreptitious glances back in my direction.

"Do you recognize me?" I asked the boy in some astonishment. "But I've been gone nine years, and you can't be more than, what, twelve?"

He gave me a gap-toothed grin. "Right on the money, you are Evie-girl. But my memory is second to none. I were only three back then, but I never forget a face." He looked inordinately proud of himself.

"Only three?" I tapped my lip thoughtfully and examined his face again. "Don't tell me you're little Howler!"

He threw his head back at that and laughed. "Oh, aye, that's what they used to call me, ain't it. But I learned to stop the howling soon enough." He puffed out his chest. "Youngest ever to join the crew, I was. I learned the ropes quick enough." He thrust out a hand which I grasped and shook. "They call me Lookout now. Ain't no one who can hoodwink me."

"Good," I said. "Then you're just the person I need to speak to."

CHAPTER 26

*L*ookout's stamp of approval seemed to give the other children confidence, and they swarmed all over me, examining my hair and clothes with eager, sticky fingers. I tried not to wince. It was hard now to believe I had ever felt at home in such grubby environs. But I had once felt far more welcome here than in the place that officially housed me.

The young boy who had tackled me and the second girl both had faces so pale they almost glowed in the candlelight—northerner parents, then. The boy introduced himself with a wink as Whitey, and the girl as Reya. They had clearly all chosen names for themselves, in the typical manner of street urchins.

The laughing girl was Dancer, and she informed me that the scornful boy was called Mastiff. The other two were apparently deemed too young to bother with.

"Where did you get this dress?" asked Reya, running the folds through her fingers.

"I made it."

"All on your own?" She regarded me with wide eyes.

I nodded. "I taught myself how to sew. It's how I made a life for myself."

"I wish I could learn to make dresses." She looked downcast, her fingers still trailing over the material as if of their own volition.

"I can teach you myself, back in Lanare, if you really want to learn," I said. "Or find you an apprenticeship in Largo if you would rather stay here. But it's no easy ride. If you want to get good, you'd have to work hard."

She looked up at me, her eyes alight. "I can work hard, if it's for something I want."

Mastiff scoffed. "What did Dancer just say about us working for no one? You just going to throw that all away for a pretty dress, Reya?" He said her name like an insult.

She glared at him. "You shut it, Mastiff. There ain't nothing wrong with learning a proper craft if you can find someone's willing to teach you. Didn't Frostbite leave just a month ago? And he ain't regretted it none. We can't stay here forever, sure enough."

Mastiff glared back but made no further comment.

I smiled at Reya, wondering what I had just taken on. "Well, you got some time to think on it. I'm here with the Royal Tour, I'm the official seamstress. We don't leave for another two weeks, so come to the mansion in two weeks' time if you want to leave with me." I didn't need to say which mansion.

"Official seamstress to the royals?" Her eyes grew wide.

"I always knew you was going to go far, Evie-girl," said Look-out. "You was always too pretty not to." He winked at me, and I rolled my eyes in reply.

"You said you was here to talk," said Mastiff. "Let's get on with it, then."

"No one knows Largo like the street urchins," I said.

"Ain't that the truth," crowed Whitey, slapping celebratory hands with Dancer.

"Well, I'm guessing then that you've seen there's something off." Their smiles fell away, the mood instantly turning grim.

"There's something rotten in Largo, and I want to dig it out and destroy it. But first I need your help to find it."

The children exchanged glances, a complex language that I didn't know them well enough to read. For a long moment I thought they weren't going to tell me anything, and then Lookout shook his head and sighed.

"Things ain't been right around here ever since the Shadow Man showed up. And things won't be right until he's gone."

The others all nodded, except for Mastiff. But he neither scoffed nor protested, either, which I took as agreement.

"Shadow Man? Who's the Shadow Man?"

Dancer looked at me and shivered. "That's just what we urchins call him. Cause he's always lurking in them." Her expression transformed into one of indignation. "But that's our territory. And we don't like him bringing so many strangers into it."

"So he's not from Largo? He's a foreigner?"

The children frowned at each other. Whitey scratched his head. "Now that's 'arder to say," he said. "He looks like one of ours."

"Sounds like one, too," said Dancer. "Only not from the streets, for all he likes to pretend."

Lookout shrugged. "I already told you as how I don't forget a face. He claims he grew up here and just went away for a while to learn to fight better, but I never saw 'im on the streets until real recent like. Just before that fool rebellion what happened up north last year."

"I guess he saw his chance," said Reya. Street urchins understood power and its workings as well as any noble—they had to in order to survive—they just operated in an entirely different power structure, that of the streets.

"He came in with weapons and men, and he took over the streets." To my surprise, Mastiff joined the conversation. "We didn't like it, then, but we don't get involved with the full-sizers. Set themselves up in a warehouse and talked a lot about everyone getting their due." He shrugged. "Sounds like nonsense talk to me, we each got what we make for ourselves. But some got real riled up by it."

"Then that rebellion happened, and we began to hear real ugly talk," said Whitey, his face pinched. "Talk about kings and thrones and the moment being ripe. That's when we knew for sure. We ain't seen no ruler of the streets who wants to be a real king before. Naw, he ain't one of us."

"A lot of new folks have come in since then." Dancer looked worried. "And not folks like us. Hired fighters from up north. And nobles' sons and merchants' sons and the like to lead them."

"But never oldest sons, you note that," said Mastiff. "If you ask me, he's gathering an army of folks who are dissatisfied with their lot in life. People who want to turn the tables on those who got more than they did."

I rubbed my head. "But Lanover is the richest of all the kingdoms. No one lives in true want here, the crown makes sure of that. Don't they care about that?"

Mastiff gave a harsh laugh. "Course they don't. You mark my words, if they got into power, us poor folk would be the last to get any good things coming our way." He shook his head. "But some folks're never satisfied."

I thought of Marcus. No wonder he had been pulled into the rebellion. I wouldn't want to live in a kingdom ruled by people like him. But were there even enough dissatisfied people in Lanover that they could convince an army's worth to risk their lives?

I considered their actions so far. Maybe not. Dancer had said they had brought northerners in. And it might explain why everything they had done so far was designed to sow chaos and dissatisfaction. They needed to upset the current balance to bring more people to their side. And then maybe, if they could strike a targeted enough blow…

I stood to my feet. "I need to return to the mansion. The royals need to hear about this."

Whitey pulled on my hand. "But didn'chya say something 'bout hiding? When you first fell in here? Who you hiding from if not them royals?"

A shiver ran down my spine. I looked around at my small audience. "Have any of you seen a newcomer? He would have arrived within the last few months. Tall, dark hair—a disgraced islander noble."

Dancer and Lookout exchanged glances.

"Marcus," they said together.

Lookout turned to me. "Aye, we know 'im. Now *he* really ain't one of us. Not that he knows it. Struts around the streets like he's the king o' Largo."

"He's a vicious one," said Dancer. "All the urchins know to steer clear of him."

"I used to know him, years ago." I paused. "And I'm the reason he got banished from the islands. He has it out for me, and he got me cornered in Miller's Alley."

"Whew, now that's what I call lucky," said Reya. "Couldn't have asked for a better spot."

I nodded. "I just don't want to get cornered again somewhere less fortunate."

They all nodded and crossed their arms over their chests, fists tight, in the street urchin sign of solidarity.

"I'd better go with you, then," said Lookout. "Back to the mansion. No one sneaks past me."

"I'll come, too," said Reya, "you can show me where to meet you when it comes time for you to leave."

"I'm not missing out on the fun," said Whitey with a grin. "I ain't strolled through the streets with a noble girl before."

I considered reminding him I wasn't a noble but decided it wouldn't be worth the effort.

"S'pose I'd better come too," said Dancer.

They all looked at Mastiff, but he said nothing, staring moodily at the far wall.

"Fine then," said Lookout. "You keep an eye on the youngsters."

And so I found myself with an escort of four as I wound my way back through the streets. Not that you would be able to tell it.

"Can't have a bunch of street urchins trailing a girl dressed like a noble," Dancer told me cheerfully. "That'll attract the guard right quick."

The children blended seamlessly into the street, some ahead of me, some behind. Only Reya, the cleanest of the lot, walked beside me, asking questions about Lanare and the life of a seamstress. I answered her almost at random, my gaze flitting around the street.

"Relax," she said quietly after we'd crossed half the city. "The others will spot him if he's here and give us a signal."

"I'm sorry," I forced myself to smile. "We have something of a history, and it's a little hard not to be afraid…"

She shrugged. "Everyone has fear. It's what keeps us alive. But you got to trust your mates. They keep you alive, too."

I stared at her and then felt ashamed of myself. I hadn't expected to hear such hard-hitting truths from a street urchin, but that just showed I'd forgotten. They had always been a canny bunch.

A sudden commotion erupted behind us, as an irate shopkeeper ordered someone away from his stall. Whitey's cheerful voice swore back at him.

Reya went stiff beside me. "He's here," she said, somehow restraining herself from turning to look. I didn't have the same self-restraint and glanced briefly backward. Dancer caught my eye and flicked her eyes upward. Following her gaze, I found Marcus on the roof of a nearby building, surveying the street. While I watched, he turned in my direction and met my gaze.

His eyes widened and then narrowed, and he vaulted from his roof to the neighboring one, moving in my direction.

"We need to run," I said, looking around for somewhere safe to go.

"No," said Reya, "best not to attract the attention."

With a tug on my arm, she led me weaving through the traffic on the street at what felt like the pace of a snail. I forced myself to look as relaxed as possible as I followed her. Without showing any sign that she meant to do so, she abruptly ducked off the main street into a lane. Material spread between the houses on either side, forming a canopy over our heads and blocking us from view from overhead.

We picked up our pace, moving at a fast walk as children materialized around us. I soon had a visible guard of four.

"Don't let him see you all," I panted. "I don't want him targeting you next."

Lookout scoffed. "Whitey here got on his bad side less than a week after he arrived. We know how to keep our distance."

I grimaced and said nothing more, promising myself silently that we would catch him this time and ensure he never had the chance to hurt anyone again.

Reya led us down another lane and then into an alley that smelled so bad, I had to cover my nose. When we reached a main street again, two of the children dashed forward as scouts, signaling when we were safe to emerge. We hurried down the thoroughfare, ducking off into another lane as soon as we could.

When we reached the next major road, all four children halted.

"There's the mansion." Lookout pointed. "You leg it as fast as you can in that direction, and there ain't nothing he can do now, even if he do find you."

I nodded and was surprised when Reya gave me a quick embrace. "You stay out of his way." She winked at me. "I want that dress-making job."

I grinned, thanked them all, and took off running. I hiked up my skirts and ignored the consternation of the people I elbowed past.

Fear for the children kept swirling in my head, but I forced myself to push it away. The streets held all sorts of dangers for a child—only the toughest joined the street urchins. And they knew the city better than anyone. Marcus, a newcomer to Largo, had no hope of tracking them back to their den, even if he could identify them in the first place.

I didn't slow until I reached the front gate. But as I panted in front of the armed guard there, I looked back down the street and into the city. Marcus stood in the shadows five houses down, watching me with fire in his eyes. I drew myself tall and met his gaze without flinching.

His eyes narrowed and then he turned away. I looked back at the guard.

"Could you open the gate, please? I'm a little out of breath."

He looked me up and down but must have recognized me because he shrugged and opened the gate without protest.

CHAPTER 27

$\mathcal{T}$he only person in the courtyard of the mansion who paid me any attention was a servant who looked at my ripped gown askance. I hurried inside, trying to remember how to get to Celine and my room. I needed a change of clothes before I sought out the royals.

But when I rounded a corner in one of the corridors, I found Celine just leaving a room.

"Evie!" she screamed as soon as she saw me, running in my direction. "Where have you been? The boys are back…" She slid to a halt in front of me, her eyes widening as she examined my dress. "Wait, what happened to you?" She grabbed my arm. "Never mind, hold on a minute, and you can tell us all."

She dragged me to the door she had just closed and flung it wide again, pushing me into the room. The luxurious sitting room had been decorated with the same slightly extravagant and not very elegant taste as the rest of the mansion. Frederic stood by one window, looking out across the city, while Cassian sat on a low settee with Tillie beside him, talking softly.

The room looked very similar to the one attached to Celine and my bedchamber, so presumably it belonged to the princes. I had heard some of the nobles grumbling the day before that with the royals in the only two guest suites, the rest of them had been forced to make do with nothing more than a bedchamber. It had made me laugh at the time, considering they had all been reasonably happy living in tents during our recent trek across the desert. Tillie certainly seemed more than pleased with the room provided for her. But obviously Largo reminded the courtiers too much of their usual accommodations in Lanare, and their expectations had been raised.

Frederic turned at our entrance and smiled, but the gesture didn't reach his eyes. "I'm afraid he got away from us. I'm sorry, Evie."

"What happened to your dress?" asked Tillie, standing to come toward me.

I gestured for her to return to her seat and collapsed into a puffed armchair myself. My legs still trembled slightly from my mad flight through the city.

"Yes, I worked out you didn't catch him," I said.

"What do you mean?" Frederic crossed to sit on the chair beside mine. He leaned forward, bracing his elbows against his knees, all his attention on me. "Did you see him? Are you hurt in some way?" He glanced at his sister. "I was most displeased with the guard for abandoning you like that."

Celine grinned. "I pleaded mercy on the poor fellow's behalf. I provoked him most terribly, I'm afraid. I told Frederic not to worry, that you knew the city better than any of us. But perhaps…"

I nodded my head. "I do know the city, you're right. And thank goodness for that. I'm afraid Marcus must have circled around because he managed to grab me." I shivered. "He had a dagger, and he made all sorts of threats."

Frederic leaped to his feet, his hands in fists. "I'm turning out the guard. We'll find him if we have to tear the city apart."

I shook my head. "Don't be ridiculous. I mean, yes, we need to find and arrest him, but that's not the way to go about it."

Frederic looked down at me, and I held his gaze, my own steady, until he at last sighed and dropped back into his seat. "I take it you have a plan, then?"

"Not a plan, exactly. But I do have some information." I bit my cheek. "But first I think I need to give you some background as to how I came by it."

All four of them watched me silently, and I reminded myself how well they had taken every other revelation about my past. There was no reason this one should be different.

"I was born in Largo. That's what they think, anyway—I never actually knew either of my parents. No one even knew who they were." I forced a quick smile onto my face, but I doubted I was fooling any of them. "So that's who I am. An orphan without home or family, just like Monique said."

Frederic frowned.

"I could have been much worse off, really," I continued. "A kind woman, who I called Mama, found me abandoned in the middle of the public gardens near the marketplace. She said I was such a cute little thing and all alone, and she just couldn't bear to leave me there. So she took me home and raised me."

I looked down at the ground. "She truly loved me, I believe that. But she worked as a nanny for a wealthy family here in Largo. They let her keep me in her small set of rooms above their stable, but she spent her whole day in their home, and I wasn't welcome there. As soon as I could walk and talk, the children stopped seeing me as a doll to play with and saw me as another child. One who wasn't like them. They started demanding she leave me behind each day."

I pulled at a curl of my hair. "She always said I must have northerner blood in me somewhere. But the family she served were originally northerners themselves, and obviously I didn't have enough to suit their children. They never saw me as one of them." I sighed. "Just like my skin was too light for the traders, and my trader eyes and ways too much for the junglers. It's my curse, I suppose, to never really fit in anywhere."

I tried to shake off the melancholy mood and get to the real point. "And so every day I went out to explore the city. I had a mother, of sorts, but I was almost as good as a child of the streets, and the street urchins took a liking to me and took me under their wing."

"Street urchins? How thrilling!" said Celine.

"Don't be ridiculous, Celine," said Cassian quietly. He looked at me. "My parents provide all of their nobles and governors with funds to provide for any orphans. If there are street urchins here, then the governor will have to answer for it. My family does not wish to sit in our palace on piles of gold while our people suffer."

I smiled at him. "I know you do not, and it is the reason the street urchins are loyal enough to the crown. There are orphanages that are never short of food or clothing for those who wish to go to them. Their doors are never closed, and they find homes for the children where they can. But they keep a strict regime." I shrugged.

"They are training the children for future jobs as servants and the like, and many are happy enough for the opportunity. I often used to play with them in the public gardens on their rest day. But I think the reason they are such a satisfied bunch overall is because those who do not want that life leave."

I shook my head. "Some children don't like the strict order they keep, and they don't want such jobs. What they want is to be free. And so they choose a life on the streets."

"Thieves, you mean," said Frederic, his voice heavy.

I frowned at him, but he didn't meet my eyes, his expression distracted.

"They're not thieves." I paused. "Well, I'm sure there are thieves among them, as there are thieves among the adult citizens of Lanover. But the ones I knew were not like that. They scavenged what they could and made up any lack by running errands and messages in the marketplace and the like. They banded together and formed their own family, as unusual as it might be. I suppose that's why they accepted me. They were already misfits, just like I was."

I ran a hand down my skirt, straightening its folds. "When Marcus grabbed me, he dragged me into an alley that I recognized." A quick intake of breath from Frederic made me look at him, but he still didn't meet my eyes.

"I managed to escape because the urchins have a bolt hole in the back wall of the alley. And then I ran, by instinct, I suppose, to their hideout. And it turns out it's still an urchins' den." I smiled at the memory of the children I had met. "And the children themselves were much like the ones I used to know. I asked them what was happening in the city, and they had a lot to say."

I related the story the street urchins had told me, telling them what I now knew of the Shadow Man and his actions and motivations. Frederic stood and walked back to the window, Cassian following him with his eyes.

When I finished the tale, Cassian frowned at me. "We need more information on this Shadow Man. We need to know who he really is. Do you think they could lead someone to this warehouse where he supposedly lives?"

"I suppose so." I considered. "But I wouldn't want to get any of them into strife. They're only children. Perhaps they could draw a map."

"Perhaps…" said Cassian, his eyes straying back to Frederic who still said nothing.

For a moment silence fell.

"So you're an orphan," said Frederic at last, in a strange, strangled tone. "But not just an orphan. You don't even know the names of your own parents?"

"That's right," I said, struggling to keep my own voice level. "When I was nine my adopted mother took ill and died. The family she worked for threw me from her rooms, and a passing caravan picked me up. I wanted to escape the place that reminded me of her, and so I went with them, hoping to shape myself into a trader and forget the past."

He spun around abruptly, and his eyes caught on mine. They held so much fire that I instinctively shrank back. Without a word, he strode from the room.

"Well," said Celine into the silence. "That was unexpected."

Over and over again during the next two days I replayed the scene in my mind. Because in spite of our expectations, Frederic did not return for the evening meal. He had left the mansion, and he did not return to sleep that night, or for any meals the next day.

Cassian told Celine and me that Frederic was occupied, and we would have to wait to hear an explanation from his own lips. And with that we had to be content, although it didn't stop Celine from grumbling about being excluded from whatever action was going on. She seemed convinced Frederic had gone off to retrieve vital information on the Shadow Man.

We downplayed the crown prince's absence to the governor and the nobles, and Cassian held off ordering any action be taken to track down the rebels until Frederic returned to give us some direction. Celine and Tillie seemed to sense my distress since they clung to me like limpets, asking for help with their gowns and hair and generally attempting to distract me. I put on a cheerful face for them—I had plenty of practice at it, after all— but alone in my bed at night, I cried.

I tried to cling to my new self. The one who had learned to trust the royals. But in the dark of the night, my old fears attempted to resurface. I had told them the final piece of my past, and Frederic had turned and run. I couldn't hide from my own heart: no one else's reactions mattered compared to his. I just couldn't understand what was behind his behavior. Why had he run? I went over and over it all again in my mind, looking for signs I had missed, and told myself Celine was right, and it had nothing to do with me at all.

But I was all too afraid it did have something to do with me. Some internal struggle had always seemed to grip him whenever we got too close. Perhaps one side of that unknown war had been tipped into victory by the truth of my past. I just couldn't understand what could possibly have made him run.

I chose to believe he would not abandon me now. But the truth was that I wanted something more from him than acceptance as the royal seamstress. Or even as a friend. And I wanted it even as I knew it was wrong for someone like me to desire anything more from the crown prince.

In the morning, I posed my worst fear to Celine and Tillie.

"Are we sure…" I cleared my throat and started again. "Are we sure he's all right? That he hasn't fallen afoul of Marcus, or something?"

They exchanged glances before looking at me. Neither asked who *he* was.

"Cassian seems unconcerned," said Tillie. She bit her lip. "He hasn't said anything specific to me, but he clearly knows where he is."

I swallowed and nodded. That was a relief at least.

He had been gone two nights when Cassian sent for the three of us girls. My legs trembled as I walked back to the princes' sitting room. Had Frederic returned? What would his attitude toward me be?

He will not abandon you, said an internal voice. *He would never do such a thing. Certainly not with Marcus looking for you. And that will have to be enough.*

Perhaps he had been injured himself? My footsteps quickened. If he had returned I would tell him that he need not go to any lengths to avoid me. I had no desire to push myself in where I wasn't wanted. I would stay out of his way, and as soon as we returned to Lanare, he need never see me again. I held back tears at the thought.

But when we entered the room, I could see no sign of Frederic. Cassian looked grim.

"We set questions in motion as soon as we arrived," he said, "trying to flush out these rebels. And I have just had word from the governor. They have discovered the traitors."

"They have?" Celine rushed over to him.

"So they claim." His look of concern remained. "The governor has received intelligence of a plot against the throne by a cabal of northerners who have been trickling into our kingdom over the last few decades and who have set up their base of operation in Largo. They covet the wealth and resources of Lanover for themselves, and they saw the weakness and instability of the recent rebellion as the perfect moment to strike."

I sat slowly on a long stool near the door. That made no sense at all, not given the intelligence I had learned from the street urchins. The only northerners they had mentioned had been a few hired as mercenaries to swell the number of rebel soldiers.

"But…" Celine looked over at me and then back at her brother. "What does he propose you do?"

Cassian ran a hand through his hair. "The suggestion has been made by some of the nobles that I issue orders in Frederic's absence to round up all the northerners in Largo. Once they are all safely under containment, we can root out who among them are traitors."

Celine gaped at him.

I jumped to my feet and joined them in the center of the room. "You cannot do such a thing! Imagine the chaos and the fear! And I am sure it's not the northerners. It can't be."

"What are you suggesting?" asked Cassian. "That the governor has invented the intelligence? Why would he do such a thing? Or are you suggesting he is aligned with the rebels himself?" He shook his head. "Come Evie, do you really think the governor disloyal to the crown?" He grimaced. "Do you even think him smart enough to head a rebellion?"

I considered his question. "No, I don't think the governor is behind the rebellion, but I do think his information is wrong. Someone has fed him bad information."

"Or someone has fed you bad information."

I let out a growl of frustration. "That makes no sense! The rebels could never have guessed I'd run to the street urchins. Why would they bother to plant false information with them? And they risked themselves to help me get away from Marcus, remember!"

Cassian ran his hand through his hair, clearly torn.

"Look," I told him, "I'm not asking you to believe them, just not to disbelieve them. Just give me time to gather more evidence, to find some sort of proof before you do anything so drastic."

I held my breath through a long pause.

Finally Cassian nodded, once. "Very well, then. I'll admit that with such a diverse population, such an action would drive a wedge down the middle of Largo. Many of the northerners here have lived here their whole lives. The anger such a move would create seems all too much like the moves the rebels have already attempted. I will wait. Only don't take too long. If Frederic returns, he may choose to overrule me."

CHAPTER 28

*T*flew straight back to my own bedchamber to change into my plainest and most sensible gown. Celine trailed behind me.

"Evie, what are you doing?"

I didn't look at her as I searched for the dress I wanted. "You heard Cassian. I have to get some more evidence. I'm going back to the street urchins."

"Not on your own!"

I straightened and looked at her. "Yes, on my own."

"I'm coming with you."

I raised an eyebrow, and she sighed. "Fine." She flounced over to the window. "Sometimes being a princess is the worst."

I shook my head. "It's not just that. You don't know the streets and the urchins don't know you. I'm sorry, Celine, but you'd be a hindrance, not a help."

She gave me a sad smile. "I know. But you should at least take some guards. What if you run into Marcus again?"

I gulped. "I have to take that risk. I guarantee you that if I turn up at the urchins' den with guards in tow there won't be a child in sight."

Celine frowned. "I don't like the idea of you going out there on your own."

"Neither do I, to be honest. But I'm not going to let Marcus and those rebels win. I've escaped from Marcus once, and if I have to, I'll do it again." I didn't feel as confident as I made myself sound, but I did trust in the street urchins to help me. I was finished seeing my past as a burden dragging me down. It had made me strong, and I was ready to use my strength.

Maybe my past precluded me from being loved by a prince, but it didn't stop me from acting to save the kingdom that I loved. Because I did love Lanover, for all the pain I had experienced in it. Revisiting my past had reminded me that nowhere I had lived had been all bad. There was much of beauty and kindness in this kingdom.

Once I had exited the mansion and reached a crowded street, I slipped into an unseen nook and wrapped my desert covering around me. Enough traders and northerners with delicate skin wore the costume here that I wouldn't stand out. And with the face wrap up, neither Marcus nor anyone who worked for him would be able to recognize me.

I moved swiftly after that, weaving through the streets until I once again entered the quieter part of town. This time when I reached the wooden board guarding the entrance to the urchin den, I knocked politely before swinging it open and launching myself in.

Apparently the knock had been enough to identify me because they hadn't bothered to extinguish the lights this time. As I unwrapped my face covering, Reya bounded over to me.

"You came back!"

Whitey wasn't far behind her. "That's a clever trick." He pointed at my garb.

I grinned at him. "Clothing *is* my specialty."

"What are you doing here?" asked Mastiff. Absence didn't seem to have sweetened him to me.

I took a deep breath. "I've come because I need your help. Someone's fed the governor the idea that this rebellion is coming from the northerners here in Largo. They want them all rounded up, confined, and put under investigation."

"What?" Reya drew back a step, exchanging looks with Whitey.

"I ain't being confined," said Whitey, his face going, if possible, even paler.

"No, exactly," I said. "It's a terrible plan and will give the rebellion exactly what they want. But if I'm to convince them of the truth, I need more evidence."

I looked at them hopefully, but they all exchanged concerned looks.

"What kind of *evidence*?" asked Lookout. "We don't got no evidence."

I sighed. "No, that's what I was afraid of. Which means we need to find some. You said you know where the Shadow Man has set up residence…"

Dancer raised both eyebrows. "You want us to take you right to them? You sure about that?"

I decided honesty was my best strategy. "No." I grinned ruefully. "But unless you have any better ideas…"

"I ain't risking my neck," said Mastiff.

"Course you won't." Lookout rolled his eyes. "But I ain't sitting back and letting them scoop up half me crew."

"No one pays much heed to us," said Reya thoughtfully. "We can get you close enough. They might pay some attention to you, though."

I grimaced. "I did the best I could to dress inconspicuously, but there's nothing I can do to make myself shrink."

"Well, come on then," said Dancer. "Let's get going."

One by one we climbed out of the den, walking as we had before, with only Reya staying beside me. The closer we got to my target, the more uncertain I became. What if I couldn't find any evidence? Perhaps I should have enlisted help after all.

And then we'd arrived, and I had no more time to waste on doubt. I had brought the darker of my two wraps and twilight had gripped the city, making it easier for me to blend into the shadows.

"It's that one," whispered Dancer, appearing beside me and pointing ahead to a large block building. "There are guards there, there, and there. All around that main entrance. It's the only door, so they're always on that side."

I bit my lip. In case I needed a reminder of how out of touch I had grown, I hadn't noticed any of the three men in their inconspicuous places. And I needed to get close enough to find some sort of compelling evidence I could take back to Cassian.

"Thank you." I nodded at them both. "Could one of you please go to the gates of the mansion at sunrise? If I don't meet you there, tell the guard you need to speak to Princess Celine. Tell them to say that Evie sent you."

"Wait, what?" Whitey popped up at my elbow. "I'm coming with you!"

"No, you most certainly are not."

"You wouldn't want me to miss out on all the fun." He grinned from ear to ear.

I kept my look stern. "I won't budge on this. I'm not putting any of you at risk."

They stared at me disapprovingly, so I softened the blow. "You want to help me? Fine. Keep a look out—from a safe distance, mind—and if you hear a commotion, if something looks off and you think they nabbed me, go straight to the mansion. Don't wait for sunrise. And make a ruckus until they fetch the princess."

After a quick exchange of looks, they all nodded their agreement and slunk off into the shadows.

"A safe distance!" I whispered after them, as loudly as I dared.

Only when I had lost sight of them in the dusk did I begin to creep forward. The location of the three guards meant I needed to approach from the rear of the building, but even out of their sight, I moved slowly. When I finally stood with my back to the building, I let out a long sigh of relief.

Inching along, I looked for a window, or a grate, anything which might give me a sense of what was within. I still hoped I might discover something of use by listening from outside. If I could possibly avoid going in, I would.

Eventually my slow steps brought me to a dirty window. I peered inside. A large, cavernous space filled the interior of the building. Men milled around inside it, some carrying lanterns, all carrying weapons. A table covered in paper and with several men bent over it sat under another window, around the corner from where I stood now.

Returning to my snail-like progress, I kept my back pressed to the wall, my eyes straining and alert for anyone around me, as I rounded the corner and reached the second window.

A small hole had been smashed in the bottom corner of the window in the time the building had stood empty, and I kneeled down, positioning my face near the round opening.

Another man approached the table and saluted. "There's been no move to gather up the northerners yet."

Several of the men rustled uneasily, but the one in the center growled at them. Confidence and authority hung around him as obviously as visible clothing. I didn't doubt for a second that he was the urchins' Shadow Man. The gray in his hair and beard supported the nickname they had given him, although his manner had an arrogance and assuredness that seemed ill-suited for the shadows.

"There's still time. They may even yet be making plans to strike the foreigners at dawn."

A man beside him barked a laugh. "An excellent strategy." A

rumble of humor moved through the men, a smile even touching the face of the leader.

"Intelligent indeed. I would hardly have suggested we use it otherwise."

"And if they don't act on our *intelligence?*" the newcomer asked.

The Shadow Man shrugged. "We move at dawn the day after tomorrow regardless. The royals are unpredictable, they may decide at any moment to cut their visit short and run like the cowards they are. We cannot afford to lose this opportunity."

Move at dawn? What did that mean? Surely they did not intend to attack the governor's mansion and the royals directly?

"You truly believe we are ready for an all-out assault? Our attempt in the desert did not go to plan," said an older man around the table. "And we wasted our only godmother object on the attempt. Its magic is entirely depleted now."

The leader's eyes narrowed, and he looked as if he would throttle the man for daring to question him. But a moment later his expression calmed.

"You heard the report our troops sent back. The caravan defied expectation and veered off into the middle of the desert. No one could have predicted such a move. We lost the element of surprise, and our men should have waited for our response rather than sending off a messenger and then attempting the attack anyway."

He grinned, sending shivers up my spine. "This time will be different. They'll be so busy dividing the city, they won't know what hit them. And this time, I will be in the lead."

His grin expanded around the table, his men clearly won over. I eased backward to rest against the wall, out of sight in the descending darkness. It was worse than I had feared. I slipped back in front of the window to try to estimate the number of men in the room. There were more than I had expected, I had to admit. Scores, at least. And an untold number might be lying in wait elsewhere.

They moved around the room, making it difficult to count, and from this angle, I couldn't see the whole warehouse. I needed to return to the window I had first used.

"Just remember," the Shadow Man was saying as I slid to my feet, "the so-called Earl of Serida is mine."

I moved away from the window, puzzling over his words. What connection did he have with the earl?

I knelt next to the first window and tried to do another count, my mind so full of numbers, I nearly screamed when a voice spoke calmly behind me.

"Enjoying the view, are you?"

I turned slowly around. "Marcus."

"Evangeline." He looked inordinately pleased with himself.

I sprang to my feet and attempted to dart to his right, but he easily stepped to block my way, a sword appearing from nowhere. I slid to a halt a mere step from being skewered and backed up again to the wall.

"Aren't you going to call for help from your buddies?" I asked, jerking my head toward the window.

His eyes glittered. "All in good time. But I'm in no hurry. Besides, our illustrious leader understands the concept of a personal vendetta."

My breathing caught in my throat, and I tried to think of a way of escape. If I screamed, I might alert the urchins, but I would also alert the rebel guards. And once they arrived my chances of escape narrowed to zero. And by the time the urchins made it to the palace and back with help, it would likely be too late anyway. If I was going to escape, I needed to do it myself.

But as I examined Marcus's face, I could feel all the blood draining out of my own. He carefully kept his distance this time, using his long blade to keep me trapped against the wall. Lazily he used its tip to pull off the wrapping over my face. Placing the edge against my cheek, he dragged it down my face without quite breaking the skin.

"Where to start…" he mused, while my legs began to shake. He grinned. "This is too much fun."

I began to think alerting the rebel guards to my presence wouldn't be such a bad thing. But then I remembered the face of their leader. Marcus terrified me, but even he didn't compare to the fire beneath the cold and ruthless exterior of the Shadow Man. There was a man who would light up a city just to watch it burn.

But as Marcus trailed his sword tip down my neck, still taunting me, I could come up with no options for escape. I closed my eyes as I desperately searched for inspiration. There must be some way, surely there must be some way.

A muffled thump and the sound of a body hitting the ground made my eyes shoot open. Marcus lay crumpled on the stones of the road, and Frederic stood in his place. He had never looked so handsome.

He held a naked sword in his hand but had evidently used the hilt to knock Marcus out rather than the blade.

"I should have liked to fight and defeat him in a straight battle," he said in a quiet voice, looking down at the body. "But I couldn't afford the noise. I only have two men for backup."

He looked back up at me, and the expression in his eyes would have made me back up if I hadn't already stood against the wall.

"Evie…" He sheathed his sword and closed the gap between us. "What were you thinking?"

He had reached me now, and he took a single curl in his hand, running it through his fingers. "Cassian must have been mad to let you go alone. I came after you as soon as I heard…"

The trembling hit me harder now that I had been rescued, and he slipped his arms around my waist to support me as if it were a matter of course. I had no idea where to start, so I said nothing.

246

His arrival, even just his presence, felt like a dream—the feel of his arms around me both the strangest and the most natural thing in the world.

I leaned into him and turned my face up to examine his expression. He had returned to the mansion and rushed straight to my rescue. Why was I not surprised? The connection I had felt between us couldn't have been all on my side.

His eyes moved from mine to my mouth. "Evie, you could have been killed." His voice trembled on the last word.

I licked my lips, and he swallowed, his eyes flicking back to mine for a moment. "Don't you ever do that to me again." And then he pulled me tight against his chest and pressed his lips down hard against mine.

CHAPTER 29

The darkness, the building, the road, everything swirled away from me. Nothing existed except this moment and this man. Every home I had ever left had been worth it to bring me to him.

My already trembling legs gave out completely, and Frederic broke off the kiss to scoop me into his arms. I thought hopefully that he might start kissing me again, but Marcus stirred behind us.

Frederic went rigid and spun around, carrying me with him as if I were the lightest of burdens.

"Men," he whispered, "bind him."

Two guards with unnaturally straight faces emerged from the gloom and made short work of binding and gagging Marcus. Once the job was done, they hoisted him up between the two of them, and we all began to move quietly away from the rebel stronghold.

I wanted to kick myself for wasting time in such a dangerous place. We should have moved out immediately. And, yet, I couldn't bring myself to regret anything of the last few minutes.

I made a half-hearted effort to signal my willingness to use my own two feet, but Frederic's arms merely tightened around me. I happily gave up and let him carry me away from the fear and tension of the last hour.

Even when we reached a more populated part of the city, he made no effort to put me down. There were stories to tell on both sides, but neither of us spoke, content for the moment simply to enjoy each other's presence.

I noticed several familiar faces coming in and out of view and smiled to myself. Apparently my urchin friends meant to see me all the way back to the mansion. The sight of them brought back some of my questions.

"How did you find me?"

Frederic's arms tightened around me. "Your young friends saw you were in trouble and were on their way to the mansion. Thankfully they ran into me, out looking for you, first."

They had been waiting closer than they should have been then. But once again I couldn't find it in me to regret their actions. I would have to talk to Frederic about rewarding them somehow. Without their assistance we might have been rounding up the northerners right now.

Celine must have been watching for us because she appeared before the gate had even closed behind us. A satisfied expression flitted across her face as she saw my position, and I blushed, but it was gone a moment later.

"You found her! Is she hurt?"

"No, I'm fine." This time I wriggled forcefully out of Frederic's arms. "And I have something I need to tell you all, immediately."

I looked up at Frederic and read rebellion in his face.

"It's important," I said, putting my hand on his arm. "Very important." Once he heard what I had to say, he would understand. A conversation about us would just have to wait until we'd dealt with the rebel attack.

Within minutes we were back in the princes' sitting room once again, the same five of us gathered to talk about the rebels. I described everything I had seen and heard, my words sending a spark through both princes. Within moments of the end of my tale, the door was open, and they were calling orders out into the corridor.

The Tour's guard captain soon arrived, along with two of his lieutenants and several nobles. The first of the nobles to arrive was the Earl of Serida, and Frederic ignored the chaos that had erupted around us, bringing him straight over to me.

"It seems you have some sort of connection to the rebel leader, Earl," said Frederic, his tone giving nothing away.

The earl jerked in his grip, his face showing what looked like genuine shock and confusion. "Me, Your Highness?"

Frederic let go of him and nodded to me. "Tell him what you heard the man say about him, Evie."

I repeated the line as faithfully as I could remember it. When he still looked confused, I added a physical description of the Shadow Man. As I spoke, a look of understanding and dawning horror filled the older man's face, and he sank into a nearby chair.

Slowly he ran a hand over his face. "I don't believe it. I just don't believe it."

"Believe what?" asked Frederic, watching him closely.

"I think I mentioned before that I came into my title unexpectedly," said the earl, slowly. "But there is more of a story to it than that. My father was the previous earl's cousin and passed away a mere month before the old earl. But I had never expected to inherit because the earl had a son. A healthy, intelligent, capable young man my own age. I had met him only once when we were both young because we rarely left the islands in those days."

He shook his head. "And then the old earl died, and the truth came out. His countess, dead some years before him, had never actually been the countess at all. She had never actually been his wife. Everyone had believed them to be so, and they had lived for decades as if they were, but it turned out it was all a lie. The various houses of Lanover have some odd succession laws—you would know that, Your Highness."

A strange flicker crossed Frederic's face, but he merely nodded, and the earl went on. "It turns out that my title comes with restrictions. One of which is that if I wished to keep the title, I was required to marry into the nobility. The earl had always claimed his wife as the daughter of a baron from a small southern barony. But she was no such thing, and a legal marriage ceremony would have required proof. So they had simply never bothered." He shook his head again. "The whole thing was simply incredible. The extended family wanted to hush it up as much as possible, so the illegitimate son was hurried away, and I was brought in to take his place. The family let people assume he had died, and I suppose I had come to believe it myself."

"Well, it seems he has not died," said Frederic. "Though how a penniless outcast managed to raise a rebellion I cannot imagine."

The earl, who had been shaking his head at the ground, looked up at that. "He may have been an outcast, but he wasn't penniless, Your Highness. Far from it. His father had left him everything in his will. And while the main estates were tied up with the title, several smaller properties and a large number of business interests were not. His legitimacy was not a consideration when it came to the inheritance of that wealth."

I found I wasn't surprised to learn that Marcus and the Shadow Man were distant cousins of some sort. Now that I understood that piece of the puzzle, the inevitability of their crossing paths seemed obvious. The rebel had merely gone looking for people who felt as cheated by life as he did. I might have even felt sorry for him if he had not been responsible for the death of so many.

Talk turned after that to strategy—to defense and attack and the possible rebel numbers. After some time, my eyes began to droop. It had been a long and intense evening.

"Come on," said Celine gently, her hand under my elbow. "They'll probably be at it all night, but there's no reason for us not to sleep. From what you've told us, we have time to prepare."

I paused at the door and looked back at Frederic. His eyes were fastened on me. I gave him a small wave before slipping out the door. Any conversation about the two of us would clearly have to wait.

I slept late the next morning, but not as late as the princes who had apparently been up most of the night. A new bustle filled the mansion, but otherwise things appeared to be continuing on as normal which confused us until Cassian finally appeared and filled us in on the plan from late the night before.

"We have decided we will be best served by defense. An attack would be foolhardy when we don't know their true numbers or whether they have other similar bases of operation. But if we are to draw them out in an attack and leverage the advantage of surprise, we need to keep up the appearance of normalcy."

But behind this appearance, there seemed to be an endless number of preparations to be made. The wall of the governor's mansion was thick and sturdy—it would create an effective line of defense. Which had led them to the conclusion that the rebels must have a way through it.

In the mid-afternoon, they got their answer, but only after questioning every guard belonging to the mansion. All guards and servants had been put under a temporary house arrest with only trusted members of the Tour permitted to leave the mansion grounds. And one of the guards had seen which way the wind was blowing and turned informant.

He and two others had the night watch that night and were to let the rebels in at dawn.

"But not before a big show of them breaking down the gates," he said. "He wants the city to see him storming the mansion."

The three guards were swiftly locked up next to Marcus, and the plans continued apace. Several nobles known for their loyalty, along with the harbormaster, were brought into the mansion only to leave after committing to return and bring their own personal guards back with them. Except they would return through the back way and under cover of night. With the guards who remained loyal to the governor, the Tour guards, the harbor guards, and the new guards pledged by the nobles, Frederic was confident they would be able to hold the wall against almost any number of attacking rebels.

Or so he assured Celine and me in the only five minutes I saw him all day. "And naturally we have sent word to Father already. He will send more troops in haste, I do not doubt."

When Celine turned away for a moment, his hand reached up to cup my cheek. But when he opened his mouth, no words came out. I understood. This was not a conversation we could have by halves.

Someone called him away after that, and I didn't see him again but for the evening meal.

Cassian sternly commanded us to get as much sleep as we could, telling us he would send someone to wake us well before dawn.

"Which is all well and good," said Celine after tossing and turning for what felt like forever but turned out to be only thirty minutes. "But how in the kingdoms are we supposed to fall asleep with this looming over us?

CHAPTER 30

Somehow, to my amazement, we managed it eventually, and the next thing I knew, I was being shaken awake by a frightened looking maid. Anyone without training as a fighter was to take up a position in a large room in the center of the mansion. A number of guards had been posted to protect the room, and despite Celine's protests we had both been ordered to wait out the attack there.

The remaining time until dawn passed more slowly than seemed at all possible. Once we had taken our places, Celine silently handed me her second dagger as she had done at the attack on the trader caravan. I weighed the hilt in my hand, glad to have it but hopeful that I wouldn't need it.

More minutes slowly passed as some around us murmured quietly and others wept. Tillie left us to comfort those traders who had accompanied her to Largo. They all either remembered the raider battle or had loved ones who had fought in it, and the recent memories made the coming attack harder for them to bear. I found my mind circling back to that day in the desert myself and kept firmly pushing it aside.

After the seemingly endless wait, the first sounds of a clash outside fell heavily into the quiet of the room. A startled child screamed and was immediately hushed by those around him.

And then began an entirely new type of waiting, one that turned out to be far more awful than the one that preceded it. The shouts and screams permeated into our inner retreat, and I tried—impossibly—to track the progress of the conflict from the sound alone.

I ran over the plan in my mind, trying to guess how long it all might take. But time moved deceptively, and I couldn't track the seconds or minutes with any accuracy. The extra guards were to have remained in hiding within the mansion and its outbuildings until the attack began. But by the time the Shadow Man realized his plan had gone awry, and the gates were not opening before him, they would all be at the wall, armed with bows and arrows, ready to cut down the attackers.

As time flowed on, I began to worry. Surely they could have shot half the city by now, if need be. What was taking so long? A moment later a new sound cut through the din of battle. The clash of steel against steel. Celine and I exchanged tense looks. Someone at least had made it past the wall.

"I can't just wait here," whispered Celine. "What if they are at our door? If any of them make it in here, these people will be slaughtered."

I looked around the room, unable to deny her point. If the plan had already gone awry, who knew what might happen now? We had guards outside the room, but would they be enough?

"Perhaps if we just take a look?"

Celine nodded, and we attempted to move through the room as casually as possible. I wasn't sure how many others had realized something had gone wrong, and the last thing I wanted was to spread panic.

When we reached the door, I fixed stern eyes on my companion. "Just a look, remember."

She gave me a tight smile. "Don't worry, I have no desire to die today."

I eased open the door and stuck my head out into the corridor. For all my fear, I expected to see a handful of alert guards, standing dutifully in place. Instead, at first glance, the hallway appeared empty.

My heart rate sped up as I searched the space with my eyes, Celine crowding behind me.

"What is it? What do you see?"

I moved slightly, making room for her to inch in beside me.

She sucked in a breath. "Where are they? Where are the guards?"

I gave her a worried look. "They should be here. I can't think of any good reason why they would leave."

Celine gripped her dagger more tightly, thrusting it out ahead of her. "Then I guess it's up to us to go see."

I hesitated. I could only imagine what Frederic and Cassian would think of my leading their sister into danger. "I don't know…I'm not sure that's the best idea."

"Wait! There!" Celine pointed down the corridor. Two legs lay on the floor, the only visible part of whoever was stretched out on the ground around the corner. "Is that one of the guards?"

I swallowed. "I think so."

While we both watched, horrified and transfixed, someone strode around the corner toward us. It took only the briefest glimpse for my blood to run cold.

"Well, well, well," said an all-too-familiar voice. "Isn't this very neat. Here I was looking for you, and here you are."

I moved to slam the door closed and paused, glancing over my shoulder. If I retreated into the room, he would follow, and then everyone would be in danger.

"You know, they really should have left more guards on the prisoners' rooms," he said conversationally as he strolled toward us.

"What do we do?" asked Celine. "Should we run for it?"

"Yes! Go—now!"

We tumbled over each other, rushing to get clear of the door and out into the empty space where we could run. I slammed the door behind us as we led Marcus away from the rest of the untrained mansion inhabitants. They weren't supposed to have been in any real danger, but apparently no one had counted on one of the prisoners escaping.

Marcus picked up his speed in response to our flight, racing after us. I glanced back and realized he was closing much too fast for us to escape. Or for us both to escape anyway.

As we ran past an open door, I shoved Celine hard. She staggered sideways into the room beyond, and I slammed the door in her face. I took off running again, but I knew I'd lost valuable time.

Marcus didn't even hesitate, letting his hate rule his head as I had hoped and going after the less valuable target. I pushed my legs harder than I ever had before, wishing I had longer legs or were in better shape. I didn't have to outrun him, I just had to make it to some of our guards. Assuming we had any left...

I almost fell as I whipped around a corner and into the front foyer of the building, catching myself just in time. I had hoped to find the large room full of guards, but it was deserted.

Something hard, like the flat of a blade, whacked against one of my legs, and I lost balance and went sprawling. I tried to recover, pushing up onto all fours and attempting to crawl, but a sword point against the back of my neck made me freeze.

"As delightful as this all is," said Marcus, "I'm not inclined to leave undone business this time." The blade pressed deeper, nicking my skin. A warm trickle ran over my neck and dripped to the ground.

I closed my eyes, but death did not come. Instead the ring of blades sounded, and the pressure eased and disappeared. I crawled forward, slipping and sliding in my haste, before pushing up to my feet and spinning around.

Marcus and Frederic stood across from each other, blades held out, a martial light in both their eyes.

"It seems I am to have my opportunity to defeat you in combat after all," said Frederic. His concerned gaze flicked to me for the tiniest instant, and Marcus seized the opportunity to lunge forward.

Frederic danced back, blocking his attack, and then pressing forward in response. Marcus easily evaded his blade.

"Don't think I'll be as easy a defeat as Julian," he said with a taunting smile. "My cousin never did like to play dirty."

"I'll bear that in mind," said Frederic, his voice ice. I hung back as he went on the defensive, wishing there were some way to help him but aware in the lightning clash of blades that any attempt to intervene by me would only be in the way.

As the thrust and parry went back and forth, they ranged up and then back down the length of the large entryway. Marcus's taunts dropped away as his breath came shorter and harder, his face intense with concentration. Frederic feinted and then lunged, coming up under the islander's guard and cutting a shallow gash up his sword arm before Marcus could stumble back and thrust his blade away.

Marcus's rhythm changed, his moves becoming sloppier and more desperate. He feinted, but Frederic saw it coming and twisted his sword up and out, sending Marcus's blade flying.

He pressed forward, placing his sword tip at the other man's neck. "I should run you through, as you meant to do to her."

Marcus, his face livid, glared at the prince. The taut moment stretched between them, neither moving. After several long seconds had passed, Marcus gave an ugly smile. "But you won't, Prince, will you?"

Frederic sighed. "No, I won't. Because I don't operate the way you do. You will receive due process under the law." His sword lowered slightly.

Marcus's eyes flickered off to the side, looking to my right. As I turned to follow his gaze, he lunged away from Frederic and leaped across the room, moving so quickly that his victim had no time to do anything but scream before he had her firmly in his grip.

Only Marcus had seen Celine enter through a side door.

He gripped her with both hands around her slim throat, a manic light in his eye. "You will not sit in judgment over me. I will release her when I'm safely away from this place."

His eyes were glued on Frederic, but Celine's were frantically signaling to me. With a start, I realized I was closer to the pair than Frederic, and I still held Celine's dagger in my hand.

I didn't stop to think it through, I just threw myself forward, sliding across the marble floor to plunge my short blade into his closest leg. He howled and stumbled, shaking Celine, as Frederic raced the last couple of steps forward and ran him through.

Slowly, almost gracefully, he crumpled and fell to the floor. Celine collapsed onto her knees beside him, both of her own hands now cradling her bruised neck. I sank down into a full sitting position, tremors running through me.

"Celine, are you all right?" Frederic knelt beside his sister.

"I'm sorry, what a terrible time for me to come in," she croaked out. "Not exactly the heroic rescue I was planning."

Frederic and I met gazes and both began to laugh. My body shook with it, the involuntary tremors subsiding, as tears leaked from my eyes. I could feel the hysterical quality to the sound, so I pulled myself back from the brink, mopping at my face.

"That sounds like our Celine."

"And you, Evie?" Frederic crossed to me, cradling the back of my head with gentle fingers. "You're bleeding." When he pulled his hand away, it was smeared with red.

I shrugged. "A small cut only. It will heal well enough."

Together we all staggered to our feet and moved away from Marcus's body. I could still feel the sensation of plunging in the dagger, and the thought of it nearly sent me into hysterics again. I had thought I would have been better prepared after the confrontation in the desert, but this had been so much more personal.

"Where's Cassian?" asked Celine, her voice little more than a whisper. "What happened to the guards who were supposed to be guarding us?"

"I was about to ask you that," said Frederic grimly. "How did you end up out here?"

With a guilty glance, we told him our story.

"We couldn't let him into that room," I said. "Who knew how many he would have killed?"

Frederic sighed and rubbed a hand across his eyes. "He was a skilled swordsman and must have taken the guards by surprise. I suspect if you had run in the opposite direction, you would have found them all around that corner where you saw the fallen guard. Most likely he drew some of them away so that he could take them on in smaller numbers. I should have known better. I should have left more guards at the storage room where he was imprisoned. I knew it was never meant to be used as a cell and wasn't as secure as I would have liked."

I placed a hand on his arm, shaking my head. "You can't blame yourself. You needed all the guards you could get to keep the attackers from scaling the walls. And you didn't even know how many you would face."

"Did they?" asked Celine. "Scale the wall, I mean."

Frederic drew a deep breath. "There were more than you saw in that one warehouse, Evie, but fewer than I had feared. Their surprise at the gates remaining firmly barred against them counted much in our favor. Our arrows disabled fewer than half before the rest surrendered. But a small handful were still fighting on when I decided to check on you." His eyes lingered on me. "And it's a good thing I did not wait to do so."

I shivered at the memory of how close I had come to death, and he placed a warm arm around me. "You're safe now, Evie," he murmured quietly. I smiled up at him.

"We should check on Cassian," said Celine.

All sounds of fighting had ceased as we passed out into the courtyard surrounding the mansion. My eyes scanned the space, seeing few wounded and only a handful of motionless bodies. Our strong defensive position had worked, then.

And as we crossed to Cassian—who stood in the middle of the space calling orders, a naked sword still gripped in his hand—I noticed that most of the small number of bodies were missing guard uniforms. And the one at Cassian's feet looked familiar, despite my only having seen him once and at night. He wasn't the sort of person you forgot.

Frederic looked between the dead Shadow Man and his brother.

Cassian looked apologetic. "I would have preferred to take him alive. But he refused to surrender. He and a small band managed to scale the wall and take us by surprise after the bulk of the fighting was over and many of us had let down our guard."

"I'm afraid the sight of me may have enraged him," said the Earl of Serida from where he sat on a large crate. A doctor bandaged a nasty looking gash on his arm. "Perhaps I should have cowered inside after all."

The earl had insisted on joining the fight, despite his age, since he claimed the whole mess had been started by his own family.

"It's a good thing Prince Cassian here is so handy with his blade," said the earl. "Or the doctor would be having a much harder time of stitching me back together right now."

Frederic clapped his brother on his back. "He's one of the best."

Celine leaned toward me and whispered. "Our brother Rafe is actually the best."

"Thank you for that, Celine," said Cassian. "But what's wrong with your voice?"

So then we had to relate our own story and the fate of Marcus. Guards were dispatched to remove his body, locate the missing guards and release the non-fighters from their inner room. With some relief we learned that Marcus had killed only one of the guards—the others were expected to survive their injuries, although one would likely lose his leg.

That we had taken losses was hard to bear after all of those we had already lost in the desert and in Medellan so many weeks ago, but at least this time the rebellion had been gutted and destroyed, with no hope of rising from the ashes.

CHAPTER 31

The doctor insisted on examining my tiny wound and Celine's neck after all the other wounded had been seen to. By the time he had finished, it felt as if one of the longest days of my life had passed, and yet, it was only just past the time when I usually ate the morning meal.

Frederic and Cassian were both kept busy seeing to the aftermath of the battle, the incarceration of the new prisoners, and in drafting proclamations for the city to inform the citizens of the cause and outcome of the chaos which had erupted in their midst.

But as soon as the most urgent things were taken care of, Frederic called the five of us together once again in his sitting room.

"It's about time," said Celine, her voice still rough. "We've all been superhumanly patient, but I want to know where you disappeared off to before all this chaos broke loose."

Frederic barely responded to her, his focus on me, and my heart sank a little at the uncertainty I saw reflected in his eyes. Surely I could not have misunderstood our interaction after he saved me outside the warehouse?

I dropped onto a seat and tried to wait patiently. Once we were all assembled, Frederic strode up the room and back again.

"You seemed greatly distressed by Evie's story about her birth and years in Largo," Celine prompted him.

He stopped and faced us, his eyes on mine. "I was distressed, greatly distressed."

All the blood drained from my face, but he shook his head at my expression, rushing forward with his words.

"I was distressed to hear that Evie did not know even the names of her parents." His eyes flicked to Cassian's, the look on his brother's face knowing. I frowned.

"I determined that I would track them down, and so I did. It took me two full days, but I managed to discover the truth of your birth, Evie." He came and sat beside me, the concern in his eyes deepening. "I hope this doesn't cause you pain."

He paused. "If you do not wish to know of them, I will not force the information on you."

My heart—which had leaped at the realization that his uncertainty and concern were for me, not about me—stuttered and slowed. Was I ready to hear the truth of my past? I drew a deep breath. I had finally taken ownership of my history, surely it was time I knew the entire story.

"I would like to know," I said.

Frederic looked relieved. "That's my Evie," he said softly, pressing my hand, his smile making me feel like the bravest person in the world.

"It wasn't easy, but I felt sure someone in Largo must know the truth. I had to search most of the city, talking to many who only come out at night, but I won't bore you with all the details. The end of my search was this: your parents were married a mere ten months before your birth in a secret ceremony. Their betrothal had been forbidden by your mother's parents who were wealthy traders in Largo. Those grandparents passed away some years ago, but an old butler of theirs confided in me. Your grandmother was a Rangmeran who had fled their hard northern life for the ease of Largo. She married your grandfather, a local, but the two of them always felt that they had no place in either the local community or the northerner community that dwelt here. When their only daughter fell in love with a desert trader who had been cast from his caravan after challenging the caravan master, they ordered their daughter to turn him away. They could not bear for their daughter to live as they had done, torn between worlds."

He squeezed my hand again. "But they defied her parents and married in secret, disappearing completely. They lived on the fringes of the jungle, only returning to the city for your birth. But the birth went wrong, and your mother did not survive. And when your father realized what had happened, he ran from the birthing room in a frenzy and was hit and killed by a passing wagon."

I had not moved throughout his tale, barely able to take in the incredible story.

"The midwife who had assisted at the birth feared being blamed for the death of your mother if she admitted your existence to your grandparents, and she had a friend who had always longed for a baby. So she took you and left you in the public gardens when she knew your adopted mother would be passing by. Thankfully for us, guilt plagued her after her friend died, and you disappeared, and she wasn't quite as tight-lipped after that as she had been previously. She let slip some comments to a few people, and I managed to get wind of them."

He looked over at Cassian again. "Despite the secrecy of their marriage, official records remain." His brother nodded approvingly, and he looked back at me. "The midwife who attended at your birth has agreed to write up a birth certificate, although she is late by eighteen years. She knew your mother, and it was part of what fueled her fear since your grandparents were well-respected in Largo. She had a girl assisting who she swore to secrecy. She is still quite a young woman, and I managed to track her down also. The details of her story matched."

"And what of her grandparents' estate?" asked Tillie, her words reminding me that she had been raised among traders with their focus on wealth.

"They died without living relatives, so the crown has been holding their wealth in case a claimant comes forward. The allowed five years before the crown absorbs the unclaimed estate has not yet passed. So it seems you are actually an heiress of sorts, Evie, although not perhaps an extravagant one."

I stood and strode to the window before returning and plopping back into my seat. It was a lot to take in. I had already guessed the mixed nature of my ancestry—my face had told that story—but of the rest, I could never have imagined such a fantastical story. What bitter irony that my grandparents had feared their daughter and future grandchildren might grow up as misfits and outcasts. It was exactly what had happened, but only because they had rejected their daughter's choice and caused her to flee.

"Being an heiress is nice indeed," said Celine, her eyes fixed on Frederic. "And it's very kind of you to track all that down for Evie. But what in the world made you choose such an inconvenient moment to disappear?"

Frederic actually flushed slightly, his eyes straying back to me. "I'm afraid I could not wait. Do you not remember, Celine, the conditions required for the crown prince of Lanover to formalize a betrothal?"

"No, of course not," said Celine. "What interest is that to me?"

Tillie snorted at her cheeky response, but Frederic continued to watch me, once more taking my hand in his. "The Earl of Serida mentioned that Lanover has some ancient and convoluted traditions on the matter of succession, and he is right. For a crown prince or princess of Lanover to become betrothed, they must present the name of their intended, along with those of her parents and grandparents, to the royal council for approval."

"A mere formality," murmured Cassian, "but still a legal requirement."

I gasped as the full import of his words crashed through me. But before I could speak, Frederic slid off the sofa and onto one knee. Still holding my hand, he looked up into my eyes. "Now that you know who you are, Evie, would you consider becoming my wife and future queen? I cannot think of someone more suited to one day rule Lanover than you—who know all parts of it. You have suffered over and over, and yet you have risen from your suffering as one of the strongest women I have ever met. You have shown courage in the face of danger and compassion in the face of suffering. And instead of using your hard-won knowledge, skills, and connections for your own advantage, you share them freely with others. Despite everything you have faced, you have grown into someone whose beautiful outside only matches your inside."

Tears welled in my eyes. Never had I imagined that someone might view my bumpy history in such a way—that they might desire the whole me, seeing value in every part. Let alone a prince and future king. It did not seem as if it could be true.

And yet, when I looked into Frederic's eyes, I knew that my days of mistrust were behind me. He had taught me how to trust, and I would trust now that he truly loved me—as I truly loved him.

"Yes, yes, I will marry you."

He laughed, rising to his feet and sweeping me up with him. When he pressed his lips to mine, Celine protested, and he pulled back, still laughing. His eyes promised me that he would finish the kiss when we no longer had an audience. But for now, we had a great many congratulations to endure.

≈

And, sure enough, when we were alone later—in the public garden near the marketplace, Celine, Cassian, and Tillie having conveniently wandered off—he completed it with all the will in the kingdoms. And he apologized over and over again for leaving me in doubt while he searched.

"I didn't even think how you might interpret my absence," he said ruefully. "Which is reprehensible of me. I just knew I could never wish to bring anyone else before the council as my betrothed. And, of course, I only knew it in the instant you told me I could never bring you. An almost madness seized me, and I forgot about my duty and about the rebellion, and I just knew that I must find the names of your parents at any cost."

After another interlude of our previously interrupted activity, he apologized again. "I'm so sorry for my confusion, Evie. I was drawn to you from the start, and the longer we traveled together, the harder I found it to hold back. And yet, I was plagued by doubt. As I told you in the jungle, my blindness in the past had led me to doubt my own judgment. So although I knew my responsibility was to marry my true love, I tormented myself wondering how I would recognize true love when it came. I kept asking myself if I was certain. How could I be sure it was true—the one the godmothers would bless?"

He shook his head. "It seems foolish beyond belief now that I could have ever doubted my feelings for you. But my duty weighed so heavily upon me that it blinded me. You are fun and lively and talented and beautiful and brave—it seemed almost incredible that I could be permitted to love you. Surely my duty could not call for something I so desperately wanted."

He pulled me close. "It was only when I forgot all about my duty that I stopped questioning my feelings for you. Only true love could so effectively lift the burden that always weighs upon me. And now I cannot believe how light it feels to know that I will one day rule Lanover with you by my side. But I hate that I caused you pain for so long. And I hate that despite all my promises, I could not prevent Marcus from hurting you again."

Another enjoyable interlude was required to assure him that I harbored no ill feelings. Even the direct involvement of a godmother could not have brought about a more perfect fairy tale ending for me. The misery that had gripped me at his disappearance was nothing to the joy I felt now. And the joy I intended to continue feeling no matter what the years ahead might bring. Because I had finally learned not only how to love another, but how to accept my past and every part of myself, and it was not a lesson I intended to ever forget.

EPILOGUE

I paced back and forth while the queen watched me placidly.

"My dear Evie, you will exhaust yourself," she said.

"But how can she not be nervous, Mother?" Celine asked, coming to my defense. "It is quite ridiculous that the proposed betrothed is not permitted to be present at the council meeting when her ancestors' names are announced."

"It's not at all ridiculous," said her mother, calmly. "Imagine how awkward it would be for everyone if the council members wished to make objections on the basis of her family, and the lady herself were present."

I stopped. "Could...could that happen, Your Majesty?"

"Please, Evie." She smiled at me. "You must call me Viktoria. And, no, of course it won't happen, it is merely a formality as I have assured you."

At her daughter's strangled yelp of outrage at her mother's contradiction, she smiled. "But that is the thing about formalities, of course. They are so very formal."

She eyed her daughter. "So you might as well cease fretting, Celine. The boys will return soon enough."

I expected Celine to protest, but she merely sighed and collapsed into a chair. I had noticed on our return journey that her second rebellion in as many years seemed to have sobered her the slightest bit. I couldn't blame her. While the old nightmares were mostly gone, I sometimes woke with new ones. But I had determined to work on that. I would face my fears and hurts while I was awake so that they did not need to always leach into my dreams.

And it was easier to face them in the daylight hours now that so much of my waking life resembled a fantasy developed especially for my enjoyment. Frederic and I spent as much time together as possible, and I had already chosen a successor for my dressmaking business, moving myself into the palace at Celine's insistence. She told me that as an heiress I wouldn't have continued to live in my small shop, even without my unofficial betrothal, and that I might as well save myself the trouble of looking for a different abode by moving straight to the palace.

I had been willing to do it because in the end Dancer had accompanied me as well as Reya, and since the new dressmaker already had a home, they were to live in the tiny apartment above my shop. I feared it would be too small for the two of them, but they assured me it was more than adequate and that they preferred to be together. It was a sentiment I could understand from my own experiences of arriving in a strange place.

The new dressmaker had been disappointed to learn that she would not inherit exclusive access to my source of materials, but she cheered up when she learned I would be a new source of royal commissions. I could hardly sew all my own dresses once I was a princess. And when she learned I still intended to design my own dresses, at least—and that she would share some of the credit for them—she had happily agreed to my one stipulation. Reya and Dancer were to be her apprentices, safe where I could keep an eye on them.

None of the other urchins had shown any interest in leaving

Largo, so I had spent some time before my departure finding them respectable places that fitted each of their interests. An easier task given my new almost-royal status.

When we had sailed from Largo, it had given me a pang. More than anywhere else, Largo had been my home. But when we sailed into Lanare, a sense of comfort washed over me. Not quite a homecoming since my new home stood beside me on the deck, but a sense of rightness. Lanare alone was free of bad memories and the taint of old fear. Here I could build a new future on the foundation of my past.

And if I could breathe more easily, if the air was a little less dense—and if the greater range of temperature allowed a broader range of dress design—why, all the better. Frederic had already promised that we could make many future trips in the royal yacht to visit my friends around the kingdom.

"Cassian wrote to his twin about your engagement, as I'm sure you know my dear Tillara," said the queen, jerking me from my distant thoughts. "And we have just received a reply from Clarisse."

Celine looked up and grinned. "Was she suitably amazed? I hope she means to come visit so she can see his transformation for herself."

"It seems—as is so often the case with twins I find—that despite the distance that separates them, their lives parallel in strange ways. She has also become engaged at the same time."

"Good for her," said Celine. "Hopefully he is a great deal nicer than her first husband who quite deserved to be run through from all I hear."

"Celine." The queen gave her remonstrance without heat, and her youngest daughter seemed entirely unabashed by it.

She looked over at Tillie and me. "I'm great friends with Lily and Sophie, the Arcadian princesses, and they heard all about it from someone who was there. It sounded perfectly thrilling." Her face turned sad. "Although not, I think, for poor Clarisse."

"No, indeed," said the queen. "But it seems her new betrothed is everything we might wish for. They are to have a quiet ceremony in Rangmere, apparently, and then she will bring him here to meet us all." She smiled at Tillie. "She wishes to be here for her twin's wedding."

Tillie didn't have a chance to respond before Celine jumped in. "Talking of Lily and Sophie and weddings, can I invite them to come for Frederic and Evie's wedding, Mother? It's been over a year since they were here last."

"Naturally all the royalty of the Four Kingdoms will be invited for the wedding of our crown prince," said the queen. "Whether they come or not will be entirely up to their own parents, however, and I would not dream of placing any pressure on them to do so."

"Well do tell them how much I am longing to introduce my friends to my two new sisters." Celine turned away from her mother and gave me a wink.

I hid a smile. Frederic had already warned me about those three together, but his words had only inspired an earnest desire in me to meet the twins who were a year younger than Celine.

"I would have thought you experienced quite enough adventure on the Tour," said the queen, watching her daughter with a resigned air.

Celine considered this. "It's true that adventures can be less fun than I used to imagine when I was younger, before I had any. But I still think I would like to have one of my own."

"You will, my dear," said her mother, looking a great deal less terrified by the idea than I suspected I would have been if I were Celine's mother.

"Do you really think so?" Celine swung one foot disconsolately. "It seems all the adventures have already been had. No corner of the Four Kingdoms has been neglected."

"Well," said the queen, "then you will have to sail across the seas and find some new lands."

Celine laughed and bounded up, crossing over to kiss her mother on the head. "Sometimes you are even more ridiculous than Frederic, Mother. There are no lands across the sea."

Her mother simply smiled at her before expanding the expression to include me and Tillie, who looked almost as nervous as I felt, despite not needing the council's approval for her own betrothal. She seemed to think she could not endure life at court and learning the ways of a princess without my support. No doubt it gave her comfort not to be the least-equipped potential new member of the royal family.

It had been fun to watch the capital's astonishment at the transformation of Cassian in the presence of his beloved. Celine in particular took great delight in provoking romantic outbursts from him in front of astonished courtiers.

In truth, I was as glad as Tillie to have company during the overwhelming transition. It had helped to arrive at court with ready-made friends.

The door across from us flew open, and I swung around. Frederic strode straight to me, picking me up and spinning me around.

"You're going to be a princess, Evie." He smiled down into my eyes and lowered his voice. "You're going to be my queen." I shivered at the words that were almost too much to believe.

Later that evening, I smoothed the soft silk of my gown with nervous fingers as I stood behind the closed double doors that led onto the landing above the ballroom.

"Don't be nervous," said my betrothed beside me, stilling my hand with his. "It is a triumph. I have never seen you look so beautiful." He leaned down to whisper in my ear. "And that's saying something since every day you take my breath away."

I rolled my eyes but smiled up at him anyway, and he stole a quick kiss.

"Frederic!" I whispered. "The doors might open at any moment."

He grinned. "I don't care." When he tried to snatch another one, I ducked away, evading him. He might not care, but this was my first proper introduction to the court, and I didn't want to start with a scandal.

Surreptitiously I smoothed the skirt again. This dress I had made myself, wanting it to be just right. The peach silk was so fine it ran through my fingers like water, the full skirt falling from a tight, ruched bodice. The top of the bodice was decorated with tiny emeralds, a clear mesh, the finest I had ever seen, allowing them to rise all the way to my neck. I didn't need jewelry with a dress like this, but Frederic had sent a gift to my room, anyway—a fine bracelet that so perfectly matched the outfit, I suspected his mother or Celine had assisted in the choice. I wore it with pleasure.

I could hear the murmur of many voices and the soft swell of music behind the doors. Then a trumpet sounded, and silence fell. Frederic tucked my hand into his arm, the warm pride in his face as he looked at me stilling the anxious feeling clutching at my throat.

The doors swung open and the herald announced, "His Royal Highness Frederic, Crown Prince of Lanover, and his betrothed, Evangeline of Largo." And together we stepped forward into our future—a journey that I hoped would be less painful, but just as rewarding, as the one we had just completed.

NOTE FROM THE AUTHOR

You can read about Celine and the twins finding their own adventures in the Beyond the Four Kingdoms series, starting with A Dance of Silver and Shadow: A Retelling of The Twelve Dancing Princesses. Turn the page for a sneak peek!

Thank you for taking the time to read my book. If you enjoyed it, please spread the word! You could start by leaving a review on Amazon (or Goodreads or Facebook or any other social media site). Your review would be very much appreciated and would make a big difference!

To be kept informed of my new releases, and for free extra content, including an exclusive bonus chapter of my first novel The Princess Companion (Book One of The Four Kingdoms series), please sign up to my mailing list at www.melaniecellier.com. At my website, you'll also find an array of free extra content.

CHAPTER 1

*B*right banners and flags flew from masts and the tops of buildings. Everywhere I looked the sun glinted off a riot of color. I gripped the rail in front of me as the ship rocked gently, pulled along by lines attached to two smaller rowing boats. The harbor already looked full, with several ships anchored further back in the deeper water, so I was glad we weren't attempting to enter under sail.

The Duchy of Marin, the city-state we were entering, was a center of trade. At least according to the Marinese Emissary who had brought us here. But I still hadn't expected it to be so busy.

Look! I didn't bother to open my mouth as I called my sister's attention to a ship with rainbow sails. Our traveling companion, Princess Celine, had gone to see something from the other side of the ship, so neither courtesy nor secrecy demanded we speak aloud.

How delightful. I've never seen such a thing before. Sophie's projected voice rang in my mind with childish delight. She hung over the railing, her golden curls blowing about in the light wind, a wide grin on her face.

I wasn't sure if the enthusiasm was for the exotic-looking

port, or the end of our long sea voyage. It would certainly be a welcome relief to feel land under my feet again. And I hadn't even been seasick like my twin.

I glanced across at the Emissary and frowned. His eyes were roving over the many ships in the port, and I found the surprise on his face disconcerting.

I narrowed my eyes and stepped toward him when a loud voice hailed us all from the pier. I swung reluctantly back toward the dock and found Sophie alternating her gaze between me and the Emissary. After seventeen years, we were attuned enough that she could guess a lot of my thoughts, even if I didn't speak them into her mind.

He looks a bit odd, doesn't he? Are you worried? Sophie projected. Outwardly, she had stepped back from the rail and assumed a demure smile for the welcoming party on the pier.

I don't know. But he's the person who gave assurances about our safety. I don't like to see him looking surprised.

We haven't even stepped off the ship, and you're already worrying about our safety. Why am I not surprised? Sophie's mental tone swung between exasperation and amusement. *You know that's the Baron and Baroness of Lilton's role, right? They're the Arcadian delegation heads.*

On the outside, I maintained the same courtly façade as my sister. But, internally, I sent her a mental image of my shaking head. *You know I trust Gregory and Helena, but that doesn't mean I won't stay alert.*

I know. Sophie sent the ghost of a laugh along with the thought. *You're hopeless. But one day you'll have to realize that we're not on our own anymore. And that my sickness was a long time ago now.*

I sent her an apologetic grimace. She was right, I couldn't help myself. Our parents had distanced themselves emotionally from us as children, and I could understand the complex dynamics behind that now. After five years of being secure in their love, I could even sympathize a little. They had meant it for the best. They never imagined that you could grow up lonely when you lived in a palace full of people. And, in a way they were right. We hadn't been lonely, not exactly. Because we'd always had each other.

How many times had we told each other as children that it didn't matter if our parents loved us, because we loved each other? Two halves of one whole. It didn't matter if we were weak on our own—as long as we had each other we were strong.

I drew a deep breath, almost shaking at the memory of how close I'd come to losing her. To facing it all alone.

I'm sorry, Lily. Sophie's apology came quickly. *I didn't mean to bring it back up. There's enough going on right now.*

I forced myself to smile. *Don't be silly. I'm fine. You're right—it was a long time ago.* So many years ago, in fact, that many of the details had faded away.

My mother had even recently assured me that I was remembering it all wrong. That Sophie had never actually been dangerously ill. A normal childhood sickness, she'd called it.

But I knew better. While the facts might have disappeared, as early memories do, the emotions still burned clearly. I knew if I closed my eyes, I could bring them rushing back, as powerful as ever. Fear for Sophie. The certainty that no one saw the danger but me. And the utter terror of being left alone.

But I couldn't afford to dwell on those emotions now. I was no longer either helpless or a child. Sophie and I would be eighteen this summer, and I had spent years learning as much about healing as the palace doctors were willing to teach a princess.

I had no time for clouded judgment, I needed all my wits about me. Because we had finally arrived in this foreign land, and something was wrong.

And for all she had laughed at me earlier, Sophie's next projection showed that she shared at least some of my concern.

Has it seemed to you like the closer we get to Marin, the more nervous the Emissary has become?

I bit my lip. *It doesn't quite fit with the idyllic picture he's been painting of his beloved duchy, does it?* I noticed the slightest tremor in my sister's clasped hands and stepped to her side.

Do you think we should have let Father send more guards? she asked.

I shook my head almost imperceptibly. *No, Alyssa was right,* I projected, referring to our brother's wife, a favorite with us both. *What would be the point? They have six kingdoms full of guards. If it comes to a fight, we wouldn't have a chance.*

But it won't come to a fight. Sophie's answering smile seemed more genuine than her previous attempt. *The Emissary has made it clear Marin wants a trade alliance with Arcadia. They wouldn't do anything to endanger our new ties.* Sophie sounded confident now, her tremble gone.

My soft-hearted sister was brave and determined—she sometimes just needed to be reminded of it. A service I was always on hand to perform. Just as she was always around to remind me that I wasn't responsible for everything.

Celine sidled up to us. "Is anyone else getting a bit of an odd feeling?"

"Absolutely." I didn't take my eyes off the people waiting on the dock. The sailors had nearly finished securing our vessel, and the Emissary had already stepped off to consult with the newcomers.

"Sounds like an adventure to me." Celine bounced a little on her toes. "It has to be better than four weeks at sea at any rate."

Sophie grinned at our friend. "It's a relief to see land again, isn't it?"

I listened with only half an ear to their comments on the unpleasantness of being cooped up for so long on a moving ship. The Emissary was now involved in some sort of heated dispute with the committee on the dock. And he looked increasingly unhappy about it.

The Emissary had led the deputation from Marin that arrived unexpectedly in our kingdom of Arcadia. He had requested that an Arcadian delegation return with him to his home. When he heard Sophie and I were considering accompanying him, he had given personal assurances to our parents of our safety in his land. I found it unnerving to see him so quickly discomposed upon our arrival. Perhaps we had been foolish to put our trust in his authority.

But the chance had seemed too good to miss. Old stories held that inhabitable lands existed beyond the Four Kingdoms, but no one in living memory had managed to find one. Any ships that tried to sail westward eventually encountered an impenetrable wall of storms of such severity that they were forced to turn back. So our surprise had been great when, two months ago, an unknown ship sailed into the harbor of Arcadie, the capital of my kingdom of Arcadia.

The Emissary explained that he came from a duchy nestled amongst another set of kingdoms. That all their attempts to sail eastward had previously been foiled by storms as well, until several fishing boats had recently reported calm seas for as far as they dared sail. His people wasted no time in outfitting their largest ship and sailing into the unknown in search of new kingdoms with whom to establish diplomatic ties.

It had all sounded exciting and romantic. And it seemed as if the High King himself must have sent his godmothers to open the way between our two lands. He ruled over all the kingdoms from his Palace of Light, helping us to keep the darkness at bay, and his laws decreed that a kingdom ruled by true love would prosper. Several years ago, the Four Kingdoms had seen a run of royal marriages that had been assisted by the godmothers and fueled by love, with the consequence that we were currently in an historic period of peace and prosperity. So, it had seemed only natural that the High King would clear the seas to the fabled other lands.

Sophie and I had begged to be included in the return delegation, and after much discussion, it had been agreed that we should go. Our southern neighbor, the kingdom of Lanover, was also sending a delegation that was to include our friend Celine, the youngest Lanoverian princess. No one had stated outright the reason for our inclusion, but none of us were foolish. We knew we were the only three unmarried princesses left in the Four Kingdoms. And a marriage alliance was the strongest bond two kingdoms could forge.

Well, the only unattached princesses of marriageable age, I conceded. Sailing away from my new niece, possibly the cutest button of a baby to ever exist, had been the hardest part about leaving home. Sophie and I had been so excited when the second child of our brother Max and his wife Alyssa had been a girl.

Three figures emerged from below deck and came to stand behind us. I felt my muscles loosen a little at their solid presence. The middle-aged couple and the older woman carried the same sort of reassuring authority as a parent. If something was wrong, they would see it put right.

Gregory and Helena, the Baron and Baroness of Lilton, were the official head of the Arcadian delegation, and the Duchess of Sessily led the Lanoverians. Sophie and I had been strictly enjoined to follow their direction in all things. The duchess was a highly respected negotiator throughout the Four Kingdoms, and everyone knew that Lanover never considered a new treaty without her input. In fact, so great was my parents' admiration for her wisdom and shrewd intelligence, that they had instructed us to take careful note of any directions she might give Celine, and to match our behavior to any restrictions she chose to bestow on her own charge.

The Emissary, who was still on the dock talking with the group who had come to greet the ship, noted the arrival of the delegation heads and hurried back on board. He bowed low before launching into a speech that only made me more nervous.

"I'm afraid there has been an unforeseen occurrence. Entirely unforeseen, I assure you." He paused and rubbed his hands together.

"I'm sure, whatever it is, we can find our way through it together." The duchess' calm tones should have given anyone confidence, but the Emissary simply threw her a wary look.

"Yes, yes, certainly. Of course, we will do all we can. Our greatest desire is to see a profitable alliance established between our two lands and we would never willingly do anything to jeopardize that."

I caught Celine's eye roll just as Sophie projected, *Gracious, he's not good at getting to the point, is he?*

Apparently our guardians shared this opinion. "Perhaps you might enlighten us as to this new development," said the baron with admirable restraint.

"Yes, indeed. It has all happened in my absence, you understand. I had not the smallest inkling. How could I?"

"How indeed?" said Helena, the baroness, with apparent sympathy. No doubt our parents had hoped we would learn from her example when they had chosen her as a joint head of the delegation. She hadn't been born to her station, as we had, but she carried herself with more dignity.

The man who had originally hailed the ship strode on board. "I'm afraid we really can't wait any longer." He cast an exasperated glance at the Emissary. "Their Highnesses will need to accompany us immediately."

"Excuse me?" A lining of steel appeared around the duchess' calm.

The man gave her an apologetic look. "You are welcome too, Your Grace, of course. But we only have room in the carriage for three. We didn't realize there would be so many. Another carriage is on its way. But we cannot wait for it. The ceremony is about to begin, and we don't know what will happen if Their Highnesses aren't present."

"What ceremony?" Baron Lilton stepped forward as if to shield Sophie and me with his body. I appreciated the gesture, but I also noticed a group of guards standing uneasily on the pier. Our small Arcadian honor guard looked equally uncomfortable, hanging back on deck and awaiting some sort of direction.

"The opening ceremony of the Princess Tourney," said the Emissary unhappily. "Apparently it is beginning even now."

The Princess Tourney? That sounds ominous. Sophie had her eyes on the Marinese guards as well.

Tourneys had long gone out of fashion in the Four Kingdoms, but our great-grandparents had apparently been fond of them. I had never heard of one with princesses, however. *They can't possibly mean us to joust with each other, can they?* I tried to picture it and failed.

"The Princesses need to come with us now." The newcomer reached forward and gently gripped my upper arm, attempting to lead me off the ship. "The Emissary will remain to explain everything. And you may follow as soon as the extra carriages arrive."

I dug my heels in and glanced back at the baron and baroness. They both looked concerned, but I could read the truth in their eyes. They could do nothing against the might of this entire land. Even the ship we stood on was theirs. We would have to acquiesce and hope for the best.

I stopped resisting and gripped Sophie's hand, dragging her along behind me.

Don't worry, Lily, you know they can't separate us. Not truly. Sophie looked at me knowingly, and I felt a renewed sense of justification for keeping our secret.

No one in all the kingdoms knew about our connection. Not since Nanny had passed away the previous year. She alone had known the true effect of the gift our godmother had given at our

Christening. *A greater bond than ever twins have shared before.* And she had always advised us to keep it to ourselves.

"Your special secret," Nanny had told us as children, and "Your special weapon," as we had grown older. "It will unnerve others, unnecessarily," she had warned. "You have no need to speak of it."

I had wondered, sometimes, if she was wrong. If we should have told our family at least. But now I tucked the knowledge of the secret close. There was no way anyone in Marin could have heard of our connection so, whatever happened, we had one unexpected advantage.

The Marinese herded Celine along behind us and within moments had bustled us all into a waiting carriage. Their attempts to shut the door were hampered by Celine's outstretched foot. "Wait," she said. "Where are we going?"

"To the Palace, of course, Your Highness," was the reply, before the door was forcibly closed. Celine collapsed back onto a seat, and I took her place, peering out the window.

The carriage jolted and started to move, and I watched the distant figures on the ship recede farther and farther away. Was it only minutes ago I had been comforted by the presence of the older nobles? It looked like I wasn't going to be able to rely on them to fix things, after all. My earlier instinct had been right. If we wanted to stay safe, we would have to rely on ourselves.

Read on in A Dance of Silver and Shadow

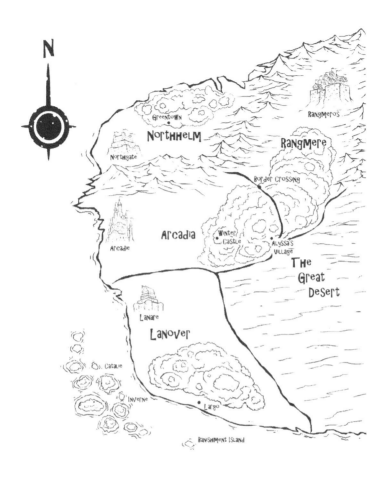

Royal Family of Lanover

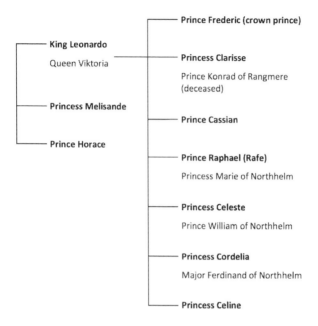

King Leonardo
Queen Viktoria

Princess Melisande

Prince Horace

Prince Frederic (crown prince)

Princess Clarisse
Prince Konrad of Rangmere
(deceased)

Prince Cassian

Prince Raphael (Rafe)
Princess Marie of Northhelm

Princess Celeste
Prince William of Northhelm

Princess Cordelia
Major Ferdinand of Northhelm

Princess Celine

ACKNOWLEDGMENTS

The Princess Search wasn't part of my original plan for the Four Kingdoms series. I intended to finish once all the princesses from The Princess Companion had their stories. But, in the end, I couldn't end it when the crown prince of Lanover still hadn't found true love. Or Cassian and Clarisse for that matter. And many lovely readers seemed to feel the same way, so I decided to add one last book. Hopefully you enjoyed the unplanned extra chapter to the Four Kingdoms story!

Of course, as always, many people assisted to bring the story to this point, and I rely on and appreciate every bit of their assistance. My lovely beta readers, Katie, Rachel, Greg, and Ber, and my editors, Mary, Dad, and Debs.

Thanks once again to Karri for the perfect cover. This time I had it before I wrote the book, and it was a fantastic inspiration in the hours I spent at my computer bringing the story and Evie to life.

As always, those hours at the computer were only possible due to the support of my family. In this case, thanks go both to Marc and to my parents who kept me fed and mostly sane while covering more than their share of the parenting duties.

And, of course, thanks to God, an unchanging rock in the midst of a life that currently feels full of change.

ABOUT THE AUTHOR

Melanie Cellier grew up on a staple diet of books, books, and more books. And although she got older, she never stopped loving children's and young adult novels. She always wanted to write one herself, but it took three careers and three different continents before she actually managed it.

She now feels incredibly fortunate to spend her time writing from her home in Adelaide, Australia where she keeps an eye out for koalas in the backyard. Her staple diet hasn't changed much, although she's added choc mint rooibos tea and Chicken Crimpies to the list.

Her young adult *Four Kingdoms* and *Beyond the Four Kingdoms* series are made up of linked stand-alone stories that retell classic fairy tales.